Pause: Everyday Prayers for Everyday Women (nonfiction)
"This book encourages us to keep striving for a deeper walk with God"
– Wanda Lee, National WMU Executive Director 2000-2016

A Stranger's Promise
"Wonderful book with a great storyline that insists you keep reading because you've got to know how it ends!" – Jeannine U.

"Betsy Lowery sure can spin a tale. Her realistic descriptions have you enjoying the company of new friends, seeing the cabin in the woods, and joining in the eye rolls and the laughter. With some unexpected twists, the plot holds your interest to the very end." – Barbara H.

No Doubt It's Love (sequel to A Stranger's Promise)
"In this sequel, the author has cleverly woven together two very different families: one with a loving and playful dynamic, and one with a history of much pain and loss. A delightful mix of characters!" – Carol R.

"A sequel that depicts realistic experiences exploring virtues such as true love, faithfulness, honesty, reconciliation, and redemption. Along the way, we are delighted with literary surprises. You will welcome every chapter of this roller coaster ride down the aisle!" – K. Dennis Anderson

Love Ever Green
"Wonderful book! I loved it. Betsy Lowery is a wordsmith who crafts a tale full of surprises. I'd been hoping for more from her ever since her first novels were released. Her eye for detail leaves no stone unturned. Life lesson undertones are so masterfully presented and woven into the story. I have no doubt every reader will be blessed." – A. Fenton

To Michelle.

Enjoy this romance :)

That Jesus be exalted,

Betsy Lowry

Love Ever Green

BETSY LOWERY

WestBow Press books may be ordered through booksellers or by contacting:

WestBow Press
A Division of Thomas Nelson & Zondervan
1663 Liberty Drive
Bloomington, IN 47403
www.westbowpress.com
844-714-3454

Interior Image Credit:
Betsy Lowery - song and cards
Connie H. Nolen - author photo

ISBN: 978-1-6642-5104-5 (sc)
ISBN: 978-1-6642-5103-8 (e)

Library of Congress Control Number: 2021924854

Print information available on the last page.

WestBow Press rev. date: 12/14/2021

Contents

Acknowledgments, Credits, Notes

Special appreciation to Auburn University's School of Forestry and Wildlife Sciences for interviews, e-mail correspondence, general on-site assistance, and access to the Kenwood C. Nichols and Family Faculty Library and to the Mary Olive Thomas Demonstration Forest on Moore's Mill Road. Specifically: Jamie Anderson, Communications & Marketing Specialist; Dr. Becky Barlow, Extension Coordinator & Harry E. Murphy Professor; Michael Buckman, Manager, Kreher Preserve and Nature Center; Alex Doss, Development Coordinator; Dr. John Kush, retired Auburn University Research Fellow; Russell Miller, Forest Systems Management (University Forester).

For invaluable and kind assistance in answering questions, offering feedback, locating resources, and/or referring me to other persons, I wish to thank the following individuals and organizations: Ginny Becker; Alta Faye Fenton; Ramona Ford; Stephanie Fuller, Alabama Forestry Association; John Harris, Harris Carriage and Caisson, Rockford, Alabama; Dara Hosey; Courtney Jones; Dawn Lowery; Jeff Lowery, retired, Manager, Large Commercial and Industrial Business Development, Alagasco/Spire; Rosanna McGinnis, Director,

Opelika Public Library; Lee McLemore, Director of Golf Operations, Birmingham Country Club, Birmingham, Alabama; Cliff O'Rear, Director of Landowner Programs, Alabama Forestry Association; McKenzie Poole, Opelika Chamber of Commerce; Andrea Lowery Satterfield; Lewis "Lew" Scharpf, Jr., birder and wildlife photographer, Auburn University retired, and advisory board member at the Louise Kreher Preserve and Nature Center, Auburn, Alabama; Ken Ward, Executive Director, Opelika Main Street; Heather Watters.

Heartiest thanks to Lamar and Felicia Dewberry of Dewberry Lands in Lineville, Alabama, for a personal, guided truck excursion through their forest acreage, which provided factual and inspirational material on watersheds, longleaf pine, planting, burning, thinning, wildflower identification, wildlife food plots, camping, retreat accommodation, timber harvesting economics, road maintenance, marking paint, and more – not the least of which was a view of the certified oldest chestnut oak in the state.

For kind assistance and providing audiovisual materials, Dr. Doug Phillips, Executive Producer, Discovering Alabama, The University of Alabama, Tuscaloosa, Alabama. Let no resident of this state undervalue the quality and extent of informational and inspirational material in the video series Discovering Alabama, first made known to me by the nonfiction librarians at Hoover Public Library and accessed for additional research on the website discoveringalabama.org. In these media gems I discovered facts, ideas, and quotes for this book; moreover, I found a greater appreciation for the natural resources of this state where I came to reside and to put down roots as a young adult in the mid-1980s.

Photography credits: front cover image by the author was taken at the Kreher Preserve and Nature Center in

September 2021; primary back cover image by the author was taken at the Mary Olive Thomas Demonstration Forest in July 2021; back cover inset image of a female pine warbler (titled "Warming in the Sunlight") is courtesy of Lew Scharpf. Interior illustrations are by the author.

Special appreciation to Janell E. Young, graphic designer, for assistance with photo image file formatting; and to music ministry staff of Dawson Family of Faith, Homewood, Alabama, for image assistance: Dan Mullis, Associate Music and Worship Minister, and Angela Roberts, Worship Coordinator.

Credits for nature quotes and references: quotes are from various poems found in *Favorite Poems Old and New,* selected by Helen Ferris (New York: Delacorte Press, 1957), as follows: "What Do We Plant?" by Henry Abbey, page 211 (referenced in chapter 2); "Strange Tree" by Elizabeth Madox Roberts, pages 208-209 (referenced in chapter 3); "The Little Rose Tree" by Rachel Field, pages 217-218 (referenced in chapters 4 and 10); "Be Different to Trees" by Mary Carolyn Davies, page 208 (referenced in chapter 7); "Under the Greenwood Tree" by William Shakespeare, page 211 (referenced in chapter 9), which comes from his play *As You Like It* (and online sources suggest that Gina's interpretation is not quite on the mark!); "Queen Anne's Lace" by Mary Leslie Newton, page 219 (referenced in chapter 9); "Trees" by Joyce Kilmer, page 207 (referenced in chapter 15).

Scripture quotations, references, allusions, in order of appearance, and from the New International Version of the Bible unless otherwise indicated: In chapter 3, "a gentle answer" quotes Proverbs 15:1. Gabe alludes to Leviticus 19:33-34 and he refers to Psalm 24:1 in chapter 4. Isaiah 40:6 is referenced, and Isaiah 40:8 is quoted, in chapter 6. Isaiah 35:10 is quoted in part in chapter 7. Emmie reads Proverbs 29:25

in chapter 8. In chapter 11, Frances mentions her brother's having referenced a Bible verse during his prayer over the Thanksgiving meal; that verse is Psalm 4:7. In chapter 11, Frances quotes Psalm 4:8. Emmie's statement in chapter 12, "God knows our needs before we ask," is from a teaching of Jesus given in Matthew 6:8 but does not represent or quote any specific Bible translation. In musing on her mother's consistent teaching to overlook insults, in chapter 15, Emmie is alluding to Proverbs 12:16 and then to Deuteronomy 6:9 (doorposts). In chapter 15, Frances quotes Luke 2:10, which is a part of the Christmas story, from the King James Version. Reference to God's using something for good that people had meant for harm, in chapter 15, is a reference to Genesis 50:20, not from any particular Bible translation, and the broader reference to Joseph's misuse by his brothers comes from Genesis chapters 37 through 50.

Additional Quotes, References, Sources

The reference to an antique tree planting spade in chapter 5 is taken from the article "A Tree Planting Spade for a Crawler Tractor" by Grant M. Powell, appearing on pages 278-281 in the April 1948 issue of *Journal of Forestry*, Volume 46, published by the Society of American Foresters, Washington, DC.

The reference in chapter 5 to a locally made soap called "Cedar & Clove" is from a product by Kudzu Hill Handmade in Auburn, Alabama, purchased at Ace Hardware on East University Drive.

The quote about outdoor recreation planting receptivity in human minds, mentioned in chapters 6 and 12, is attributed to Aldo Leopold in the article "Summary – Outdoor Recreational Skills and Education: Responsibilities, Ethics, Successful and Needed Programs" by Edward L. Kozicky. It appears on page 132 of *Transactions of the Fiftieth North American Wildlife and Natural Resources Conference*, March 1985, Washington, DC, edited by Kenneth Sabol.

The hymn lyrics in chapter 7 for "The God of Harvest Praise" by James Montgomery (1771-1854) are public domain. Source: hymnary.org. Additional song credits in chapter 7: the public domain tune of "My Country, 'Tis of Thee" is known as America and also as God Save the King (per hymnary.org) and its title and lyrics are by Samuel Francis Smith (see also loc.gov); Jay Livingston and Ray Evans for the tune of "Silver Bells" (source: Wikipedia); Richard Storrs Willis for the tune and Edmund Sears for the first line of "It Came Upon the Midnight Clear" (public domain per hymnary.org); and James Pierpont for the tune of "Jingle Bells" (also public domain per easysonglicensing.com).

"Hit Parade" in chapter 7 is a reference to an old-time radio and television program that showcased popular music. Source: https://en.wikipedia.org/wiki/Your_Hit_Parade

The "ancient" and peppy chorus "Keep Me on the Straight and Narrow" depicted in chapter 7 exists only in this novel and was invented with the utmost fondness for songs of similar ilk in the spiral-bound *Youth Sings: A Praise Book of Hymns and Choruses* (Glendale, CA: G/L Publications, 1951). My family used *Youth Sings* at church and in singing around our piano many a Sunday night in North Dakota in the mid-1960s. The fictional song that might have appeared in such a book is shown in one of the illustrations following chapter 15.

Quoted in chapter 7, "all's right with the world" is attributed to poet Robert Browning (1812-1889). Source: Wikipedia.

The quote of a song lyric in chapter 8 is from "Do-Re-Mi" with lyrics by Oscar Hammerstein II.

Dialogue in chapter 8 about bringing children into the woods to increase their observation skills is suggested by the Discovering Alabama video "A Walk in the Woods" (segment 19).

The fictional app used to identify plant species, in chapter 9, comes from real app information shared and demonstrated by Dr. Adam Maggard, Extension Specialist and Assistant

Professor, Forest Systems Management, Auburn University School of Forestry and Wildlife Sciences.

Cole Porter is the composer of "Don't Fence Me In" (tune is mentioned in chapter 10).

The quote about more of something not necessarily being better, in chapter 10, is from the 1995 film *Sabrina* starring Harrison Ford and Julia Ormond.

The quote in chapter 10 about looking up to the trees' Maker was inspired on July 29, 2021, during my project to transcribe handwritten journals kept while using *The One Year Bible* Arranged in 365 Daily Readings, New International Version (Wheaton, IL: Tyndall House Publishers, Inc., 1986).

"He's the One I Love" song lyrics quoted in chapter 11 are public domain according to hymnary.org. Song appears as selection 34 in *Youth Sings: A Praise Book of Hymns and Choruses* (Glendale, CA: G/L Publications, 1951). The arrangement, only, is credited to Merrill Dunlop; hymnary.org credits the tune to him as well. Additional source: chicagotribune.com.

The statement in chapter 11 about having confidence in God for future provision as well as having thankful hearts for realized provision is suggested by the August 22, 2021 sermon "The Privilege of Prayer" by Dr. David Eldridge, Senior Pastor, Dawson Family of Faith, Birmingham, Alabama.

Source of two recipe ideas that Gina and her mother try together in chapter 11 is butterwithasideofbread.com.

In chapter 11, Gina browses and quotes from the website of Dewberry Lands, which is dewberrylands.com.

Sources of song titles and any quotation of their lyrics in chapters 13 and following: "Holly Jolly Christmas" (Johnny Marks, per Wikipedia); "What Are You Doing New Year's

Eve?" (Frank Loesser, per Wikipedia); "Sleigh Ride" (Mitchell Parish; Leroy Anderson, per Wikipedia); "O Tannenbaum" (origin provided on Wikipedia).

The definition of *patsy* in chapter 13 is from google.com.

A "desperate resolution forming," mentioned in chapter 14, is from a phrase used by Jane Austen in a climactic chapter of *Pride and Prejudice* (1813).

The lengthy quote Gina reads in chapter 14, about the importance of character and self-respect as assets in the business world, is part of a filler item that appears on page 504 in the April 1948 issue of *Journal of Forestry,* Volume 46, published by the Society of American Foresters, Washington, DC.

Rev. Blake Jenkins, Dawson Family of Faith, Homewood, Alabama, preached a sermon on July 11, 2021, that included the definition of *revenge* that is paraphrased in chapter 14.

In chapter 15, *White Christmas* refers to the 1954 film of that title by Paramount Pictures.

The reference in chapter 15 to God and sinners being reconciled is from "Hark! The Herald Angels Sing," lyrics attributed to Charles Wesley and George Whitefield (public domain per hymnary.org and Wikipedia).

The quote that summarizes this book's theme, in chapter 15, is spoken by Everett E. "Rhett" Johnson (Director of the Solon Dixon Forestry Education Center in Andalusia, Alabama 1980-2006) in "Longleaf Pine" (segment 29) in the Discovering Alabama video series produced by The University of Alabama. Mr. Johnson's words and name are used with his permission.

The dialogue in chapter 15 about "only one answer" is adapted from a line spoken by Nelson Eddy to Jeanette MacDonald in the 1935 film operetta *Naughty Marietta.*

American Canopy by Eric Rutkow (New York: Scribner,

2012) contains a statement on pages 347-348 that is the springboard for Discussion Question 3.

Grace Livingston Hill is the author whose influence must be acknowledged and hailed above any other inspiration for this book. If my novel *No Doubt It's Love* was a tribute to Hill's body of work, *Love Ever Green* is even more of an effort to reflect that beloved author's hallmark standard in Christian romance fiction.

Betsy Lowery

The forest experience has been connected to words and phrases including mental health, reason, faith – and resiliency. For escaping the spaces and entrapments of hurried and noisy lifestyles, the resource that is Alabama forestland is of a size, complexity, and heritage unique in this nation. Its enormous majesty, its beauty in minute detail, and its ability to host myriad life forms both plant and animal enrich those whose irrepressible quest for retreat – be it a brief disengagement or an extended one – takes them not just into contact with nature, but into an immersion in sight, sound, and scent for which there is no substitute.

Chapter 1

"*Order for Mary!*"

Good. Gina was getting pretty hungry after deciding what she wanted for dinner and then driving the thirteen or so miles to Panera Bread. She left her temporary seat in the restaurant's dining area and headed to the pickup counter, holding her car keys in the hand that was also gripping her Panera loyalty card and her dessert choice in a bakery bag given to her by the cashier. When she reached for her dinner plate, somebody else's hand was coming at it from the other side.

"Oh." The girl, who was a little taller than Gina, stepped back. "That's right. Mine was to go." She smiled. "Is your name Mary, too?"

As Gina fit her bagged cookie on the edge of the plate and tried to manage everything else, her keys fell to the floor. *Honestly!* This was so typical of her. Unable to go for the keys yet, she answered, "Yes, it is, and I don't know why I've never bothered to update my app settings to the name I go by." She paused and nodded to the other, who had picked up the dropped keys and was miming a request for permission to set them into Gina's shoulder-strap purse, the top of which was unzipped. That done, Gina spied a likely table and moved toward it.

"Same here. Maybe I set it up that way to keep my brain at the ready." The other Mary laughed and drifted toward Gina. "Or merely to keep life interesting. I don't remember." She wore a somewhat official-looking name tag whose rather informal style of lettering spelled "Miss Emmie." Like Gina, she had the name Mary but didn't use it. How funny!

"Order for Mary!"

"Miss Emmie" stopped in her tracks and headed toward the pickup station. Meanwhile, Gina carried an empty plastic cup to the beverage area. Catching up, Emmie dispensed ice into her larger cup. "Mary's my first name," she said.

"Mary Emily?" Gina nodded toward the name tag.

"No. It's actually more complicated than that." Emmie chuckled. "My mother is obsessed with the Christmas story in the first two chapters of Luke, so I'm named for that Mary and her cousin Elizabeth. By middle school, though, I was completely over *Mary Elizabeth* always being spelled so small on name tags and monogrammed pillows to make room for all of the letters. So, I turned the M and the E into *Emmie* and stuck with it until even my family adopted it."

"Nice going." Gina carried her water to the table, followed by Emmie, who apparently wasn't super hungry or in a hurry. And that was okay. Gina didn't have any friends in Auburn, and she'd been alone all weekend. It was good to chat with someone nice, who appeared similar in age. She invited Emmie to sit, and the invitation was accepted. "Very assertive of you. That's a characteristic I wish I had more of. Anyhow, Mary Georgina here. But I've gone by Gina from the start. My parents' decision. Are you just getting off work? I mean, the name tag." Emmie wasn't wearing scrubs. What job had her working on the weekend?

Emmie's hand went to the tag. "Oh, yeah. I always forget I have it on. I guess that's why they gave me an odd look, when my name didn't match what they'd called out." Emmie sipped a dark pink liquid through her straw for a second. "I scheduled a meeting with a new student and parents for this afternoon, and they needed to be at their church right after, so we met there in a Bible study classroom."

"You're a teacher?"

"A speech pathologist. Pediatric."

Gina swallowed a couple of spoonfuls of her creamy tomato soup, then said she didn't want to keep Emmie if she needed to be going.

"No, I'm good. In fact, tomorrow is a school holiday, so I grabbed the chance to get to this side of town for the margherita flatbread pizza" – she tapped her Panera bag – "and some specialty tea. 'Me' time. After this, I'll stay up late and catch up on some reading. What did you think of that game yesterday? Were you there? We saw it on TV. A sad time in Jordan-Hare, for sure. And the mourning goes statewide, compliments of a banner day in College Station!" She laughed. "Couldn't resist throwing that in."

"I didn't catch any football yesterday. Were you watching with your fiancé? Assuming that's an engagement ring. It's beautiful."

"Thank you!" Emmie angled her left hand. "June wedding coming up!" Her eyes sparkled. "Yes, Dillon was over at the house, with my mom and me."

Emmie must live with her mother. She probably had no monthly rent payment to make, in that case. Must be nice. Gina sipped her water. "As for why I didn't see any football this weekend, I was busy getting settled in. I just got into town on Friday."

"New job? Or grad student?"

"Um, neither one, actually." Gina looked down at her food, trying to remember exactly what she was supposed to say and what she was supposed to keep confidential. "I'm between jobs, to be honest." And that much was true. Well, sort of. Her job here in Auburn was a temporary thing, an unusual opportunity she'd found posted online and had applied – and was chosen, even over some candidates who probably had college degrees, unlike herself.

Emmie seemed to sense an awkwardness in Gina's silence. *Is she seeing me as down on my luck? That's probably how I sounded. A stranger's perceptions can be so different from how you see yourself.*

"I spy your dessert." Emmie pointed at the orange-iced, pumpkin-shaped shortbread cookie peeking out of the view window of the bakery bag. "I love their cookies."

"Me, too. I'll have to make that big decision in a minute, whether to gobble the whole thing right now or save half of it for later. I'm ashamed to say which direction I usually go, of those two, when it comes to dessert."

"You should let me send you my spreadsheet of local cookie sources."

"What?" Gina's eyes opened wider. "You have a spreadsheet for that? And I thought *I* was a dessert person. Do you need to go to therapy?"

Emmie laughed. "It's a work thing. I've somehow ended up being the person who usually orders food for meetings, at school and in our family business. So, I've taken the guesswork out by getting organized. And I try to follow all of the local bakery accounts on social media so my document doesn't fall out of date."

"I'm impressed. Maybe I need to keep a spreadsheet for my pattern numbers and who I've given which things to, for Christmas and birthdays, instead of keeping it all in my head."

"What kind of patterns?"

"Sewing. I'm addicted to it. And it's not just paper patterns anymore, but downloads, too, and the notes I take while watching video tutorials that don't give you anything in writing. Yeah, I seem to be talking myself into spending some computer time to get my files better organized. I'm much happier at the sewing machine." Gina pulled her fall-season handbag forward from where it hung by its straps on the back of her chair. "This is from a class I taught a few weeks ago. I work at the JOANN store in Montgomery." Gina frowned. *Worked* is what she should have said. Having turned in her notice to take this temporary and undercover thing was still quite surreal. Fortunately, Emmie didn't seem to notice the sudden silence. She was exclaiming over the purse, which gratified Gina.

"My mother can sew. I'm sure she wishes I had taken to it better. She'd be impressed with this work. It's so professional!" Emmie reached out to touch the purse with its exterior zippered pocket sections and tailored details. "Do you mind?"

Gina, saying that of course she didn't mind, showed Emmie some of the interior features. This wasn't the first time she'd wowed a friend or a stranger with something she had made. Far from it. Sewing really was her thing. And her store manager knew that. That's what made this new venture not quite as risky. Gina's comfort level was bolstered by the promise that she would be welcomed back at the craft store at any time. "Anyone can learn to sew. I've never considered the basic concepts very difficult. It just takes lots of practice to do them better and better." Gina was neglecting her supper, and her stomach knew it. She picked up her spoon. "I'm letting your food get cold, rattling on this way. Next to sewing, I guess being chatty is my strongest feature. I've been told I never meet a stranger."

"People say the same thing about me." Emmie smiled and pushed back the end of a blonde ponytail almost as long as Gina's darker one. She gathered her food bag closer. "Look. Would you consider texting me the pattern info for your purse? Maybe I could hint to my mother about making me one for Christmas."

The new acquaintances exchanged phone numbers and wished each other a good week. "Good luck with wedding plans!" Gina called.

Emmie's departure left Gina free to finish her soup and baguette. As for dessert, was she going to gobble? Or conserve? She unwrapped the cookie as parts of her conversation with Emmie replayed in her head. The two of them seemed to have things in common, and if Gina had a reasonable question as a newcomer – cookie information included – it appeared Emmie would not mind being asked. Still, Gina must be more guarded than usual. She had to remember that! Being the type that never met a stranger wasn't exactly an asset in what she was here to do. It *was* a bold move, packing up and coming to Auburn, a big, busy college town, and during the thick of football season, too. Of course, since most of her time would be spent in a cabin in the woods, getting into a lot of social situations like the one just now wasn't to be expected.

Mmm. The thick, sweet cookie did not disappoint. And there was a lot of it. Better to save some to have tomorrow with morning coffee or after lunch. Gina gathered dishes, trash, keys, phone, and purse, managing for once not to forget anything or drop anything.

In the car, she adjusted the fan and temperature settings a bit. Grocery run next. The welcome basket and the pan of homemade chicken and rice casserole Chip and his wife had brought when they'd met her at the little cabin two days ago were running low. Gina started making a mental grocery list, but decided as the list grew longer that she'd better keep a record of it on her phone. That expense allowance was a huge bonus. Imagine it: a great-paying job *and expenses!* This was a sweet deal, and she still couldn't believe her good luck at landing it. The decision to apply had been a sudden impulse, and she'd been nervous in the interview, probably talking too much, in her typical fashion. The people who had interviewed her had been really nice, though, putting her at ease and seeming to find reasons she was a good fit for the job – reasons Gina hadn't even thought of.

And so they had chosen her! All she had to do for the pay was to come and stay as a guest at some unknown, fledgling retreat site for a few weeks and return ratings data in the manner that a food critic would evaluate a restaurant experience unbeknown to the owner and staff. Was it clean? Were the workers helpful and professional? Stuff like that, the kinds of questions Gina had answered what seemed like hundreds of times on customer feedback surveys. She had lots of online reviews to her credit – on restaurants and lodgings, on sewing machines and related gadgets, on all kinds of products and services. And her reviews, with their punch of personality, always got lots of views and frequently were marked "helpful." Once Gina had completed her user report on this cabin site with its trails and recreation, she would e-mail it to Ms. Floyd, the administrative assistant. She would get her nice stipend, pack up, head back to Montgomery, and that would be that.

Meanwhile, her cover was almost nothing to remember at all: just somebody between jobs who wanted serious personal time to search for answers to some of life's questions. When she'd explained that to Chip, the man whose name Reuben gave her during the phone call letting her know she had the job, he'd been very open to her proposal. In fact, he'd seemed taken aback at the good timing of it. How exciting! Not in any of her different jobs had she been given the chance to do something as interesting as this.

Gina finally started the motor and drove to Walmart on South College Street, ambling first through the produce section. How much to buy before driving out this way again... that was the question. She pictured the cabin's small kitchen with its minimum of cabinets and its cute, little, one-person-sized refrigerator. When she would come to the frozen foods aisle, last, she'd better look at Talenti gelato tubs or quart cartons of other brands. No more ice cream than that would fit into the small freezer. Which was fine; she'd probably never finish a half gallon.

As for the retreat's outside, what she'd seen thus far was okay, though it didn't look like much. But that was understandable since it was a start-up deal. Reuben, when leading the interview, had told Gina to look at the place impartially and to send back a "believable" review. If she rated everything a 5 out of 5, the data wouldn't really be any good. "Medium ratings will fly better," he had told her. "No facility or restaurant is 100% perfect or 100% awful. Everybody knows that."

Driving back, Gina was glad some daylight remained. This was the first time she'd ventured out since arriving on Friday, and she didn't want to make any wrong turns. Not with ice cream among her purchases. Her destination being somewhere off Biltmore Lane, basically out in the country, she was relying on satellite navigation to get her there.

Chapter 2

M*onday morning, October 11.* Gina's journal account was gradually expanding as she sipped hazelnut-flavored coffee while relaxing in a furniture grouping on the cabin's side porch. *A secluded and beautiful place to be.* It was too early in the day to be forming nice, complete sentences inside the light brown book she'd bought with her employee discount. The cover and interior design were all about nature, with cute quotes, and that was exactly what had caught her interest.

Nice autumn color in the trees. Last night, those same trees must have had millions of crickets or whatever in them. The noise kept me awake a long time. A text message interrupted Gina's thought process. Emmie wanted to know whether Gina could eat supper with her and her mother tonight. "My brother is out of town and I don't think my mom knows how to cook for only me and her. It'll be oven-roasted chicken along with vegetables frozen from the garden's abundance, what with so much rain all summer. Plus, I've already been baking on my day off. Espresso chip brownies! ☺"

How sweet! Gina decided immediately to accept, and Emmie added a heart symbol on the reply. Then, "Great! 5:30

if that works." The rest of the message contained an address on Frank Drive. Gina answered that she'd find it and added, "Thanks so much."

Satisfied that later she could extract from her journal anything she needed to put in what ultimately would be her review of this place, Gina closed the book and mulled over Emmie's invitation. It was a good reason to wash her hair today and fix it down, after wearing it in a ponytail all weekend. She smiled. Espresso chip brownies! That was something to look forward to. She tried to imagine what kind of house it would be, automatically picturing nice mother-daughter time in the kitchen. Her smile faded. Emmie hadn't mentioned a father. Gina didn't have one, either. And she hadn't had mother-daughter fun in the kitchen in forever.

To cheer herself up, Gina decided to take the government holiday off, same as a lot of the working world was doing. Panera had been right across from the Auburn Mall. It would be nice to venture that way again to look for something cute to wear tonight, and she ought to get a hostess gift, too. Good plan. First, though, she dunked the final one from a package of four breakfast protein cookies into her half-empty cup of lukewarm coffee and pulled it out again pretty quickly so it wouldn't topple over into mush the way the first one had done. *Cookies.* The pumpkin one – the remaining half of it – was safely sealed and set aside. Probably because Gina had told Emmie of her tendency to overindulge in a large cookie all at once, she was trying hard to prove herself capable of doing otherwise. *Ping!* Another text alert, and, practically on top of that, a chime reminding her to do her daily abs and arms workouts. The text was Emmie again, sending that spreadsheet she'd mentioned on Sunday night. Cookies in the future, maybe. But first, brownies tonight! It was promising to be a good day.

Her breakfast trash cleared away and coffee things washed, Gina exchanged outdoor-soled house shoes for sneakers. The crunches and hand weights she could do later on. It was practically a crime not to get out and enjoy the weather and the quiet scenery by day, now that the summer heat seemed to be really, truly gone at last. She started down the widest trail at a brisk pace, but not so aggressively that she missed the surrounding beauty, including a patch of yellow wildflowers she stopped and captured in some pictures to post on social media. This content should be safe enough. Her location she had disabled on day one of this adventure, on instructions from the hiring company. Flowers in the woods could be found a lot of places, and most of her friends would see pictures like these, scroll right past or maybe take a second to "like" them, but hardly ever comment. Even if they did comment, it would be "Nice" or "Pretty," but not "Precisely where was this?" Not for average-quality pictures of a sight fairly common.

Hours later, having taken her sweet time getting dressed and out to begin with, and having explored the full mall before deciding on anything, Gina had no option but to head directly to her dinner appointment. She used the boutique's dressing room again to change into the clothes she had just bought, then set out on East University toward the given address, which was somewhere near Beehive Road, which was...*somewhere.* As long as the app knew the way, Gina could admire the sunset as she drove.

Frank "Drive" turned out to be more of a quaint, country lane lined on both sides with trees of very even height. When the trees stopped, a two-story, white frame house was visible in a large clearing nicely landscaped and surrounded by woods. Inside, Gina met Emmie's mother. Mrs. Madison said that the note cards Gina brought as a hostess gift were beautiful and that she certainly would use them. Emmie complimented Gina's outfit.

"Thank you!" Gina looked down to admire her straight, teal dress and brown leggings, glad all over again that she'd bought them. "I decided to go shopping for the occasion. It's so nice of you to have me over." She moved farther in as her hostesses led her through a large living room. "I love this house!" Her eyes landed on a family portrait of four, posed on the front steps of the house and obviously taken some years ago. If this was the Madison clan, blonde-haired Emmie didn't look to be older than eleven or twelve. Her mother's hair had essentially the same style as now, but the color was darker. The brother was taller than Emmie. And the dad was handsome.

Another picture, over on the piano, caught Gina's attention. It was a framed eight-by-ten engagement portrait. She pointed. "That's so pretty of y'all, Emmie. A June bride! Oh, to have a thousand dollars each for just the *June* brides we get in the fabric store!" Gina heard her usual talkativeness coming out and immediately went silent as the three moved into the kitchen. Wouldn't it be nice if she could remember to at least pretend to be shy among new people, instead of showing herself not to be, and then backpedaling? It was awfully important that she not accidentally say something that opened the subject of her real purpose in town. If Reuben and the others had stressed that point once with her, they had stressed it three or four times. "You never know who you may be talking to, especially in a small town." That was how Kristyl Floyd had put it.

"I understand you met my daughter because the two of you have the same first name." Mrs. Madison turned toward Gina after peeking into the oven and closing it again.

"Yes, that's right." Gina commanded herself to speak in

short sentences. "A funny coincidence." She couldn't help herself, though. She kept talking. "I'm glad it happened. It was a nice way to meet somebody worth meeting."

"Aw, that's sweet." Emmie looked at her mother as though communicating something only the two of them would understand. Maybe Emmie was telling her parent she'd raised a good daughter!

"It was difficult for me to give in on the nickname, I confess. In my heart, my daughter will always be Mary Elizabeth."

"It *is* a pretty name, and Emmie told me how you came up with it."

"Yes. I found out on a Christmas Eve that I would be having a baby – which turned out to be my son, Gabe –"

A loud alarm sounded, interrupting Mrs. Madison. Gina hurriedly pulled her phone from its dedicated purse pocket and silenced it. "I'm so sorry. I tend to stay pretty connected to my phone, for alarms and reminders. Sometimes I set too many of them." She apologized again and asked Mrs. Madison to continue telling her story.

"And so, that night when Frank and I read the account in Luke's gospel of the angel Gabriel's announcement to Elizabeth's husband, and then again to the virgin Mary, I felt very moved. That has always been a favorite Bible story for me. I told Frank then and there what I wanted to name our children." A smile broke across her face. "I guess he had too much wisdom to argue with the woman carrying his child. I got my way. Gabriel blessed us first, and Mary Elizabeth three years later."

"What a beautiful story, Mrs. Madison. In fact, names come up in the fabric store a lot, with customers sewing things they plan to monogram. But I do have to side with Emmie a little. My name, *Mary Georgina*, is as old-fashioned as *Mary*

Elizabeth is." Gina realized what she'd said and exclaimed, "Oh! I didn't mean that the way it sounded. I'm sorry!" Was she ever going to conquer the curse of putting her foot in her mouth, blurting right out whatever came to mind? She felt her face going red.

Emmie's mother set a spoon down beside a steaming pot, wiped her hands on her pinafore apron, came straight to Gina, and administered a quick hug. "You mustn't worry another second, Dear. If I got over my daughter's belief that her name was too long, I certainly couldn't be upset with you for considering it old-fashioned – which, to me, is not even an affront. So, it's no big deal, truly. Okay?"

Gina nodded, fighting to suppress tears of embarrassment.

"I hoped you would be carrying this purse again tonight. Mother, take a look. Can you believe Gina made this?"

Credit Emmie for a graceful change of subject. Gina pitied whatever family had been next in line after this one when tact was handed out, because these Madisons had been given their rightful portion and somebody else's besides.

"You don't mean it! Gina, this is very impressive work. I sew, and have for many decades, but I don't often attempt items this detailed."

Gina glanced at Emmie. *Oops.* Maybe that idea about Mrs. Madison making a bag like this as a Christmas present wasn't going to work out. "Well, when you factor in the time – and sometimes the frustration – of working the machine, and people not being happy with the fabric they chose, it can be smarter and cost less to buy ready-made. Still, though, sewing is a great skill for when you can't find something in the exact size or fabric you want. And also to be able to do your own alterations and repairs. It costs a lot to have somebody else do those for you."

"So true, Gina. I've never thought of myself as short, so

maybe it's that I'm low-waisted. Anyhow, Mother saves me a bundle by hemming pants for me."

"A labor of love, Dear. And don't be so modest. I make alterations for you at the waist, too, you with your young, trim figure, just like our new friend here."

"One of my favorite classes to teach is on how to open the sides of a skirt or a pair of pants and add in-seam pockets." Gina's hostesses looked duly impressed. Finally, a topic she could talk about passionately without getting herself into hot water.

"Right. You told me last night that you teach sewing classes." Emmie was pulling silverware out. "At your store, I'm assuming?"

"Yes. I love it. People don't learn sewing from a parent as often as in the past, and not even in school, where it used to be taught. But that doesn't mean those who cherish the art are going to let it go away without a fight. The people who love it or make a living in the industry have to market it differently now. If a mom is working all the time and doesn't or can't teach sewing at home, and the kids are too busy playing soccer or video games to want to learn it anyhow, we try to fill the gap with classes in our store. It might not be dresses or shirts a kid wants to wear to school, but it can be adorable cases for their earbuds, or head wraps, or phone totes – I've recently come across a great pattern for phone belts in various styles – or fleece blankets, or curtains for the dorm room in sizes and colors nobody anywhere is manufacturing and selling." Gina took her phone out and opened an album of pictures. She showed the two Madison women a part of her sewing portfolio including some of the items she had just named, plus baby bibs, dog and cat clothes, lunch totes, wine bottle bags, and gift card holders. Emmie and her mother looked, pointed, and exclaimed.

"I have so many friends at school who would love these things! You should have your own online shop, Gina, if you don't already. Seriously!" Emmie moved away and opened a large upper cabinet door, revealing dinner plates. She reached for three and held them out to Gina, nodding toward the pedestal-legged table. "I can see why you are successful at your job." Emmie looked confused for a moment, no doubt because Gina had talked last night about being *between* jobs.

Setting the table conveniently closed that conversation, and Mrs. Madison described the size of their summer garden and said how many years she and Emmie's father, who'd been gone fifteen years now, had tended the soil together. Gina complimented the looks and aromas of the squash, the corn, the sweet potatoes baked in their skins...and the roasted whole chicken now coming out of the oven as the crowning touch.

They bowed their heads as the mother prayed, then partook, naturally with a little less conversation than before. Gina gathered impressions from what she saw. "Who plays the guitar?" The instrument, a basic acoustic model in light-colored wood, rested on a stand in the corner beside a chair that matched the ones around the table.

"My brother plays. When we can get him to." Emmie glanced at her mother. "He works long hours."

"And we appreciate all that Gabe does in managing the timber business Frank started. But we also miss the fun-loving side of my son that we saw more of when he was younger. He gets glued to his computer, running analysis tools and such, when he isn't on the land itself."

Gina nodded sympathetically. "He's become a sort of Mr. Workaholic, has he?"

Mrs. Madison nodded rather solemnly, but Emmie laughed, though with an edge to it. "Exactly. But I'd say *Mister* is not a strong enough title, Gina. Gabe is, like... *President* Workaholic!"

Gina found Emmie's remark extraordinarily funny even though the subject clearly wasn't a happy one to the sister and the mother of the person in question. "I'll have to remember that one, Emmie. Still, I'm sure it's not easy to watch and worry over something you can't control." Feeling herself to be among friends who had just exposed something rather personal, Gina reciprocated. "I've watched my mother live her years with a sadness that just won't leave her. We lost my dad when I was very young."

"Oh, Gina." Emmie laid a hand on Gina's arm.

Gina wanted to give her hostesses an out so this delicious "company" dinner wouldn't get clouded by gloomy topics. She asked about Emmie's wedding venue.

A small ceremony would take place at the little chapel across College from Samford Hall, Emmie said, followed by a reception south of there at the art museum.

"How did you and your fiancé meet?"

Emmie replied that she and Dillon met on campus when both were undergrads. "He came from the Birmingham area, but he lives here now. It's the kind of place a lot of grads stay and work, which is nice. Especially nice for me!"

Mrs. Madison added that a lot of other people were settling in Auburn as retirees. Between that boom in the real estate market and the expansion of classroom buildings and student housing, the landscape was changing significantly, she said. "'We plant the house when we plant the tree,' as the poet Henry Abbey has put it."

"*Sustainable forestry* is a term you'd surely hear from my brother if he were here to hijack the conversation away from softer topics. It's been nice to have 'girl time' for a change, with talk of sewing and fashion. And baking!" Emmie moved as she spoke, bringing her special brownies to the table along with coffee. "Although, truth be told, Gabe comes in late from work half the time, and we have our dinner 'just girls,' anyway. But it's been fun tonight to have a third voice in that mix, hasn't it, Mother?"

They gravitated to the living room after tidying the kitchen a bit, many hands making light work. Emmie told Gina about a certain downtown costume thing on the last Friday before Halloween. "You ought to go. Unless you have other plans. And, of course, the Kreher Preserve's Enchanted Forest event is the weekend before that. A lot of the kids at our school go with their families. My teacher friends and I will be at both events wearing simple black outfits and 'cat' makeup. They'll have to do mine for me. Even when I have a tutorial to go by, I'm basically a disaster at makeup."

Her mother interjected, "I'm not sorry. I had the usual motherly concern about my daughter wanting to wear makeup before *I* wanted her to," she told Gina. "So, maybe I'm to blame for what she now considers a lack of skill. At any rate, I've always said less adornment simply means a woman's face is beautiful just the way God made it."

"Your lipstick exempted, Mother. Be honest, now!"

Gina laughed with them. "I haven't been wearing much makeup while here, but I normally put it on for work so my eyes will at least show up and not look sleepy. My manager is great at doing eyes. She's shown me some good tips." Gina leaned back against the large, upholstered chair and sighed, full from the big meal with dessert. "It's been nice just hanging around doing nothing these days, not having to dress up."

"Sounds like a dream," Emmie commented, and Gina sat up a little straighter, suddenly more alert.

"I am so glad Emmie ran into you, Gina. Will you be in Auburn long?"

Gina felt she could read through the lines in those words. She'd walked right into this, not being careful what she'd said. Again! "Hanging around doing nothing" sounded like the life plan of someone this mother might not be thrilled to have her daughter become friends with. Gina plunged into some damage control, trying to choose her words carefully. "I…uh, I came across the opportunity for some R & R in a rental house here. I'm not truly unemployed, unless I actually do decide to resign the store job. My manager considers this a leave of absence. She wants me to come back. I just want to, um…" How should she say it? "I don't know. Uh…iron things out for a few weeks."

"Ah! A great *sewing* pun, if you'll forgive the interruption." Mrs. Madison smiled. "Please go on. I'm very interested."

Gina shrugged and tried to explain that she was kind of tired of rooming with two girls she'd gone to high school with, managing by splitting rent, utilities, and community groceries three ways. "I didn't go to college, and I've tried different jobs like temping at a call center, restaurant work, and lately the shift lead at JOANN." Uncrossing her legs and stretching her toes, she thought for a second before attempting the cover scenario she had rehearsed. "It just seemed to hit me all of a sudden, one day. Where am I really getting?" She didn't tell them, of course, that her frequent job changes had given her the habit the skimming daily alerts of employment apps, which was how she had found this opportunity in Auburn. Nobody but Gina was supposed to know that she actually did have a paid position here. She finished simply, "So I started looking for a place to spend some quiet time."

"Well, it's clear to me that you're highly talented and smart," Emmie said. "I'm also sure you're impacting people in a positive way through your retail job. But I understand, too, that work needs to be something that feeds *you*. I'm glad you have this chance to come aside and think things through. What a great opportunity!" Emmie was tenderhearted and sympathetic, Gina could tell. And that would go right in line with her chosen profession, working with little children who had issues in their ability to speak.

"I emphatically agree," Mrs. Madison tacked on. "More people should have the courage to do exactly what you are doing, Gina. And I pray the answers you're seeking will come to you as clear as a bell."

Chapter 3

W*ednesday, October 13. Let's hope today is not unlucky based on the date.* Gina wrote that much and stopped. Her journal book, styled with a green ribbon bookmark and with inspirational nature images and quotes every few pages, offered her for today a whimsical bit of poetry that made her smile. It seemed to counteract any thoughts of bad luck: "When I stopped and turned to see, the tree was leaning out to look at me." The source given was "Strange Tree" by Elizabeth Madox Roberts. Gina wrote in response, *A childlike viewpoint on being out among creation. And maybe a viewpoint more adults need to understand.* She set the blue-ink pen aside. Last night, she'd sat among two adults she felt would get that; would look at a tree and imagine it to have eyes, a will, and a personality. But she'd also heard about another adult, of the same household, whose work life might leave him little time for such play-thought outdoors even though he spent time among trees virtually every day. Mrs. Madison had said "timber business."

Gina stood up from the desk chair in the little office nook – a nice feature, given the cabin's small size – and refilled her after-lunch coffee in the kitchen area a few steps away. She grabbed the rest of Sunday's shortbread cookie as well.

"Lodgings" obviously was one of the categories she would assess during her assignment. The cabin, for sure, should be rated high. It was built with simple-looking wood siding in a light color. The wood smelled good (yes, she'd smelled it up close...speaking of childlike curiosity), and the cabin seemed to be fairly new, snug, and solid. Of course, it wasn't decorated like a hotel suite or anything, probably by design. Simplicity away from the normal patterns of life, and all of that. Still, Gina hadn't been able to resist making one easy improvement. She'd used some straight pins from her travel sewing gear to gently tack a large, lightweight batik square to one of the bare walls. The fabric's tiles and swirls in vivid shades of coral, gold, rust, and turquoise had drawn her some weeks ago at the store, and it had been quick work to put a narrow hem on the two sides without selvage.

"Outdoor recreation" wouldn't be as easy as lodgings to evaluate. She had received no information on recreation, and she hadn't found any equipment for fishing, hunting, or boating in hidden storage spaces inside the cabin, nor outside in a shed or on a rack. As for navigability in general, the trails didn't have any directional signs. Gina had spent yesterday, in fact, exploring a little more in that regard, tentatively enough not to get lost, and cleverly enough to use some bright fabric strips to mark her way. Some distance off the trail, other color spots were visible here and there. They appeared to be lengths of plastic tape tied around certain tree trunks. Some of the ties were pink; others, lime green.

Gina adjusted a couple of the windows, leaving them open enough to admit some of the cool air. Another gorgeous autumn day! She put her long, straight hair into a ponytail and dressed in basic workout wear, idly considering her looks as compared with Emmie's. Gina's hair was darker, but not as thick. Length and cut were roughly the same. Emmie had a wider face; Gina's was more oval. It was funny how the two of them and Emmie's mother had laughed and talked on Monday night as if all three had known each other a long time. The hostesses had treated Gina as a valued guest and hadn't asked her an excess of personal questions – at least, not in a way that had made her feel awkward or judged.

Outside, she looked, listened, breathed deeply, and finally sat on the one structure out here for sitting: a simply hewn wood bench, extra-long, symmetrical, and without a back. What kind of impression had she really made on the Madison women? If a disastrous one, in spite of the nice things they had said, she would know it eventually if she never heard again from Emmie, who had promised to send links to those costume parties, with dates and times.

From here, the cabin looked as inviting as it did on the inside. It was a basic rectangle with a double window either side of the center door. The front porch that wrapped and went down one side of the building required only a small step up. Too bad this place was hers for such a short time. The detail of her departure date had been left kind of open-ended, actually. Gina's report did have a deadline, shortly before Christmas. If she did a good and thorough job quickly, she didn't even have to stay until then. But, if she was finding more things out, she was free to stay longer and include that information.

Suddenly, the sturdy bench seemed to call to Gina in a new way, not unlike that "bending, looking" tree described in her journal. Smiling, she stood up on one end of it. It wasn't a bench now. It was a balance beam, and wide enough for anybody who'd never trained in gymnastics! Gina walked its length gracefully, pretending she *had* trained in gymnastics and picturing some of the elite athletes featured in Olympic Games coverage during the summer. She pivoted on the balls of her feet, extended her arms, and traversed the length again. Now, she stepped to the other end, each time dipping slightly and extending her free foot out to the side. "I'm a baby bird!" she called laughingly, imagining such a creature learning to walk along a twig of a tree before it was old enough to fly. Though that's probably not how it really worked in the bird world. A chirp sounded, and Gina giggled. Something out there knew it was being thought of! Squirrels were close by, too, where the trees were especially dense. They scurried into hiding, it seemed, the minute she looked that direction. Stepping and turning, Gina relished the feeling of abject freedom to act any way she felt like, with no one to see or hear her for miles around. This was the intangible benefit of a truly secluded retreat, whether in the woods or wherever else anybody might create a site for it.

"Hello – ? Miss?"

The voice from out of nowhere startled Gina so badly she couldn't move or speak except for turning automatically, in a panic state, to locate the source. *A man!* Her heart pounded and her hands were suddenly trembling. Rooted to the spot, she had a flash of gratitude that this "beam" wasn't four inches wide, and higher, else the fright probably would have had her on the ground right now, possibly with injuries. *What's going to happen to me?* Being nicely dressed did not mean a man wasn't a threat. Everybody knew that.

"I would have said something sooner, but I was hoping not to startle you."

Mission not accomplished!

"But now that that's no longer the issue, do you think you could interrupt this...playtime, or whatever you would call it, long enough to tell me *what* you are doing here?"

Tall, dark-haired, he planted his arms across his chest and stepped apart a little more for emphasis, effectively resetting his form – a nicely-put-together form, Gina couldn't help but notice, in spite of her fear level – into a totally "Brawny paper towels guy" kind of pose. Just add lumberjack gear in place of the slacks and lightweight sweater. *Navy sweater. Nice fit. Nice face. What self-defense do I know?* Her mind awhirl with impressions and safety alerts, all Gina could do was stare. Who *was* this, acting so bossy? If he owned the place, wouldn't he be dressed like that Brawny guy instead of like this? Add to her confusion having had an audience without knowing it. It was so embarrassing that he had seen what he obviously had. *"This playtime."* As if she were eight years old!

And so here they stood, warily eyeing each other, he on the ground a good distance away, she still up on what had been her apparatus of sheer freedom. *Scratch that.* Cautiously, Gina stepped to the ground, keeping the bench between herself and the stranger. She visualized what she might do if it became time to run. Could she get to the cabin door before he could get to her? Get inside and lock him out? *Right.* All of the security features helped when a person was inside. That flaw definitely was going on her report. What should the owners add for safety out here, though? A tree spring noose trap, which she could sidestep so the pursuer would be swept up by his ankles? Not likely. That probably happened only in the movies.

Wait. In the movies, it usually worked to get the enemy talking. Not to mention, she had as much right to be here as he did. "Look, whoever you are, and assuming you have legitimate reason to be all high and mighty, didn't Chip tell you about me? I mean, what I'm doing here? It never occurred to me there would be anybody else involved in the arrangements."

He didn't move, except that his expression changed. It went from annoyed to something darker. "Chip? You know my uncle?"

Gina relaxed a little. *Okay.* If this guy was a relative of Chip Ensley, her contact person, then that made some sense. Chip must manage the retreat, but maybe his nephew had a hand in it, too. "Yes, I do," she answered. "If it's the same Chip. *He* was very *nice* to me," she added pointedly. "Not a family characteristic, I gather?" She folded her own arms. *Where is this coming from? There must be an easier way to learn assertiveness than a plunge into mortal danger!* That was it. It had to be adrenaline. No matter how it had happened, Gina congratulated herself for speaking up. But was it wise to antagonize somebody this way who already seemed hostile?

"Gabe Madison." Identifying himself, the Brawny man in business casual ducked his head in what might be interpreted as the merest hint of politeness. "Chip Ensley is my uncle."

Madison? Madison! Well, no wonder! Something clicked in Gina's mind. When she'd driven home on Monday night, it had turned out to be a very short distance compared to her errands during the preceding 24 hours. Gina smiled to herself. So, it would seem that this Gabe Madison guy *was* a lumberjack. The house where he lived with Emmie and Mrs. Madison must be fairly close to this cabin but accessed off a different road. How funny!

"I'm glad you think this is funny, miss. Actually, *not*."

"Wait. I think I can explain. I know your sister. And your mother, too. So, which direction is your house? I had supper there on Monday." He answered Gina by pointing, evidently with confusion and annoyance. As for Gina, more light was dawning. "Are you the one with the torn jacket and the shirt pocket practically falling off…in the closet?" She inclined her head toward the cabin. "You know the old saying: 'A stitch in time…'" She delivered the line a smidge sneeringly, maybe to pay him back a little for having startled and embarrassed her so. She wasn't about to tell him she had mended those wardrobe problems out of the goodness of her heart on her first day in the cabin, not even knowing whose things she was repairing!

"You've been going through my clothes?" He might have moved a step closer.

Gina stood her ground. "Yes, but only to gently slide them aside," she fudged, "when that *nice* man and his wife helped me get checked in for my retreat, which, by the way, you are greatly disrupting."

Gabe Madison – who, Gina suddenly realized, hadn't asked *her* name, because it must be of zero importance to him – was now looking toward the cabin as though he wanted to barge in and inspect it to see how seriously it had been invaded.

"Look." Gina leaned forward a fraction, and he turned his head toward her. *"I haven't been using your toothpaste or anything!"* She wanted to add, "So ease off, would you?" This time, though, she held her tongue. Anyway, she maybe shouldn't be bragging too much on this topic, because she hadn't been able to resist opening and smelling the bottle of Old Spice body wash that must be his, "Steel Courage" variety. It had smelled very nice, and very masculine. It was so difficult to keep a straight face right now.

His loud sigh had unmistakable exasperation in it. Nevertheless, his volume was checked a bit as he said, "Chip and Claire helped you settle in." He was nodding. "To my cabin. For a 'retreat,' whatever *that* means. Huh." Now, he was shaking his head. "And I thought my return flight atrociously early today was a nightmare." He sighed again. "I feel like 'Allen' in Wonderland, everything gone completely wacky!"

Almost seeming unaware of Gina, he was shaking his head again. Yeah, this "get him talking" ploy was spot on. She figured she could easily bolt to the door right now. But, for some reason, she didn't.

"I might have known. I go out of town *for the first time in two years,* and things absolutely fall apart here. Chip probably set this up, this...whatever you are doing, intentionally timing it for while I was away." He muttered, "And how my mother and sister got in on it is anybody's guess."

The guy obviously had some issues with his uncle. An internal power struggle in a small, family business? Gina tried another strategy, the one about a calm and gentle answer defusing an angry rant. She unfolded her arms, stepped in front of the bench, and sat. "Actually, Mr. Madison, I don't think it's possible he did that. Your uncle was quite surprised when I contacted him and asked to stay here. *Pleasantly* surprised."

"I see." He nodded, but suddenly he was doing the opposite again. "No, I really don't see at all, since you don't have permission to be here. At any rate, I mistook you for a teenager lost in the woods and seizing the opportunity to practice beginner gymnastics on a triple-wide, a.k.a. *cheater's,* balance beam, but which in reality is a $1,500 solid elm bench we installed last month in my father's memory."

"Whew!" Gina nodded and looked into the distance. Okay. Hmm. *Calm* was one thing; doormat was another. "Right." She bit her lips for a moment, then gave Gabe Madison a deliberately cool stare. "And *you're* the one who's named for an *angel.*" She exhaled a staccato laugh. "Remarkable." Good. She'd managed a nice level of sarcasm. She glared, and the not-angel Gabriel glared right back. Now, he was looking at the cabin again. Now, back at her.

He moved at last. But not toward her. Territorially, he practically stamped up onto the porch, stopping short and immediately fingering one of the little bags Gina had tacked – gently, with straight pins – to the support posts and along the handrail.

"That's fresh basil. Your mother gave it to me. So sweet of her. And I sewed the muslin bags on my portable. I bring it with me everywhere."

"And the purpose of these is…?"

Venturing closer, Gina explained that the basil served as a natural mosquito repellent. "I honestly wasn't sure how bad the mosquitoes would be, but I figured to be on the safe side. Besides, your mother said she had more of that herb in her garden this year than she could use."

"Well, whatever. I half expected you to say something different, such as it repels vampires."

"Oh!" Gina suddenly understood what books meant when they said somebody *bristled,* because she was bristling at what the guy had just said. Her forehead wrinkled and her head nodded a little. "I see." Some first impression this Gabe Madison had of her! Maybe she should make up a story about various anti-vampire methods given in a little book of superstitions kept under her pillow. "Well, thanks at least for not yanking them down."

Gabe gave her a sharp look. He reached for the knob, opening the door slightly. He stopped. He turned his head and looked at Gina. "*May* I?" His tone was phenomenally slathered in sarcasm.

That did it. Gina took a deep breath. "Since you asked, then *no.* You may not. This cabin has been legally rented by me, and I'd much rather you speak with your uncle than intrude on my belongings right now."

Appearing to struggle for self-control, Gabe finally closed the door and did an about-face. "Granted. Some colossal mix-up has happened, no doubt due to more bad decision-making being done without my input. All I know is, when I flew out a week ago, there was *no rental property here.* No 'retreat' site for others to use. Just the retreat of *my* cabin, which my friends and I built by the sweat of our brows, for family use only, and which I expected to find empty and a welcome place to unwind after a grueling work trip where the food didn't agree with me and I had to skip the evening festivities to work on contracts in my room, not to mention being worried about things back home, which, *clearly,* was warranted." He shook his head four or five times. "A little kid screamed literally the entire flight, and I honestly couldn't blame her much, based on the turbulence." Gabe expelled a harsh laugh, and the force in it sent Gina toward her former fear mode for a second. "After all of that, is it too much to expect to finally crash on *my* bed, in *my* cabin?" He put his hands on his hips. "As for my uncle and what he has 'legally' arranged with you, there is only *one* decision-maker on Madison land, and you're looking at him!"

As that tirade seemed to echo through the clearing, Gina zeroed in on a part of it. *"By the sweat of our brows"? Oh, my! Cliché guy.* For the moment, she took to coping by means of derision, giving internal vent to things she would not stoop to voicing out loud. What else could she say to him without this clash turning into fisticuffs? If she were a guy, it probably already would have! That being the case, maybe it was time to try the soft approach again. "I don't blame you, Mr. Madison. I'm sorry you've had such a bad time. If there *is* a mistake, I'm sure a solution can be worked out." Gina hoped that solution didn't turn out to be her eviction, meaning her utter failure at what was supposed to be a cushy and fun assignment. "Regardless, what a promising retreat your family does have! Such a beautiful and relaxing setting to enjoy every day of your lives! Maybe, when you're feeling better, you'll pause and be thankful." *Whoa.* Gabe Madison was growing unhappy – in slow motion, it seemed. Apparently, Gina's conciliatory and gentle words were having the opposite effect of what she'd meant for them to have.

"You're dead wrong there, miss, although I suppose it's nice, for those who can, to get away with such a simple way of looking at things. This forest is our livelihood, and that means a whole lot of hard work. When I land here at the cabin, it's so I can rest, not play. As manager of Madison Timber Farm, I frankly don't have the time to get all fuzzy-feely over this place, jumping up on benches and pretending I'm a baby bird."

Suddenly, it was hard to swallow. A measure of sympathy for this man's terrible experience notwithstanding, Gina felt a surge of disappointment. Some unfortunate mistake *had* happened, and it was probably going to lose her her whole, sweet setup. If they sent her away, she wouldn't be able to do the job she was hired for, the role that she had assumed would be a matter of small effort for great money. *If something sounds too good to be true...* The wise, old saying taunted her. A complete and total failure she would be in that case, not even a week into the assignment. She blinked several times and almost whispered, "Any normal, decent human being, *with managerial skills,* would have stepped away from this situation ten minutes ago, to go find out what the miscommunication was."

Evidently, it was Gabe's turn to bristle. Gina had learned a minute ago what that word felt like. Now, she was seeing what it looked like. In living color, some eight feet away. "I'd rather you put your energies into packing instead of crying."

Gina almost couldn't believe her ears. *Insensitive, rude, hateful–*

"But you're right about what I need to do next. I'm going to get in touch with my uncle and get this mess straightened out ASAP."

Gina felt the sting of those words deeply, undoubtedly much more deeply than the speaker of them could possibly understand. She fled past him and into the cabin as her tears came. Quietly she shut the door, daring him to have expected her to slam it. But no door was handy for shutting out the hurt. *Looking at life simplistically. Get this mess straightened out.* That was all she amounted to in his eyes. Not a person. Just a problem. Clearly, he had no interest in understanding *her* situation, nor even in hearing about it. Gina remained just inside the door. *A mess!* Yes, that's exactly what she was right now. And he'd called her a teenager, besides! What right had he to be deliberately insulting, just because he'd had a bad day? Hadn't he ever heard of simple coffee therapy?

Gina's injured feelings begged her to strike back. So, with full knowledge that she was about to act immaturely, like the teenager Gabe had claimed to mistake her for – and with no plans to regret it, ever – she opened one of the front windows a little more. Good. In spite of saying he planned to go resolve the mix-up right away, there Gabe Madison was, standing by the bench he thought she had so disrespected. Maybe he intended to phone his uncle from right out there. Or, maybe her dig about his lack of managerial skills had hit home, slowing him down. Maybe it had *rankled,* to use another great word often applied to such moments. Yes, this thirteenth day of the month was living up to its reputation (speaking of baseless superstition). Gina bent until her face almost touched the screen. "Hey!" she yelled. "Angel guy! Have you ever heard of the capybara? It lives in a type of forest far away from here and is considered the world's largest rodent." Gina paused for effect. "After meeting *you,* I know different!" She shut the window with just enough force to make a decent noise, then flung herself onto the bed.

Chapter 4

I'm back. It's still Wednesday, October 13. PSL cold brew emergency brewing! Theoretically. But I'm in no mood to go in search of coffee at markup prices. Gina set her pen down and closed the journal, using the book to shove aside a pile of wadded-up facial tissues. Of all of the things snarled at her before the good cry she'd just dried away, Gabe Madison's mention of his father was what had her attention at the moment. No wonder it had made the son angry to see her here, a trespasser as far as he knew, treating like a plaything something that had deep personal significance – the bench dedicated to the father he must have lost during his teen years. Such a tough age to lose a parent! Gina hardly even remembered *her* father, she'd been so young at the time. Yes, she missed having a father, but her situation was different. Missing someone you could barely remember was different from missing someone you had more and stronger memories of. Mrs. Madison said the other night that her husband had started the family business. Gabe must have learned a lot from him. The son held a position of tremendous responsibility at a fairly young age.

And what was that about Chip making bad decisions?

Wow. Gabe must have a lot on his plate, or in places less obvious, and Gina imagined he might not even remember, later, all that he had said to her. He really hadn't intended to tell those things to *her,* of course. They were just complaints he needed to voice. A wall would have done fine.

That took care of the feelings involved. Gabe's, and hers. But what about the facts? It was easy to step back now and try to see that man's point of view, and all, but where did that leave Gina? She was tempted to text Taylor, "You might see me back at work much sooner than you expected." Gina shook her head. Was this all that her special chance for a change of scenery was going to amount to? A week off and a big mistake? And, besides that worry, now Gina had a new one. Assuming she did get to stay, the circumstances were suddenly more complicated. She was secretly evaluating a place owned by people she now had met and liked – well, with one major exception.

It was time for Gina to get some comfort, and not the temporary kind from caffeine and sugar. Unable to think on anything but her stormy encounter with Gabe, she sent a message to his sister: "I think I need some cookies!" She explained, "I just had a horrible run-in with a guy that apparently is your brother." She could have added, "The guy you called President Workaholic…and someone I would say holds another title, the Baron of Bad Manners." Instead, she gave a straightforward account sufficient to clue Emmie in.

Emmie got back to Gina a couple of hours later. "No cause for further worry. We've had an account of things from my brother first, and then from Uncle Chip. Phones blowing up with texts, as you might imagine! Gabe came into town fully ignorant of a few key facts, unfortunately for you. My brother has now been straightened out. I'm so sorry your first impression of Gabe was him at his worst. I have a hunch he will try to make it up to you. Now, go get some cookies! Or take a bubble bath. You'll find a secret store of spa supplies in a zippered case behind the extra blanket on the closet shelf. Some of the rest of us use that cabin when my brother isn't looking!"

As Gina got ready for bed, Emmie sent another message. "Can you meet me at Pannie-George's Kitchen on South College for lunch tomorrow at 11?"

~

"An old legal issue took a new twist recently when we learned an appeal had been filed to overturn a verdict that went our way against a certain land developer. What won us that decision was my uncle's filing documents, on advice from our attorneys, officially declaring plans for a future retreat site. The appeal is based on our having done nothing since that time to actually *launch* a retreat. Connelly, the developer, filed his appeal on the Friday afternoon right before spring break, counting on our lawyers' being out of pocket, looking for any angle that could possibly give him the upper hand. He doesn't miss a trick! Truth is, we haven't made much headway in proving we have a retreat. Chalk that up to managerial conflict, I guess. It's difficult to achieve progress when the persons needing to make decisions can't agree." Emmie paused, and a worried expression flitted across her face. "Then, suddenly, you contacted Chip about *wanting* a retreat place, and that has been a needed spark. In fact, the sooner you could get here, the better for us, as my uncle may or may not have mentioned when you called him. I think my Aunt Claire was cooking chicken within the hour for your welcome casserole!" Emmie's smile returned. She pointed at her plate. "Speaking of chicken, isn't this place so good?"

"Yes, amazing! I've eaten at the one in Montgomery a few times. It's near the riverfront." Gina looked down at her selections. "This boiled okra is so tender!"

"And the people who run it are sweet." Emmie turned her head toward the front door, and Gina automatically did the same. The lunch crowd was growing. "Anyway, your arrangement with Uncle Chip happened while my brother was away, and when you met Gabe he had come straight to the cabin from the airport, with his phone not charged and basically everything else going badly. He hadn't checked in with any of us – not that Mother or I would have known to mention you to him in connection with our cabin. That is such a funny coincidence, that you and I met totally apart from the other! Anyway, none of what I'm telling you is an excuse for how my brother acted, but please know that that had mostly to do with a tiring trip, a bad mood, and some troubled water connected with Uncle Chip." Emmie paused to take a long sip of water through her straw. Gina waited, all ears, barely able to concentrate on her meal. She could take leftovers home for later.

"First, Gabe wanted the role of manager before he was really mature enough and experienced enough to take it on. Second, there is the matter of a handshake agreement Uncle Chip made a long time ago, to sell some of the company's land. It has turned into a stressful court battle. Undoubtedly, Silas Connelly has been stewing ever since his verbal agreement with Chip fell through. He wants the land, and he wants it at the price it was *then*."

Gina exclaimed, "Oh! That's awful!"

"Yeah. It hasn't been smooth sailing, to say the least. Gabe was barely out of graduate school and my uncle, who was running things, considered the sale necessary for our financial position. Though he wasn't yet free to put any of his own philosophy into practice, Gabe believed more modern methods and technology would turn the cash flow tide without any loss of land." Gina nodded as Emmie checked her phone and started tidying her plate, plasticware, and trash. "I have to head out shortly for an appointment."

Gina looked at her own phone. Taylor had texted a "have a good day" meme. And Josh had sent some kind of funny video or something. He was probably working up to a more serious conversation, which she dreaded having.

"In Chip's defense, it was his decision to make at the time, and he felt our company would do better with the money than with the land. He didn't even know until very recently that Gabe has been working with a friend in the school of forestry to replace harvested product with longleaf pine plantings on that very tract. Uncle Chip, who is a truly nice man, is sensitive to the fact that Gabe didn't bother to communicate about the plantings. Longleaf is a scarcer commodity that requires more time and effort than other pines. My brother is super diligent about keeping and managing *all* of our acreage, of course. Land is very valuable in this area just now."

Again Gina nodded. "It sounds pretty complicated."

Emmie noted the time again, wound up the conversation, and headed out, promising to be in touch when she knew more. And she didn't keep Gina on pins and needles for long. Late that afternoon, as Gina was moving clothes from the washing machine to the dryer in a miniature laundry space, her phone pinged. "Heads up. You are going to have a caller tomorrow afternoon. And I assure you, you will see a marked change in my brother when he arrives."

~

"Gabe shared his location with me. He should arrive in about eight minutes." That message from Emmie had popped in at exactly 1:41. It was now 1:48. Not that Gina was trying to time her readiness. Or manage her nervousness. She stepped outside. And here her caller was. Bringing flowers, yet! *This should prove interesting.* Gina folded her arms and leaned against one of the center posts on the porch.

Gabe moved as close as he seemed to dare to, given what had happened in this very spot two days ago. "My mother made me bring these." He assumed a rather silly-looking cross between a grin and a grimace.

Gina gave up trying to look however *she'd* been trying to look and held both of her hands out for the vase. "They're very pretty." *Emmie was right. At least, so far. She said I'd see a total turnaround.* The peace offering prompted recall of something Gina must have been impervious to earlier, a quote in her nature-themed journal. She had barely glanced at it, too much on edge to give it any thought. It spoke of flowers having "their heads thrown back to sing." She wished for the boldness and the right opportunity to share a fanciful thought such as that with a certain forestland manager who worked too hard. Right now was not that opportunity. Gina said nothing, but turned and set the vase of mixed blooms on the little table between two ladder-back rocking chairs, all three pieces made of wood similar in shade to the light-colored cabin itself.

"I understand from my family that it's advantageous for us to have you here."

Hmm. Was this Gabe's idea of an apology? Gina nodded, then did her best to look as though she expected a little more.

"And that my sister has given you some backstory as to why that's the case."

"Yes, she has."

"Yeah. Good." He hesitated. "So it seems that if you are willing to let us show you around, and maybe even go so far as to participate in some discussions on making this place an honest-to-goodness retreat site, the authentic nature of your input, as a guest, would give credence to our case."

"I'd be happy to do that." Gabe looked relieved at Gina's answer. "In exchange for…" He stopped looking relieved. "… an apology, maybe?"

Gabe closed his eyes for a moment. His shoulders sagged. "Yes, you're right. I do owe you a large apology, and I hope you'll accept it. Do you have a few minutes? I could show you the finer points of the area and maybe answer any questions you have about the trails or whatever."

"Sure," Gina answered. "My time is my own. For the moment, at least."

"Good. Okay." Gabe sighed. Not moving from where he stood, just off the porch, he gestured. "Well, your cabin here is right at 500 square feet plus the decking. It's intentionally a one-person residence, for the odd occasion...at least, until now." He looked at Gina then, but she was slightly distracted, marveling at the fact that he had just said 'your' cabin! "And it makes for a little nicer 'necessary' stop on a workday than a porta-toilet does."

"I imagine so. And that is especially true now, with my Glade automatic freshener plugged in, Cashmere Woods scent. I figured that was an appropriate choice." Gina's mention of this nicety earned her a wary glance through narrowed eyes.

"The clearing is roughly a fifth of an acre. I assume you're already familiar with the cabin's motion-sensor lights, keypad lock, deadbolt, and security alarm, since you've been living here, what, a week? Of course, all of the surrounding woodland is securely fenced and gated. Shall we go inside?" Obviously, he wanted to move through this obligation as fast as possible. Or else he was nervous.

"Fine."

Gabe's unrehearsed tour of the cabin's interior wasn't

likely to reveal anything Gina hadn't been told at check-in or discovered on her own, but it did hold a surprise for her reluctant companion right away. He spotted her temporary wall hanging, pointed at it, and frowned. "What's that?"

Gina shrugged nonchalantly. "Just a piece of fabric I carefully put up with four tiny sewing pins. The place needed an accent wall."

Gabe stared at the colorful cloth. Finally, he moved toward the kitchen, sounding a tad defensive as he said the place hadn't been conceived as a bed and breakfast.

"No, I'm sure that's true. But I can't see any harm in making a few little improvements."

Gabe looked at Gina and opened his mouth as though to retort, but he appeared to think better of it. "Noted."

Things definitely were still touchy! And that apology he had acknowledged owing hadn't been issued yet. Gina forged ahead, telling Gabe that no guest information document had been provided to her, and that she thought one should be developed without delay. "If my understanding is correct, you're building a dossier of evidence that this is really going to happen." He nodded solemnly. "Before I started my retreat, I looked at several websites on how to do that. I'm sure you can find ready information on how to *create* one. That might jump-start things for you."

"Right. Good thought." Gabe looked at Gina a moment, then walked into the combination bedroom and office. From a drawer of the desk he took a legal pad and a pen, then sat and wrote, narrating for Gina's benefit. "Decorative touches." He paused. "Within reason. And guest info. What else?"

"I've actually started a list of what might go in a guest information list or policy for this place, from how to operate the coffee pot to where the extra bed linens are, to how long it usually takes the water to run hot and what to do with your garbage when the can gets full. It could be a useful starting point if you're interested in having it."

Gabe nodded. "I'd appreciate it."

"Fine. I can airdrop it to you right now."

"Okay."

That handled, they stepped outside, and Gabe mentioned a few more facts including the cabin's age, the direction and distance from this clearing to the nearest work road, and the length of the circular trail Gina had already discovered and had been using for her frequent walks. They gravitated in that direction, Gina explaining about the bits of cloth she had tied to branches at intervals to mark her way. The legal pad in his grip, Gabe took the pen from behind his ear. Gina watched him add "VISIBLE TRAIL MARKINGS" in neat, all-cap letters.

As they kept walking, their pace gradually slowed. Gabe pointed to some of the trees and informed Gina that pine, hickory, and oak dominated the area, but pine was planted as the primary species for harvesting.

"This is a beautiful place," she replied. "And I've noticed virtually no litter, which is even better."

Gabe's quick answer, that there had better not be any *virtually* about it, seemed full of bridled outrage. "I have a strict policy about that on this land." Gina could sense the stress he apparently was never out from under.

"For the record, I'm sorry about the hoops you're having to jump through on this. I'm sure it must feel a great intrusion to suddenly have to be thinking of your own, private land being opened up to guests." *Guests who might litter?*

Gabe stopped short and stayed silent for a few moments. "Well, there is one voice in the company management to whom the scenario you just described isn't all that unwelcome."

Was that a reference to his uncle? Looking at Gabe, Gina suddenly noticed the color of his eyes. She quickly moved her gaze elsewhere, sort of to his shoulder and sort of to the trees beyond it. "Whose voice do you mean?"

"My mother's. To use a portion of our land as some kind of benevolent outreach, with a community or an educational function – whatever you might call it – has been a dream of hers for years."

"That doesn't surprise me at all, of her. You know, Gabe, you don't often spend an evening with someone in their home without getting a fair glimpse into what drives them; what kind of person they are."

Eyes averted, he nodded. "This dream I think she had hoped to talk my father into, but that never happened."

Gina murmured, and Gabe continued, "She doesn't take it lightly, references to sharing one's bounty with the stranger and the foreigner, nor the fact that everything on the earth belongs to the Lord. That woman knows her Bible."

"She could have spoken of these wishes on Monday night when I had supper with her and Emmie. My comments on what I hope to gain here would have been the perfect opening. But she didn't. And I suspect that had less to do with her passion and more to do with patience and sensitivity. She gave me plenty of opportunity to talk about myself and didn't try to monopolize the conversation. Your sister is the picture of tact, too." Gina paused, then added gently, "And I can tell you something else."

"What's that?"

"Your mother and your sister care an awful lot about *you.*"

The silence hung there until it became awkward. They resumed their stroll. "At any rate, to summarize, your being here is a convenient 'test guest' situation. I hope that term doesn't bother you. My mother would say our need and your need converging this way was a divine appointment. That being the case, we want you to have a good experience."

Gina smiled. This was a great moment for a segue. Would Gabe see it?

"To that end, will you please accept my humble apology for the other day? I had no business acting the way I did. I have no excuse. A lot of reasons I could give, but they don't justify my behavior. I'm truly sorry. To tell you the truth, I'll probably spend the rest of my life trying to live down the reputation of being a hothead. I wish I could say those blowups are all in my past. Clearly, they are not."

Gina was touched! "That was a beautiful apology. And I'd be an awful person not to accept it, especially given the fact that I said some pretty unkind things to you, too."

"But I started it."

"Yes, you did," Gina smiled, "but the funny thing, though it's really not *funny,* is that I wish I had enough courage to *act* like a hothead more often. I've always been afraid to speak up when I maybe should. You know, too timid to stand up for myself."

Gabe stopped walking and turned toward Gina, who stopped, also. He looked utterly puzzled. "Uh…that's a *problem* for you? Are you sure of that? Hmm." He angled his head the other way. "Because…you weren't doing too badly the other day, from where I stood."

Gina looked down, embarrassed, but smiling.

"I shudder to think what you could achieve if you were really on your game!" Now, he had her laughing. He actually set his hand on her arm! "Promise me – you won't go enrolling in any classes on how to stand up for yourself?"

Gina shook her head. "I won't," she tried to say, cracking up even more.

Gabe started out again, and Gina fell in step beside him. He kicked at a length of fallen limb on the trail and muttered, "You could *teach* classes." Now, Gina almost had to hold her sides.

"Oh, yeah." Gabe sounded serious again. "We haven't talked about the little lake and the canoes. Off that way." He pointed.

"You have that? Good. That's something I need to cover." He looked at her oddly. *Oops.* "I – I mean, it's something I would want to do." She had to keep her guard up! No matter that they were getting better acquainted; she was still working undercover. The owners were calling her a test guest, asking for her feedback, and even considering her somewhat of an answered prayer. They had no idea she was already filling the test guest role for somebody else, for pay. And they'd better not find out.

By now, Gabe and Gina had covered the entire loop and were back in the clearing. She said, "I could see the other day that you felt really protective of your beautiful memory bench, and I'm sorry the way I was using it offended you."

"No need to apologize. In fact," he laughed a little, "I admit that how you were interacting with that inanimate object helps me get this whole retreat notion visualized in a way that's not just impersonal plans on paper; not just a sterile report for the court to assess." He moved toward the cabin's entrance, and she followed behind him. "If you like, I'll take my clothes out of your way now."

"Whatever you want." They entered the cabin, and Gabe went straight to the desk to leave his supplies except for the top sheet of paper, which he tore off, folded, and pushed into a back pocket of his jeans. Gina wondered whether he would notice what she'd done to his blue flannel shirt and to his camo jacket.

He noticed, practically as soon as he had pulled eight or ten hangers from the closet. "Oh." He looked at her, then at the clothes again, and back at her. "Uh, it appears some rips have been mended. I imagine I have you to thank for that. Mother and Emmie have been telling me you sew like a dream."

Gina nodded, too honest to deny that fact. Then she smiled. "You're welcome." *What else has his family been saying about me?*

Outside, Gabe seemed reserved. "I'll see you."

"See you."

A few steps out, he stopped and turned. "Thanks for the mending, Gina." He soon disappeared into the trees.

On the porch, Gina sat down slowly, looking at the vase. She reached to gently touch the petals of sunflowers and roses. She must remember to thank Gabe's *mother* for these. She shook her head. At least the brown-eyed deliverer of them had finally called her by her name!

Chapter 5

Saturday, October 16. I don't know what I thought this job was going to be like, but what it is like is not what I would have thought. I guess, for anybody, a retreat (real or fake) takes them to new surroundings which may or may not include new people and new thinking, but

Gina stopped writing in the middle of her sentence. It wasn't easy to jot down a summary of what she was feeling and imagining. Not every retreat site was going to have a host like Gabe Madison. If it did, there surely would be a sudden spike in the number of young women signing up! Add to that the extraordinarily nice people in his family: first of all, Emmie, whose invitation to coffee and shopping around town today might be an add-on to her brother's attempt at making amends; Mrs. Madison, who had had somebody bring over a little bundle of zucchini-cinnamon muffins after the dinner hour last night, and Emmie had told Gina in a text message to go look for them on the front porch; Uncle Chip and his wife, as caring as the others, but evidently preferring to stay in the background. The people at Three Points in Montgomery, who had hired Gina, knew nothing of particulars here, and they probably never would. They must hire dozens of people and assign them to go all over the place to hotels, restaurants, spas, and grocery stores. It was just routine work to them, checking boxes and routing piles of numerical ratings to company execs or consulting firms who would plug them into their slide presentations and spreadsheets.

Sitting cross-legged on the bed with her hair in a towel, Gina rotated her neck a bit and looked toward the office nook where a double window on the front wall of the cabin showed the prospect of a slightly iffy weather day. If the Madisons were serious about hosting more guests, even building additional cabins for couples or families or small groups, and if they dealt with all of those guests as kindly as they were treating her, they would have something very special. According to Gabe, that type of situation was what his mother had long wanted.

Half of a muffin last night was Gina's only sample of that food gift fresh from the happy Madison kitchen. She had been saving up carb indulgence for this morning. Emmie had specifically raved over the huge and decadent cinnamon rolls at the place where Gina planned to meet her in what now was less than an hour.

The open journal needed closure. "New people and new thinking" was the last thing on the page. There was one "old" person Gina needed to do some new thinking about, and, in the back of her mind, she had already decided the conclusion of that thinking. Former boyfriend Josh had never quite gone out of the picture, and the vagueness of that relationship status was part of Gina's current unrest. Possibly, the part that had most influenced her decision to seek this job.

~

The rich greens and golds and turquoises inside The Bean's large space had Gina almost too distracted to think on what kind of coffee to order along with her cinnamon roll. "This place is cute!" Plenty of students and regular townspeople must think so, too, judging by the long line between the door and the bakery case.

Emmie ordered after Gina did, then carried the silver stand holding their number. They chose a square table on the end of the coffee shop that faced a side street. By the windows stood an old media cabinet with antique record albums on top of it. Sofas and easy chairs with crocheted or knitted afghans draped over them made groupings in the front and back corners, along with mid-century modern coffee tables. On the other end, beyond the bakery case, a bookshelf held a collection of boxed games. "I've never actually seen anybody playing cards or Rack-O, but I guess it could happen," Emmie told Gina. "It's nice they have a space for it."

"Fun. And I guess some of these old-fashioned knick-knacks on display are a teaser for this great antique mall you're taking me to?"

Emmie nodded as two cinnamon rolls were delivered to their table, each on a white serving plate. The generous icing was practically pooling. Real flatware forks were provided. "Wow!" Gina stared at her plate. Her "Fall in a Mug" latté tasted good and very sweet. "Lots of sugar to fuel our shopping!"

After asking a blessing over the food, Emmie said, "Angel's Antiques is so massive I'm not sure we can even cover all of the booths in a single visit. But it's arranged so you can pretty much see and pick the kinds of stuff you want to look at, skipping glass goblets and baseball cards and kids' toys if those aren't on your radar. As for me, I'm on the lookout for something appropriate and priced right that I can buy enough of to give to my students right before Halloween.

It's not antiques exclusively. There are stalls with all kinds of handmade craft items."

~

Angel's was a huge retail space whose hundreds of booths held small appliances, dishware, jewelry, books, repainted furniture, ready-to-hang porch swings, decorative signs reading WELCOME or any number of orange and blue "spirit" phrases for Auburn fans, Christmas stockings made from old quilts, and much more. Gravitating to some huge shelves along the back wall, Gina zeroed in on a book of sewing methods and looked for the publication date. It was 1972. She dropped it into her cloth shopping bag, one of two that Emmie had brought along. A much newer book, larger and thinner and more colorful, offered a number of little craft sewing ideas. It sparked a thought, and she asked Emmie, whose shopping bag was almost empty, how many student gifts she needed. One thing led to another.

"That would be so great!" Emmie gushed. "Would you really do that for me?"

"Sure! I can polish off the little bags for you in as many autumn cotton prints as you find, and I want to look at Halloween costume patterns, anyway. All you will have to do is decide what treats to put inside the bags."

"Perfect!" Emmie gave Gina a little side hug. "Thank you!"

Gina's gaze roamed again. "Don't you love looking at old books?" She reached for a volume on architecture because it brought her father to mind. Not that he'd been an architect. A wave of sadness swept in. She looked at Emmie – sweet, sympathetic "Mary Elizabeth," named on a Christmas Eve years before she had even existed, named by parents who surely had had no idea they wouldn't be growing old together.

"Books of a certain time period draw me," Gina said, "I guess because they show what was going on in the world when my dad was around." Emmie nodded. And waited. "It occurs to me just now that I am almost as old as he was when he died." Gina shook her head. "Hard to believe."

"What happened to him, Gina?"

"Construction accident, when I was three." The noisy antique mall seemed far away now. The setting might as easily have been a deserted beach or the inside of a car as the two who had experienced a very similar loss looked at one another. "How old were *you?*"

"Twelve."

"How did he die?"

"Heart."

Gina gave an expression of regret. "How did you manage?"

Emmie looked to the side. "I remember a lot of talk about being thankful for what we'd had for as long as we did, and I remember...well, not exactly pretending he was still with us, but knowing his life mattered and would always stand for things that lived on in the rest of us. I know my mother said things like that a lot in the beginning. We sit down every so often and look at pictures and say how we all still love him. Mother and I, mainly. Gabe feels his way of honoring Dad is in the work he does. Less nostalgia in his case, and more focus on succeeding."

~

Emmie's phone rang as she was pointing to some of the fabric bolts on a featured table where autumn décor and costume patterns – some of the costumes made up and suspended from plastic chains – begged customers to literally buy into the season. "Hello?"

Gina stepped away to let Emmie field her call. She opened a pattern book and soon came across something that ought to be easy to put together. She could make the hat as given, then mimic the rest using leggings and other regular clothes from Target or wherever, and wear her fall boots.

Emmie came over, stowing her phone. "Mother needs us to find some stuff for her while we're here. Grosgrain ribbon in brown and orange, and a new measuring tape. You'll probably find those faster than I would, even though this is Hobby Lobby and not JOANN. When I told Mother you're going to sew bags for me, she said she'd love to have you over on Monday. You can try her old Singer that she says runs better than any newer model. After all, this project of mine ought rightly to be putting wear and tear on our machine instead of yours. Y'all could visit while she does her weekly ironing, and she'll make tea and show you around the house a little more, and all of that good stuff. If you're interested."

Gina nodded. "That's so nice. I'd like that. I'm so used to my portable machine, but to have a real, permanent workstation...yeah!" And the Madisons' house, too, with its large rooms!

At the checkout, Gina's phone, debit card, hand sanitizer, purchase receipt, and shopping bag proved too much for her to manage successfully. It was the phone that went down this time. "Uggh. Trying to hold too many things at once is a habit I wish I could break. If it's not that, I'm setting my phone down somewhere and then not remembering where it is. You wouldn't think so, would you, when this purse has convenient pockets for everything?"

Emmie laughed. "Operator error?"

"Exactly."

They zipped through Whataburger for a milkshake, getting the Auburn game on radio just in time to hear a touchdown take Arkansas up 17-14. "Uggh," Emmie groaned. "Come on, Tigers!" They headed back toward Auburn on Frederick Road, passing Jim Bob's, the place they had lunched after the antiques marathon. At Kroger, Emmie parked near Gina's Ford Escape, left there after breakfast. "Sometime, I'll drive you a couple of routes where the better sidewalks are. Nothing against the woods, but if you would rather walk on solid pavement for a change..."

~

Stepping across the threshold for her second visit to the big, white house, Gina's first impression was of something sweet baking in the oven. Mrs. Madison identified it as a cinnamon-pecan coffee cake they would have along with "a little fruit and some ham salad to make a nice brunch." Saying she would need Gina to help her keep an ear out for the kitchen timer, she led the way through open French doors to a room she described as having never been a dining room because they'd always used it for their office.

"Oh, I brought you a little something." Gina took her purse and a separate tote bag of sewing materials off her shoulder and reached into the latter, presenting her gift unwrapped. "For being so nice to me. It's a glasses case. I hope you can use it." Mrs. Madison exclaimed over the bound-edged, padded eyeglasses case in a cotton print of small gold, orange, and red leaves on an off-white background. "I had some extra fabric after cutting out Emmie's bags yesterday." She watched the recipient turn the item over in her hands. Gina was proud of the attractive accessory, though with her expertise it hadn't taken her half an hour to make it. Besides having the extra fabric, the supplies purchased for her Halloween costume had given her a spare length of fleece batting for the required thickness. The bias tape edging made from the project fabric was a breeze to turn out with that handy secret weapon, a metal gadget that cleverly made three ready-to-press folds when you ran your strip of diagonally cut cloth in one end and pulled it out the other. Pressing on the go sometimes posed a challenge, but her mini steam iron and a piece of fabric placed on top of a folded bath towel had sufficed.

"I assure you this will be used well, and cherished. I always have more pairs of reading glasses than I can keep up with, none of them protected by anything as pretty as this." Mrs. Madison set the case on the front area of a large desk which also appeared to be used well, judging from the piles of file folders amid a clutter of ballpoint pens, color print material, three-ring binders, and somewhat a monstrosity of a hole punch device. Still, the edges and corners of the work surface showed a mild accumulation of dust.

"This office is for your timber operation, I guess?" Gina ventured, hoping she wasn't being nosy. She had never seen a home office for a family-run business before.

"Yes, although what you see represents more the history of management – somewhat – than the basis of current work. My son tends to be more paperless and mobile. He accesses this office but little, preferring to work in his room, or out on the land, or in the cabin." She pointed toward some shelves. "All of these industry journals would already be in a dumpster if Gabe didn't show enough respect to simply ignore them. To him, they represent the old ways, not just of disseminating information, but of forest management." Gina looked at the rows of periodicals whose spines were about three-eighths-inch wide. (With so much experience measuring seam allowances, she knew widths at a glance!) A series of journals with tan covers had a title that was something about "wildlife conference;" another set, white, dealt with soil; and another, with beige covers, concerned weed science. There was a lot to know if you were seriously growing timber! Gina stepped closer to look at some kind of antique tool mounted in a glass-front display case on the wall above the bookshelves. The implement resembled a hatchet, but the engraved plate identified it as a tree planting spade for a crawler tractor, dating from the late 1940s.

"Chip and I are gradually working through these periodicals to capture and save the articles he or I find valuable so we can go ahead and dispose of the rest before our children find themselves burdened with that chore. Not to mention folders full of printed e-mails. Like my brother, I am very much interested in the family business, and I try to make a contribution when and how I can." Mrs. Madison made sure she had Gina's eye. "By the way, we haven't brought attention to what records management we are doing in here because we don't want Gabe getting his hopes up that it will happen quickly. And, to be blunt, also because my brother feels it is better to keep a low profile where my son is concerned."

Gina nodded solemnly. "I've heard the basics about your troublesome land deal, if that's what you mean."

"Yes, that is a large part of it, but there is more. Gabe waited a lot of impatient years to assume the lead role, and he felt excluded much of that time, when it is possible he could have been invited to learn by participating, to a gradually increasing degree, as he got older. Gabe feels that certain professional organizations are the ones where our membership dollars should go, versus some of those that his uncle considered more advantageous or more personally fulfilling. The two of them haven't reached the point of civil conversations on such topics. Plain talk apart from one's baggage doesn't come easy for some, whether young or old. This matter with Silas Connelly has put a pretty big rift between my son and my brother. Gabe blames Chip for having promised Silas he could buy the land from us, for how stressful it was to get the verbal contract nullified after Silas began pressing for his rights, and for what we have to do now to meet the court's conditions.

"Chip is rather an academic, and Gabe is more aggressive about methods and science. My brother would justify a pilgrimage to the great Northwest just to see a lodgepole pine, even though such a trip might not directly benefit the business here. Gabe uses apps, video meetings, text messaging, downloads, and e-signatures on contracts. His uncle still prefers conferences, print materials, phone calls, lunch meetings, and handshakes. In one colossal case, a *regretted* handshake. As it happens, my brother and Silas Connelly were friends once upon a time." Mrs. Madison shrugged. Clearly, the woman did have her worries in spite of the angelic and serene image Gina had been building up, so different from how she saw her own mother. And there went the kitchen timer.

As Mrs. Madison silenced the alert, Gina washed her hands with a beautifully crafted soap that had tan, brown, and army green swirls in it. "This smells wonderful!" Mrs. Madison told her the soap was made locally and had the scent name Cedar & Clove. Gina said the colors reminded her of the woods. "Camouflage, you know?"

Over the food and hot, spiced punch, Gina surveyed the kitchen as she had done during her first visit. This time, though, she wasn't noticing layout, colors, and items so much. She was thinking of what must be many happy times this family had spent in here, and probably in the living room, too, where open piano books suggested that somebody actually played sometimes. But they had had sad moments, too. In Gina's family, her mother had borne the burden of loss mostly alone, and Gina had grown up not knowing family life to have been different at an earlier time.

"How did the cake turn out?"

Suddenly afraid she had been lost in thought too long, Gina answered, "It's delicious! This is such a treat! I guess you find a lot to do, between kitchen time and office time and ironing...and music?"

Mrs. Madison smiled broadly. She was pretty, like Emmie, whose face had the same square shape. The medium-length hair might have color on it. It wasn't exactly blonde, or brown, or gray. "Yes, I have a variety of chores and pleasures, enough to make life interesting. But I don't keep house all day, every day. I have church, exercise classes, and I also volunteer at the Kreher Preserve and Nature Center a few times a month. But my heart is here, at the hub where family life and business life used to be more consistent and more harmonious. At least, it seemed that way to me. My husband and my brother managed the company, and I managed the home. The children had their school lives, and our little ship of status quo sailed along. But then Frank passed." Mrs. Madison sipped her punch for a moment. "Chip took the reins then, while Gabe grew up and finished his education. Over time, a difference in managerial priorities and in basic personality has driven my brother and my son apart. As you might imagine, I want that situation resolved."

Gina nodded.

"You're a good listener, Gina. Now, how would you like to put my marvelous antique machine through its paces? I will do my ironing, and we can chat, or just each do our own thinking."

Upstairs, an oversized landing opened to the family bedrooms and bath. The room of destination, very large and with bright, white walls, featured a four-poster bed and night tables in the far end. Nearer the entrance stood an antique wood and marble washstand Mrs. Madison said was curly maple, and, still nearer, the setup for sewing and ironing.

"I pull these holiday tablecloths out every year to wash and iron them ahead of time so there is less work to do once everyone is gathering in for the food side of the preparations. And it seems my pile of regular Monday ironing never gets smaller." She nodded toward a basket where skirts, shirts, and pillowcases were neatly stacked. "Have a seat and let me know whether you need help finding any of the controls. It is so good of you to offer to do this project for my daughter. I hope the bunch of us aren't imposing too much. We just really enjoy having you around!"

Gina smiled and started pulling her supplies out, seating herself gently on a padded, rectangular stool. "It looks as though somebody already has the perfect thread loaded. How did that happen?" The answer was that Emmie might have mentioned what color thread Gina planned to use on all of the several cotton prints which had similar oranges and rusts and greens in them.

"And you aren't imposing on me, Mrs. Madison." Gina answered the earlier comment with her eyes down as she expertly judged the depth of the casing she was folding and pinning. "After years of apartment living, with multiple roommates, I am loving these bigger spaces and new people to talk to. It's as if I woke up suddenly in the middle of a family life I never had before. I'm probably imposing on *y'all.*" She raised her eyes to find Mrs. Madison shaking her head "no." Gina resumed her task. "We lost my dad when I was only three, and I don't think my mother has ever gotten over it, the way you seem to have." Gina faltered and lifted her hands from her work. "I mean, I'm sure you miss your husband and of course you wish it hadn't happened, but..." No, that wasn't any better. She looked at Mrs. Madison, then lowered her head again, embarrassed. "I'm sorry. I shouldn't be rambling this way about something so personal." *Me and my big mouth!*

Mrs. Madison set her iron upright and told Gina about the grief support she found in the early days, and how God can gradually fill painful voids with new sources of joy "if we have eyes of faith to recognize them." She lifted a forest green tablecloth from the ironing board and began folding it in thirds, lengthwise. "By the way, my brother certainly could have phoned Gabe to alert him concerning you, but obviously he did not. Nor did he let *me* know of the arrangement. Possibly he'd intended to do both, but something prevented him. The cabin is used sporadically, and Chip couldn't necessarily have foreseen that Gabe would have discovered you there before some discussion had happened among us about the sudden availability of a retreat guest. Regardless, I am very sorry about my son's rudeness toward you."

Gina laughed. "You heard about that?"

"Oh, yes, during supper last Wednesday night. And, knowing my son, Emmie and I were given only a summary version, and likely a cleaned-up one. Someday, I would love to hear *your* side." She grinned. "Anyway, I'm glad you children worked it out."

Gina bent her head and folded a long rectangle right sides together, its upper edges already neatly sewn into a split casing. She smiled to herself at the old-fashioned language. *"You children."* It actually sounded sweet, the way it had been said. She and her hostess each kept working, and silence prevailed for a while, except for the rhythmic stitching of the sewing machine and bursts of steam from the iron.

"Oh!" With a straight pin inserted halfway into her fabric, Gina stopped and looked up. "I'm not sure whether Gabe was being serious or not, that you made him bring me those flowers, but I wanted to thank you. They are beautiful." Mrs. Madison simply smiled, and Gina continued pinning a bag's side seams. "I get the impression that the three of you typically stay in fairly close communication."

"Yes, we do, at least on easier topics, and I'm so grateful for that. It's wonderful to have both children close at hand."

"I imagine so." Gina engaged the foot pedal, and the old machine's motor gave off its particular hum, its version of what long had been, for her, a comforting and satisfying sound. "I honestly don't know how rare that is, but I do know it's not the case in every family."

"Undoubtedly, it is a result of having lost their father when we did. Naturally, we have had our rough patches, but all in all we have rallied together."

A door opened and closed downstairs. "Mother? It's me." Footsteps and other sounds said Gabe was probably dropping lunch or coffee things off in the kitchen. And washing his hands.

"My, where has the time gone?" His mother smiled at Gina. Gina couldn't exactly reciprocate, and she knew why. She kept sewing, trying to hold her fingers steady.

Calling ahead as he ascended the stairs, Gabe told his mother he was going to grab a shower and go catch the Bills and Titans game with "the guys." Gina pressed the foot pedal a little harder. When the footsteps stopped at the doorway, Gina's sewing ceased. Gabe was looking directly at his mother, seeming to know exactly where she would be, there at her Monday ironing. "Hey."

As Mrs. Madison answered, Gabe caught sight of Gina, and their eyes held for several seconds.

"Gina," the mother's voice broke in, "I've been meaning all afternoon to invite you to our Madison family night. We gather on a Sunday evening once a quarter and have an old-fashioned time with food, a Scrabble game more often than not, and ice cream, which – this time of year – will probably have some warm bread pudding under it."

Gabe closed his eyes and clapped a hand to his forehead. "Ah, she attempts to lure another victim into our unique ritual! Be strong, Gina."

His mother laughed. "Just for that, *you* will be the one to sit out of the first round of Scrabble."

"I'll survive, Mother. I'll survive."

Mrs. Madison sobered and told Gina the date and the time. "I hope you will be able to join us. With Dillon, there will be five. This tradition comes from my parents, and I have refused to give it up. It's the authentic deal, complete with the reading of a Bible story."

"And singing, if you can believe that."

"Singing that will be accompanied by guitar this time."

Still seated at the sewing machine and watching, Gina caught a meaningful look passing between mother and son. It seemed the mother had just barked an order! "All done." Gina ran the spool and bobbin threads over the cutter blade and showed off a finished bag. In truth, she was all done with that bag and several more, but not with all of them. The remaining few she would sew on her own machine. In view of everything, it was time for her to move on. "I'll show Emmie how to run two separate ribbons opposite ways through the casing, although she probably already knows that's how it's done."

"I doubt it." The brotherly jab was delivered drily.

"I'm going to tell her you said that." Gina gave Gabe a slightly saucy look, then quickly lowered her eyes. *Good grief!* What was she doing? She said toward his mother, "I've really enjoyed myself. And your machine. How it purrs!" *Rambling awkwardly.* She repacked her tote bag, which also held the green felt, green thread, and new pattern still in its envelope. "Would you let me come back another time to work on my Halloween costume?"

"Nothing would please me more, Dear. Whenever you need to, morning, afternoon, or evening."

Gina carefully lowered the presser foot onto the square of woven blue fabric that had been there at the start. She turned the wheel until the needle's tip was down in the fabric, out of sight and unable to scratch any unwary hand that might wander by. She gathered her things and stood.

"Son, I must place these linens very carefully over hangers, to minimize the wrinkling between now and when we will need them. Would you mind seeing Gina out?"

Gina's pulse rate elevated even though there was no reason for it to do so, Gabe's having been put up to this escort task by his mother, same as why he'd brought flowers on Friday. Halfway down the stairs, she said the only thing she could think of, which was that she hoped he would enjoy watching the football game.

"Thanks. I'm sure we will, aided by cornhole and fajitas." Gabe opened the front door and turned toward Gina. "From what I can tell, you've made my mother a happy woman for the last little while. Thanks for spending time with her."

"It was time well spent. I mean it."

Gabe smiled down at her. This was the closest they'd ever stood to one another. "Look, I remember what you said about getting out in a canoe. Would you want to do that this Saturday? With me, I mean?"

Gina's heart began beating faster again, this time for good reason.

Chapter 6

Wednesday, October 20. I met Gabe Madison one week ago today. His mother clearly has shown signs that could be interpreted as an effort to nudge him and me together. More on that later…??

Got my Halloween costume hat made yesterday afternoon at the family home, mainly in order to use the iron and ironing board there. Tried the whole outfit on, here in the cabin, and snapped some selfies to share with Taylor and folks. If the pattern is still for sale a year from now, I'll offer my hat to the store as a display model. Did a little armchair research on canoe outings; watched video of people stepping in and out without tipping; learned what gunwales are (pronounced "gunnels").

This was a weird experience: Kristyl at Three Points texted me three days ago requesting a status meeting yesterday, which I assumed would mean a quick trip home, and that had me thinking I might go see Mom and possibly also pop in at the store.

No way could this whole account go into the journal without writer's cramp. Gina closed the book and took her commuter water bottle into the kitchen to fill it. Outside, she set the bottle on the ground next to the memorial bench and pushed against the apparatus for some mild resistance while stretching. *Apparatus.* Thinking of the bench by that term brought to mind the first impression she'd made on Gabe. Smiling, she picked up her water bottle and headed down the loop trail.

It wasn't only the mistaken expectation of a trip home that had started Gina visualizing her next visit with her mother. It was different things Mrs. Madison had said, which had led unavoidably to comparing the two women. And it was… just thoughts about – how had Emmie put it on Saturday? – being thankful for having had a dad even for a short time. How much bravery would it take to tell Mom any of this? Of course, none of it had mattered on Tuesday because the status meeting wasn't in Montgomery. Reuben and Kristyl had to be in Auburn for other interviews, looking to recruit students for short-term things during Christmas break, similar to what Gina was doing. So she had met with them at that large university hotel in a first-floor conference room. Reuben and Kristyl had sat behind a narrow table with Gina in a chair facing them. The first time she had met them, all three, plus that other man, had sat at the same table.

Maybe some of those other interviews this week hadn't gone so well, or maybe Gina had been enjoying the company of her host family so much that, by comparison, her employer and his assistant hadn't come across very friendly yesterday. Kristyl had seemed stressed and distracted. Picturing the woman, Gina suddenly halted on the trail, frowning. At Angel's Antiques on Saturday she had seen another shopper at a distance that had reminded her of Kristyl Floyd. *Hmm.* Maybe it had been her. Since she was in town on business soon after, that could make sense. As for Reuben – Gina started walking again – during the original interview he had smiled a lot, but not this time. On Tuesday his questions had been a bit odd, and he had been more intense. He hadn't mentioned the ratings at all; hadn't asked Gina to give a preliminary report on things like cleanliness, accessibility, and value for the cost. Instead, Reuben had asked more than once whether the owners seemed to suspect her of duplicity, and also whether she had been spending more time indoors than out. What was up with that? Did they think she had gained weight? Did she look paler than last time? Gina took a deep breath and released it in an utterance of perplexity as the clearing came into view.

~

"You know, don't you, that outdoor recreation in areas like this was frowned upon, back in the day, by some who didn't want the pristine land trampled on unnecessarily?" Gina glanced at Gabe as he escorted her toward the lake.

"Sorry? You want to run that by me again?"

Maybe he wasn't quite awake yet. Or maybe he had stuff on his mind, such as what the two of them might talk about while out on the water. This outing had been his suggestion, after all. The pressure was on him. She repeated her statement, adding, "But the eloquent rebuttal to that view goes something like this: 'Don't look at recreation development as building roads into lovely country, but as building receptivity into small, unlovely human minds.' How's that for a nicely phrased quote on this spectacular autumn day?" If Gabe *weren't* quite awake yet, her perky chattiness and its deep subject matter might not be landing. Yeah, based on this extended silence...

"And here I was thinking we would discuss SEC football rankings." Gabe looked at Gina curiously. "Where did you run across that bit of wisdom? And yes, it's very nicely put."

Pay dirt. "Your mother let me borrow a few of the industry journals in your company office. You know, the not-dining room?" Her goal was to share something relevant from the material Gabe apparently considered nothing other than future recycling. "One Aldo Leopold wrote that. He died in 1948. And a younger man not quite his contemporary said outdoor recreation plants the seed of nature conservation. I think he meant that if you don't get people outdoors for fun and exercise to begin with, how are they going to appreciate how important it is to preserve the forests and streams and all?"

"Gina Wright, nature philosopher extraordinaire," Gabe remarked mildly. "Is she going to step into a canoe as planned, or will she stand on the shore of the lake and deliver oratory? Inquiring minds want to know."

Gina laughed. "Oh, I'll be getting into a canoe. But don't you just love old books? I do." Lest her strategy be too obvious, she added, "Emmie and I browsed a number of them at the antique mall last weekend."

Downhill they trekked. Ahead, through the trees, Gina could see the colorful canoes stored upside down. After that strange status meeting on Tuesday, she had wandered this way to unwind and to get her bearings so that nothing today would be needlessly unfamiliar. Gabe told her he'd heard good reports of last night's Halloween event at the nature preserve. Gina couldn't resist telling him her Robin Hood costume had gotten its share of compliments. "Of course, it was attended mostly by parents and grandparents with little kids. But I learned as much as any of them about animal behavior, thanks to presentations by costumed teenagers stationed along the trail."

Gina cut her account short and hurried to help Gabe lift the red canoe he had hold of. Following his lead with little verbal instruction necessary, she got her paddle and life vest. From there, his clear directions soon had them in the vessel, away from the low dock, and out on the lake.

"Are these solid wood?" Gina used a fingernail to tap her paddle near its handle. As Gabe was starting to answer the question, her phone broke in and interrupted him. "I'm sorry." She canceled the "Redo toenail polish" alarm and put the phone back into the waterproof caddy belt around her waist. She twisted her body and sent an apologetic look toward the lead paddler.

"Yeah. So, yes, they are solid wood. Hardwood. Made locally." He smiled. "Wood's a handy commodity, you know."

Gina smiled back, nodding, then faced front again. She dutifully paddled on whatever side Gabe told her to, and the canoe glided smoothly toward the middle of the water.

"Could you ski on this lake?"

Gabe laughed gently. "No, probably not. Regardless, we prefer man-powered, quiet watercraft here."

Perversely on cue, Gina's phone gave off another alarm, a "Wake up right now!" sound with notes of sci-fi. "Oh, goodness!" She got it squelched and immediately honored the polite suggestion that she might put silent mode on.

"I do like to ski, though," Gabe volunteered. "My college crowd used to go on the Alabama in your neck of the woods. Which, come to think of it," he paused, "was when I probably should have been at home paying attention to business matters."

Gina turned and looked at him, taking care not to rock the canoe. He had stopped paddling. "Gabe." She watched his shoulders sag slightly. "Please don't do that." She deliberately softened her expression almost into a smile. "I'm sure it is easy now to second-guess, to look back and doubt the value of fully immersing yourself in college life. But don't forget that having done things differently then might only have brought you a different set of regrets now."

Gabe seemed to consider her words, nodding his head

a couple of times. He lifted his oar entirely out of the water and laid it across his lap. "Tell me something, Gina. How did you happen to reach out to my uncle? That's something I've been wondering. He and I did have a conversation about it – well into the process, as you know. But that's a point we didn't cover."

Gina nodded. She imagined that Gabe, tired and distraught that Wednesday, had not felt like engaging in a long discussion with his uncle. *Calm, now...* She had been carefully coached for this moment! She rotated her shoulders to indicate that she needed to get more comfortable after having her upper body turned the way it was, and that provided the perfect excuse for facing front again so Gabe couldn't see her uneasiness. She pulled her paddle out of the water as he had done. "Um...I, uh, I did some looking online at places to go, and I started noticing a common denominator in photos and stuff. Basically, it seemed the deeper one could get into the trees, the better." *Careful!* She'd fallen into ad-libbing, as per usual. "Um, so, to me, the obvious step was to phone the AFA office over near the Capitol." Thank goodness for those elementary school trips downtown to the hub of state government. Gina hoped this made her story sound more authentic – the fact that she knew where the Alabama Forestry Association office was. "They put me on hold and came back a little while later with Chip's name and phone number." She held her breath. Would Gabe buy that? She heard his paddle hit the water.

"Paddle left," he said, and she obeyed. The canoe started turning right, so he must be working the left side, too. "That stands to reason, I imagine. Word gets out in these circles, and our court case with Connelly is a matter of public record. Not to mention, a matter of private gossip. Those in my uncle's age group probably still think of him as the person to go to."

Gina exhaled her relief. She nodded without turning her head, hoping to show Gabe she was listening and comprehending. The important thing was for him to focus on his baggage about company management and not to press her for any more details concerning that phone call, which she had actually made, so that part wasn't a lie. The misrepresentation was that making the call had been her idea and that she'd called "cold" to the main switchboard at AFA. In truth, Reuben Marks had given her a name and a direct phone number, and he had specified the day and time she was to call.

"Switch, please."

Gina moved her paddle over and decided that Gabe had no real destination in terms of covering the lake or seeing its shoreline. His mind must be miles away. "Tell *me* something, now, please."

"What's that?"

"How long has it been since you pretended to be a baby bird?" Gina stopped paddling and grinned at Gabe.

He seemed to be trying to return her smile. Trying and failing. "If I ever did that, it was certainly before I was fifteen."

When his father had died. That had to be why he said that specific age. Gina nodded solemnly, hoping Gabe would keep talking.

"I have an indelible memory of the funeral. I was holding Emmie's hand, with our mother standing on Emmie's other side. Of course, she was still Mary Elizabeth then. I'd forgotten that..." His voice trailed off as he was likely visualizing a scene he'd relived many times. "The minister said people are like grass. 'The grass withers and the flowers fall, but the word of our God endures forever. Isaiah chapter 40, verse 8.' I'll never hear that Bible passage without being reminded of the funeral. Afterwards, people were standing around with my mother and my uncle, speculating on who would step up and manage the family business. I heard them talking about me. 'Gabe will come right along into it,' my mother told Uncle Chip, and he said, 'But that won't be for *years,* Frances. The boy is only fifteen.'" Gabe was staring at the water, his oar held idle. Now, he met Gina's eyes. "'The boy is only fifteen.' Those five short words have driven me to prove myself ever since. But Chip didn't seem to be in any hurry for it to happen."

Gina pictured the scene Gabe had described. *Yes. For teenagers, years can feel like decades.* She gazed at him sympathetically until a distant humming noise cut in. Gina pressed a hand against her accessory belt. Was her phone vibrating? She'd been told to get back to Three Points promptly if they did happen to call her. It wasn't her phone.

Gabe was looking around, too, now, as the sound grew gradually louder. Gina scanned the sky. A helicopter, maybe? Actually, it sounded more like a swarm of killer bees. (Not that she'd ever actually heard a swarm of killer bees.)

"Look. A drone." Gabe was pointing somewhere between the canoe and the place they'd started out from.

Gina spotted it. "Oh," she laughed, "this reminds me of one time my roommates and I were driving to Dairy Queen and we saw this weird, gray thing in the sky, with lots of lights. We thought it was a drone flying low, but it turned out to be an old military plane higher and farther away than it seemed. It was making some kind of special flight across the state."

"Yeah, weird." Gabe was only half listening. He kept watching the drone. "I don't know why someone would have that thing flying there." He turned and slowly studied the shoreline, presumably to see whether he could spot person or persons running the device's controls. "Paddle right, please. No, don't. Let's have a quick lesson in the cross-bow draw."

Gina did her best to follow instructions, and they got the canoe facing in the opposite direction. By then, the small aircraft had disappeared.

"I've not seen that out here before. Paddle left. Though, I haven't come down here lately."

Gina's exuberance sharing her load of the rowing was starting to make itself known in the form of tired arms. And her ponytail had loosened quite a bit, thanks to a new type of elastic band that wasn't doing its job. She begged a personal moment and pulled her gray ball cap up, off her forehead, disengaging it from the ponytail that had been sticking out of the space in back. She removed the loose accessory and started smoothing all of her hair afresh, the elastic held over the fingertips of her right hand. "Believe it or not, I considered having my hair cut short before taking on this uh…uh, this *endeavor.*" She'd almost said "this assignment." How easy it was to get the two stories mixed up! One more stretch, twist, and around, and the job was done. She fed her long ponytail through the opening first, then situated the cap on her head and straightened it the best she could without a mirror.

"Gina?"

"Yeah? I'm done. Awaiting your orders." Eyes front, she held her paddle ready.

"I, uh…I need to move up that way for a second."

Gina twisted around, puzzled.

"Just stay where you are. There's something I need to check on, okay?"

"Um…okay. We don't have a hole in the canoe, do we?" She faced front again and scanned the bottom, the sides, and the front corner. Gabe was already moving, she could tell.

"I won't tip us," he said. "I promise."

"Whatever you say." And now he was right behind her.

"Just be still for a second."

Gina felt something on her right shoulder. Gabe was vigorously brushing away a spider – a *humongous, hideous,* yellow and black SPIDER!! A sharp intake of breath was as far as Gina's startled reaction went before Gabe had his hands on her shoulders, keeping her still. "You're fine. It's gone. All gone now. Don't be scared." He relaxed his hold and might have taken his hands entirely away. Gina wasn't sure. "You okay?"

Gina's lips were pressed together. She eased them now and took a shallow breath, expelling it loudly. "I'm fine, thanks. Thanks for…for that."

"I would have said something specific, but I didn't want you to panic, and I thought it best to intervene before you detected mister spider on your own. He's a fairly harmless variety in spite of his creepy looks." Gabe was getting back to his end of the canoe now.

"*Fairly* harmless?"

"Yes. No worse than a bee sting or a small poison ivy rash, as irritation goes."

"Well, what *was* he? So I can tell my friends what I've just survived."

"Paddle right, please." Once they were underway again, Gabe talked more about the banana spider he said was also known as a golden orb weaver. "Don't get creeped out again, but it's a fair bet you had it somewhere on you practically from the time you left the cabin. You could have brushed against its web. That type is known for building grand webs, and it does serve the useful purpose of killing insects and smaller spiders for you."

"Uh, okay. Well, *thanks for being a good neighbor!*" Gina called across the water in the direction she thought Gabe had flicked the frightening creature. "I guess." She took a deep breath. "Wow!"

She followed Gabe's steering prompts and realized he was driving them toward the dock. Once the excursion was over and the equipment was stowed, he said casually, "By the way, I'm glad you didn't do it."

"Do what?" Was he referring to her maybe having panicked about that spider in spite of how capably he had managed the situation? (Gabe's management she would debrief later, complete with how it had felt to have him so close and touching her that way.)

"Cut your hair."

Gina couldn't answer beyond a quiet "oh." Her pulse had quickened, and she made sure Gabe, walking beside her, wasn't able to see her face. Of course, it wouldn't do to assume he meant her hair was pretty. Maybe he thought her face type wouldn't look good under shorter hair. *Uh, no. Not likely. Guys don't have conscious opinions on stuff like that, do they?* She heard herself say, "Yeah, I guess that would have killed the chances of anybody dipping my pigtails in ink. Or in tree sap." *Stop! Are you trying to give him ideas?*

Gabe merely chuckled.

~

Arms sore. Head swimming a bit. But the rest of me did NOT go swimming! Meaning, I stayed in the canoe thanks to expert guidance. On the side porch, Gina looked up from her writing and noticed a high corner spiderweb. Its weaver did not appear anywhere near as large as that horrible thing that had been crawling on her for who knew how long. She closed her eyes and indulged in reviewing every detail about the first part of that incident. Then, she turned to a new page of her journal and wrote:

Invited to the Madisons' yet again, tomorrow night, for the old-time family shindig Gabe's mother is so into. At that time, Gina hoped to see and hear Gabe proverbially letting his hair down to honor his mother's request that he play guitar. *Hair.* He'd said he was glad she hadn't cut hers short. Yes, the canoe outing had been memorable for several reasons. Had Gabe been thinking solely of Gina's benefit when he'd suggested it, or was he now interested in the great recreation opportunity right here on his own land that he'd been failing to enjoy? He had said almost that very thing. And he'd definitely let his guard down, opening up about some lingering dissatisfactions.

His mother had talked a lot about him that afternoon while ironing her holiday linens, letting *her* guard down with Gina as well. *She did call me a good listener!* "I think my son is the one Frank's death has taken the greatest toll on," Mrs. Madison had said. "Gabe sometimes seems on the verge of being willing to verbalize his thoughts. Instead, I feel he almost watches *me* in puzzlement, as if he thinks my grieving path has been easier than his, which is not the case. Mine has not been easy, but I did have the advantages of age and a more seasoned faith. Perhaps for my son it's a matter of gender, too, his suddenly losing that primary male role model, in life generally, and also in the business. Needless to say, Gabe compares his uncle with how he remembers his father. At such a tender age, a boy naturally sees a strong and beloved father as a giant of a man, and one nobody else could ever measure up to."

Those words from Monday's visit seemed to echo until Gina's phone vibrated, prompting her to take it off silent. Answering Taylor's texts, Gina gave an animated account of that huge, diabolical-looking spider. "This was crawling on me. I kid you not!" She found and pasted in a screenshot representative of the species, shuddering again as she got a decent look at its color-banded legs and its... *"Ehhh!"* She couldn't look at it any longer. Would she have nightmares tonight?

Gina did not share what she had felt and thought as Gabe was rescuing her, but she did eventually admit to her friend that she had "met someone interesting." The two chatted and laughed about that with plenty of emoticons flying.

Chapter 7

Gina spotted a new and huge wreath on the Madisons' front door upon arriving for the much-talked-of Sunday family night. One week before Halloween, it was the thick of fall décor season, undoubtedly to the delight of craft and fabric stores everywhere. Gina paused on the porch and gently fingered the decoration's loops of wide, orange-and-green plaid ribbon, its plastic pumpkins in various small sizes, and its artificial leaves in shades of orange, yellow, and red. At the same time, she caught whiffs wafting from around back – the mouth-watering and smoky scent of meat on the grill. She knocked and was met by the lady of the house, who offered a warm greeting and a mug of hot cider.

In the kitchen, Emmie proudly introduced the love of her life to Gina, explaining happily that the pressure of Dillon's accounting work hadn't kept him away tonight, even though fiscal year end loomed for many of his clients. Blond-haired Dillon was taller and less muscular than Gabe. His present task was allaying his future mother-in-law's concern over his missing a regular Sunday night Bible study in order to be here. "All of the sessions are recorded so nobody has to fall behind if they need to skip a week."

Gabe handled the gas grill with Dillon on call, and the ladies managed the salad greens with an assortment of optional, tasty toppings (the sampling of which had not been forbidden!). Besides that, there were potatoes almost finished baking, yeast rolls on standby, and the dessert just gone into the oven so it would bake during dinner, reminding everybody by its aroma what they still had to look forward to.

As dinner plates gradually showed less food and more of their lacy design in royal blue on a white background, Mrs. Madison appeared to be anticipating what would come next. As if this delicious dinner were not enough to make the evening special! Everyone helped to clear the table. Everyone except Gabe, that is. He washed his hands and went for his guitar as his mother announced how much she appreciated the prep time her son had managed to work in during the past few days. "The rest of you wash your hands, please, and gather back around the table. We're starting with a harvest-season hymn I'm honestly not sure I have ever heard sung anywhere. So, to make it easier, our tune for it will be 'My Country, 'Tis Of Thee.' These lyrics call to mind Thanksgiving; and, with the patriotic tune suggesting July fourth; *and,* as we are singing it shortly before Halloween, we have three holiday sentiments rolled into one."

"A hearty 'Merry Christmas' to that, Mother! You've outdone yourself again." From his chair set back from the table enough to give him room, Gabe picked out the first few notes of "Silver Bells" to punctuate his joke. The others laughed as they took the half sheets of white paper Mrs. Madison handed out. Gabe strummed some intro chords, and the five sang:

The God of harvest praise;
In loud thanksgivings raise

Hand, heart, and voice;
The valleys laugh and sing,
Forests and mountains ring,
The plains their tribute bring,
The streams rejoice.

The God of harvest praise;
Hands, hearts, and voices raise
With sweet accord;
From field to store the grain,
Bearing your sheaves again,
And in your glad refrain
Now bless the Lord.

"Lovely! Thank you all for joining in. You've done my heart good." The hostess then said they were going to do another number, with Gabe leading.

"Right. Next up is a peppy chorus Mother has selected for us from our grandmother's ancient songbook." He played the chords through once, tapping one foot in a steady beat. "Now, I'll do my best with it. Y'all follow the words on your page and join me on the second go-round."

Keep me on the straight and narrow, Jesus,
Lead me in the path I ought to tread;
See me over ev'ry sin and sorrow,
Feed me with the living bread.

"Again!" They sang it a second time, and again Mrs. Madison appeared very gratified by their participation. Gina was intrigued. Given the way she loved old novels and other books, she would probably find Gabe's grandmother's antique songbook full of captivating names, titles, dates, and poetry.

"We're going to change it up now, getting into the spirit of the season of jack o' lanterns and such. We all know, of course, what a jack o' lantern was before it got carved. So here we go, to the tune of 'Jingle Bells.' And this one's not on your song sheet, FYI. Listen closely and try to sing along the second time through."

Pumpkin seeds, pumpkin seeds, roasted to a turn.
Get yours now and salt them good,
The treat for which you yur-EARN!

Pumpkin seeds, pumpkin seeds, roasted to a turn.
Get yours now and salt them good,
The treat for which you yearn!

It was hard to sing along with Gabe the next time through while also laughing at his delivery of the silly lyrics. The guy sure had talent and a charismatic stage presence! No wonder his mother and sister had sounded the way they had on that Monday night two weeks ago, regretful that they didn't see this side of Gabe enough. The laughter at his antics was subsiding now. Emmie looked astonished. "You wrote that? Who *are* you, and what have you done with my brother?"

Dillon said, "Nicely done. However, I don't think it's a song to make the Hit Parade." He leaned toward Mrs. Madison. "See what I did there? I threw in some old-fashioned language to go with old-fashioned family night." More laughter.

Scrabble was next, with Gabe sitting out per his mother's prescription from the other day. He put his instrument aside and played cheerleader, commenting on the good and better words placed on the game board. Dillon eventually took the lead, his score propelled upward by the luck of being able to use all of his letters to spell STOLIDER around a T already on the board. He explained, "More stolid," and nobody challenged him on it. The best they could do was to tease Emmie's fiancé that the word revealed something of his own personality. "Label me if you will; it's envy, pure and simple, as I see the scores."

In the corner, Gabe took up the guitar again and softly strummed chords, his head bent.

"Your turn, Gina."

Gina looked at Emmie, self-conscious. "Oh. Sorry." She studied her tile rack and hastily added E and D to change the nearest possible word to past tense. At least she got one of the two new letters on Double Word Score to save face.

"I do have one more song if it won't interrupt the game too much."

"Gabe, you really are making up for lost time!" Clearly, his mother was having a grand and memorable evening.

Gabe strummed, starting into a Christmas song in his clear and rich baritone. Gina loved his voice, his smile, his eyes...and even more so as the song took a surprise turn.

It came upon the midnight clear
The scariest spider of all;

Gabe was looking directly at Gina. Automatically, her mouth's corners turned upward.

Its legs of yellow and black brought fear
As close...and closer...it crawled!

The rest of the family laughed lightly at Gabe's silly Halloween carol, and a couple of them applauded. But Gina's reaction was more personal than the others could know. Gabe had written those lyrics with her in mind! The knowledge warmed her heart in a way that none of the evening's other pleasures had done.

Mrs. Madison passed her turn at Scrabble in order to set vanilla ice cream out of the freezer, removing the white chocolate bread pudding from the oven on the same errand. The dessert's aroma made for a range of conversation trails as Emmie used all of her remaining letters to end the game. The collective mood seemed exactly what a mother like Mrs. Madison would want her quarterly tradition to build. That is, until one trail of banter got into a tangle, naming an inescapable current issue of the day and threatening to turn things somber. Gina wished for the return of those good feelings from earlier, especially the ones she'd had as Gabe sang. Emmie raised a hand. "'Banned topic' alert! Mother's standard rule for family night is no discussing things that stir up tension." The others nodded, somebody murmured that they'd forgotten that rule, and the room became quiet.

"Why, that's the doorbell." Mrs. Madison rose, but Gabe was closer, and he said he would go. He headed toward the living room. Moments later, some higher tones started mingling with his deeper ones, and both voices grew louder as a tall, slim blonde preceded Gabe into the kitchen. Gina quickly formed impressions of a shapely figure, salon-tinted hair in a blunt cut with bangs, and expensive clothes with jewelry accents that seemed dyed to match. Set off by low boots, her snug jeans might be dark purple and might be brown. A white T-shirt under a red, white, and gray plaid flannel shirt, tucked in, completed the ensemble.

"Well, Olivia!"

While her mother greeted the unexpected guest, Emmie whispered aside to Gina, "So much for not allowing tension on family night!"

After Olivia Boggs was introduced to both Dillon and

Gina for the first time, she rather ungraciously declined a serving of the bread pudding, saying her dietary standards were "too refined" for any dish containing what was bound to be a ton of sugar. Eyes sweeping the room where signs of the pre-dessert fare remained, she slid smoothly into an empty chair at the table and set perfectly manicured fingernails out, presumably for them to invite compliments. "Though, if you have an extra steak, I'd love to take one home. I love how Gabe grills them."

Gina watched and listened, unable to miss how pushy the new arrival's manners continued to be. But she noticed that the answers the Madisons gave to Olivia's questions seemed vague and light, if not amused, as if she were a child whose yakety-yak peppered with immaturity wasn't important enough to get folks rattled. Good for them, if that was their approach!

In a side tête-à-tête, Emmie was showing Dillon some pictures on her phone. "Here is Isaac with his buddy; kids from my school. This strap on the lion costume" – she pointed – "broke during the s'mores and hot chocolate, and Gina saved the day with her sewing kit."

Olivia pushed her way in so she could see the pictures. "Where was this party?" she demanded.

With obvious pride, Mrs. Madison described the annual Enchanted Forest event at the Kreher Preserve and Nature Center north of town.

"Oh." Olivia nodded. "*Kid* stuff."

"Yes, precisely, Olivia. Teaching children to love nature lays the groundwork for perpetuating the conservation mindset that matters to all of us. We are very proud of the 'kid stuff' and of the adult education we do at the Center." Wow! Gabe's mother had fended off the girl's derision like a pro. *Hashtag shutdown.*

"Show Dillon pictures of your costume from that night, Gina," Emmie urged. "More people will get to see it at next weekend's party downtown. And, oh, before I forget to tell you, I gave the treat bags to my students on Friday, and they were a huge hit. Bless you for sewing those!"

"Nice." Dillon's response to Gina's photos sounded sincere, yet at the same time appropriately conservative.

"It is adorable," Emmie added, and Olivia once again insinuated herself in order to make assessment. And, once again, her expressed opinion sounded scornful. "Peter Pan. That's a throwback."

Gina removed her phone from view. "It's Robin Hood, actually."

Olivia shrugged. "Same gender. If that's what you're going for. Some of us aren't built for a male character costume." She moved her shoulders back and straightened her torso in an obvious effort to showcase her figure.

Seriously? Gina was on the verge of disgust, but umpteen self-cautions to hold her tongue came rushing at her, competing with the desire to more consistently stand up for herself. She attempted to fashion a response after the kind of poise the Madisons had been exhibiting ever since Olivia's arrival. "Robin is more often a girl's name nowadays."

Emmie said Gabe had a toy bow and arrow somewhere around here, and Olivia responded, before anybody else had a chance to react, "Good idea. That ought to help clarify who you're supposed to be, at least."

Gina's phone vibrated. Emmie had texted a feline image and "CATTY" plus a string of exclamation marks and cringing faces. Gina longed to laugh out loud!

Mrs. Madison was handing something foil-wrapped to Olivia. "You'll need to rush this steak on home and put it in your refrigerator, Dear. We need to conclude some family business and get on to bed." Gina smiled. While Emmie had displayed the knack for issuing instant encouragement by modern means, her mother could probably write a book on how to take control without being rude. Undoubtedly, Madison family night would get journal space tomorrow.

Though Gina heard no such sound, a collective "sigh" of relief was evident following the close of the front door. The hostess of family night lost no time in resuming charge of her special event. She directed everyone to turn their song sheets to the reverse side, where a passage from the Bible's book of Isaiah was printed. Mrs. Madison read the words aloud as the others followed silently. In the final sentence from verse 10 of chapter 35, "sorrow and sighing will flee away," Gina caught a key word that had been in one of the songs they had sung earlier.

~

The interloper was even flirting with Emmie's fiancé, from where I sat. Gina shook her head, remembering still more about last Sunday night than she had covered in recent journal entries. She set her book aside now, stood up from the bench where she had been writing, and stretched. Suddenly back in time to the moments right before her ridiculous confrontation with Gabe Madison, Gina walked toward the edge of the woods. Not since those silly moments treating the bench as a cheater's balance beam had she behaved with random freedom in this place of blissful privacy. A prompt in one of her journal's nature quotes leading her, she moved right up next to a nearby tree. It wasn't only the quote driving this. She'd read on some webpage about hearing things going on inside a tree and even listening with a stethoscope. Gina had no such tool, so she meant to try the maneuver unaided.

Closer, and closer still, she moved her head until her ear was touching the bark.

"What on *earth?*" The shrill interruption startled Gina so that she actually scratched herself uncomfortably while reacting. In spite of her words, Olivia Boggs didn't look puzzled so much as smug, presumably for having successfully discomposed the one unaware of her approach.

Gina stared, all annoyance and little confident she could regroup and display the kind of composure Mrs. Madison had used to finally move Olivia on her way that other time. Gina had never put stock in notions like kismet, but right now it was as if the name written in her journal a few minutes ago had magically summoned the very person.

Somewhat recovered from her initial fright by now, Gina searched her imagination for some way to regain control. She looked at the tree, then shushed Olivia by holding up a hand and pretending some urgent situation was afoot. Out came her phone from her sleek utility belt. She put a finger to her lips, then pretended to video something highly interesting or important on the bark's surface for as long as she could get away with it. What foolishness. Out of the corner of her eye she could see that Olivia wasn't going away. Frustrated, she finally gave up, stowed her phone, and turned. Folding her arms to match the pose being modeled across the way, she said, "I'm the only one here, in case you were looking for somebody else." Gina had no idea from which direction Olivia had come, nor how long she had been there spying before making herself known.

"No, I wasn't looking for anybody in particular." Olivia scanned the area as if she were some kind of inspector. "However, I've heard you are pretty competent in a canoe. I wandered this way with an outing in mind after Frances got tied up with Chip in the company office, and it occurs to me I'd make quicker time with a paddle partner." She cut her eyes toward the cabin, then fixed them back on Gina. "Well?"

Gina tried to manufacture a convincing excuse. "I'm in the middle of...pondering something. 'Those who will not hearers be will never hear from any tree'." That was the best paraphrase she could produce under pressure, slightly abbreviating the actual quote.

"What kind of nonsense is that? And what kind of a 'retreat' is so taxing and regimented that you can't interrupt one activity – if that's what you would call listening to a tree – to do a different one, like relaxing on the water? Unless you'd truly rather spend more time with your ear and your hair touching tree bark that's probably *crawling* with tiny mites. *Ickhh!* Not me! And your hair looks nice. I'd want to keep it that way."

A compliment now? What was up with these mixed signals? Gina ultimately gave in to Olivia's request because resisting hadn't gotten her anywhere. All too soon, the two were suiting up in life vests and deciding who would steer. It didn't make much difference to Gina. She was doing this only to be polite. She was unenthusiastic and distracted. Olivia must be close with the Madisons, speaking with them often. Why else would she feel she could just waltz in at dinnertime on the weekend and act so at home? How else would she know Gabe's level of expertise in grilling steaks? And how else would she know Gina could stay in a canoe and was here on a retreat? On Sunday night, Gina had been introduced to Olivia as the Madisons' "guest," not as their "retreat guest."

They hadn't maneuvered their yellow vessel a third of the way across the lake before Olivia started complaining about discomfort from the neck opening of her safety gear and saying the outing had eaten further into her available time than she'd realized it would. "I waited forever thinking

Frances would stop her work and visit with me before I gave up on that idea." In the back, Gina rolled her eyes. "Whatever," she mouthed, and the two did a sloppy job of getting the craft turned around.

"Don't I remember that tonight is when your adorable green costume comes out again?"

What could Gina do except say that it was? "Paddle left." She was running a little short of time herself by now, thanks to getting pulled into this ridiculous situation. True, her hair was done. She'd put it in one long braid wound around her head. But she needed to freshen up – especially now – and do her makeup.

At the dock, Olivia secured the bow and got out. As Gina stepped over, the canoe tipped. She called out and managed not to strike the side of the dock as she went down. Instinct took over, and she got her head out of the water quickly. Now, getting her bearings, she determined she wasn't in any danger, nor needing to swim or tread water. She stood up and wiped her eyes.

"Oh, no! What happened?" Olivia's words sounded concerned, but her tone did not. And she wasn't moving an inch closer to where Gina was standing in the waist-high water. "Goodness! I didn't know you were that unsteady, after we did so well out there. What a shame. I hope your phone isn't ruined."

Sloshing carefully toward land now, Gina suspected that in reality Olivia would be delighted if Gina's phone were ruined – the phone that held pictures everybody but Olivia had been admiring on Sunday night. "It'll be fine. I designed this belt with an inner lining that's waterproof." Gina was ahead of Olivia now and didn't look back as she spoke. To explain the nature of any of her sewing projects didn't require special courage. She could talk on this subject easily, with anyone. *Oh! The canoe.* Well, it didn't matter right now. She wasn't going to initiate a cooperative effort to get the canoe out of the water and stored on the rack. It would just have to wait.

"A *homemade* caddy. How quaint."

Gina sighed. "The correct term for my accessory is *handmade,* Olivia. And my phone's working fine, FYI." Right now, Olivia's footsteps sounded closer. Gina grimaced as she made her way toward the cabin.

"Hey, I have an idea that might help. If you don't have time to dry your hair before tonight, you can always explain – I mean, if anybody cares – that Robin Hood has to manage *all kinds* of hazards in the forest, such as the occasional waterfall or cloudburst."

Gina would not rise to the bait. Even though the water by the dock was comparatively shallow, the sunshine today had been spotty, and Gina was shivering. She endured her soaked clothes and sneakers all the way to the cabin's porch, immediately crouching to undo her shoelaces. Olivia was just standing there watching, Gina could tell. Probably with a smirk on her face.

"I hope you know that the Madisons are being this nice to you only because they're in panic mode right now on this retreat thing." Olivia Boggs delivered that parting shot and sauntered away, nice and dry.

Leave it to a much nicer girl to lift Gina's spirits, hours later, after Gina confided her earlier trouble and the delay it had caused her in finding Emmie and her friends. Above the music decibels reverberating through Toomer's Corner, Emmie managed to convey how offended she was for Gina, which was very sweet and gratifying. Emmie hugged her and shouted over the Saturday night cacophony, "I have the strongest hunch that if you fell into the lake with Olivia Boggs nearby, it was not your fault." Added to those warming words, images of victory toilet paper waving in the wind to signify the defeat of Ole Miss had Gina feeling "all's right with the world."

Later, before they went their separate ways for the night, Emmie told Gina, "Mother and Uncle Chip and Gabe do their best to tolerate Olivia politely, but only because her family is connected with people in the same industry as us. Personally, I do my best to avoid her!"

~

Emmie was so sweet about the canoeing mishap. Made me feel much better. Downtown, I got called Kiera Knightley twice!! Besides my costume, my favorite was the girl in a green T-shirt and boyfriend in a white one with ENVY lettered on it, therefore "green with envy." But the contest winners for originality were an older couple wearing matching orange shirts lettered in black to spell Happy HalloWeagle. They carried a stuffed eagle toy that wore an Auburn logo kerchief around its neck. Clever! Emmie in her cat face and Dillon with a dog mask were adorable. Such a cute couple! He seems the perfect blend of serious success and easy fun.

Gina's pen left the page and automatically stayed at the ready for any new sentence that might emerge. Images of Emmie and her fiancé gave way to thoughts of the Madisons' friend Olivia. The things Emmie had told Gina made *friend* seem like the wrong word, though. Apparently, the Boggs family was connected and wealthy, with business interests that somehow intersected the Madisons' enterprise. That made sense. How else would Olivia know enough to have snarled that remark about Gina's being important to the Madisons only because of their legal situation regarding the development of a retreat site?

On top of that, Emmie had said of Olivia, "Her single mission in life seems to be making entrances and exits and filling the interim with superficial talk and impertinent questions. And she has been trying for years to get her hooks into my brother." Gina found that last idea a depressing one to end the day on. She wanted to believe that if trying for Gabe "for years" hadn't worked for the polished socialite, then maybe it never would.

Chapter 8

This was the first time Gina had been in the Madisons' home in the early morning. Even though she had been duly invited, right now she felt almost like an intruder. She heard someone upstairs brushing their teeth. Next, Gabe's voice mingled unintelligibly with Emmie's and with a partial minute's hum from a hairdryer. It wasn't likely Emmie's hair would dry that quickly. Mrs. Madison bustled about between the kitchen and the office, brewing plenty of coffee and getting a few supplies set out.

For today's agenda the company office had been outfitted with a rectangular, folding table and five compact classroom chairs with armrests made into their frames. Probably these were stacking chairs kept in a storage closet or maybe in an upstairs loft of the large, detached garage. Gina had chosen a place at the table by best guess; if necessary, they could ask her to move when they got their big meeting underway. Biding her time right now, she took to holding her feet off the floor, alternately pointing and flexing her toes.

"Five minutes, please," the mother called toward the stairs. She wasn't exactly ignoring Gina, but her determination this morning definitely had a different air than the normal southern hospitality.

Footsteps descended the stairs and entered the other side of the kitchen. Then, a collision evidently happened during the process of coffee-getting. Emmie apologized. The refrigerator door shut, and Gabe muttered, "It's a lot simpler to just drink it black."

"I'll wipe it up." That was Emmie again.

"This is really cutting into my work week."

Over the sounds of oven door and baking dish that had to be the breakfast casserole she had mentioned to Gina, Mrs. Madison answered Gabe. "It can't be delayed any longer. I would have scheduled it for yesterday, but you had other commitments."

Now, the three gravitated toward the office where Gina sat waiting, her empty coffee cup on the table in front of her. The smell of French vanilla liquid creamer lingered. Gina was with Emmie, not with Gabe, on that debate!

"You're not the only member of this family who works, Gabe. This was the best day for me to take vacation, remember." Gina had never heard Emmie sound cross, but this was getting pretty close. She, as much as her brother and mother, would wish this whole situation away.

"Right, right."

"Oh, good morning, Gina!" Emmie smiled brightly and set her things on the table at the place next to Gina, who answered shyly and was afraid to look at Gabe. It seemed as though he would have said something more, a second ago, when his sister had cut in to say hello. So, naturally, Gina believed herself to be the source of disruption. "I'm glad you're here." Emmie's morning manners were livelier than her brother's, maybe because she always had to be with teachers and students who needed that positivity from her. "We'll have breakfast casserole in a few minutes. Mother said it needs to cool a bit before she cuts it." Gabe said "good morning" then, and Gina answered with the same two words, barely getting them said before Gabe clipped, "We seem to be missing somebody." He looked pointedly left and right. "The person we're gathered because of."

"Son, it doesn't accomplish anything to continually blame your uncle for this." Mrs. Madison took a seat at an end of the table. "He meant well. He is a good-hearted man." A knock sounded on the front door. "And here he is. I would appreciate your being civil to him." She rose.

"Just in time to eat." Gabe lifted his coffee mug to his lips and shifted his body on what probably wasn't the kind of work chair he preferred.

"All of us need to enter into today's work with a positive attitude," his mother called back.

Chip Ensley joined the group with reciprocated greetings around the table. He told Gina he hoped her retreat was going well. Emmie offered to serve the food; her mother thanked her before getting things rolling.

"Let's be clear on what today's goal is. As I understand it, it is to compile substantial data on this retreat plan, which we will submit to the court soon. Within one week is what I prefer. If filing a document when Chip did was – for lack of a better analogy – a chicken wing," she laughed lightly, "our task now is to make significant headway in constructing the whole bird." Her picture of what lay before them received a couple of small laughs. "It's a job we can do, and thank you, Gina, for sitting in and giving us your thoughts. And thanks in advance to the rest of you for putting forth your best efforts. I know all of us have things we might rather be doing with our time." She turned her head. "Emmie?"

Her daughter nodded and read from her phone, "Fear of

man will prove to be a snare, but whoever trusts in the LORD is kept safe. Proverbs 29:25."

Without missing a beat, Mrs. Madison prayed aloud for God to give them productivity during the business at hand and also to lead them to a true resolution of their dispute with Silas Connelly. It was clear that she had done some thoughtful preparation for today, involving Emmie to a degree. It didn't look as though either of the men had arrived planning to present. Otherwise, from what Gina understood about Chip's practices, he probably would have had a file folder on the table in front of him. It was impossible to read the uncle thus far, but Gabe, from the time he had come downstairs, apparently wanted to be anywhere else in the world.

"First of all, I'll throw this out. Just as any real or theoretical retreat guests might examine the level of status quo in their lives, we as a business are wise to do the same. This challenge will stretch us and will make us stronger as a company, as individuals, and as a family."

Sitting right here as a "real" retreat guest (at least, as real as an undercover reviewer could be considered), Gina pondered Mrs. Madison's words. Vague dissatisfaction with *her* status quo had brought Gina here, and it wasn't going to be long before she would have to decide whether to return to her previous job or to look for something entirely new. She was intentionally staying away from job posting sites right now so specific openings wouldn't influence her in that or distract her from the task at hand.

"So, let us get to it. Let's start at the very beginning, as a famous song puts it." Mrs. Madison smiled. "People can go off on a retreat to a number of different venues anywhere in the world. What distinguishes the *Madison* site? What does a place with woods like ours offer that no other venue can? Chip?"

Automatically, everyone looked toward Mrs. Madison's brother, who presented a smile. "Yes. A lot of people from many walks of life could quickly offer a general answer about getting folks away from their desks or their recliners, away from their phones and their computers, and into the great outdoors. Fresh air and exercise. But that is a stock answer, way too general for us fortunate enough to know and to live in the realm of forestland."

Gina felt herself nodding. She had been here long enough to understand the difference between staying for a time in a forested area and, say, merely availing oneself of a nicely placed sidewalk loop in a corporate park with fountains and ducks nearby. She looked at her lap, amused. She had been wrong about Uncle Chip's preparation. Obviously, he had things in his head, and in his heart, that he hadn't needed to bring to the table on paper!

From there, the family immediately got into the issue of expansion, of clearing land for more cabins or for other structures including pavilions or storage units of any type. Gina watched and listened. At the word *acreage,* Gabe visibly stiffened, answering in terms of square footage. His mother reacted by playing the diplomat. "Yes. Small acreage with maximum impact. I think we are all agreed on that. And keep in mind that we will see beautification happening that we will enjoy personally, whether anyone else is on our property or not. A wildflower area, for example. We are not speaking exclusively of man-made additions. Goldenrod, boneset, and thistle, to name a few possibilities. I want a color variety!"

"I guess if we have to give up some of our land to keep Connelly from getting *another* part of it, so be it."

Gabe's mother eyed him for a moment as his remark hung in the air. She raised and lowered her shoulders and exhaled with obvious control. "It might serve us to take the attitude that we have before us an opportunity to be changers rather than merely having change forced upon us. In other words, we can satisfy the court's requirements while at the same time being proactive, choosing to make more of our land than what it currently is." Gabe knew his mother's longstanding dream was to use Madison land for outreach. Evidently, he wasn't interested in championing that dream right now.

She went on, "So. I mentioned wildflowers. Let's put something down officially about that under the heading Flora and Fauna, since we can focus on flowers that naturally attract birds and butterflies, the way it is at the Kreher Preserve. Not to mention intentionally attracting larger wildlife. We can plant natural feed plots for deer in warm and cold seasons. Clover, rye grass, and such."

They listed bee balm, sage, and trumpet vine, and Mrs. Madison said she had someone in mind who would probably love to be consulted about hummingbird presence. "I'll ask her this Sunday at church." She wrote herself a note. "And add coneflower to the list." She wrote again, then looked up. "That's one of my favorites because it grows tall and stands out from a distance." She said it would be easy to create natural wood signage identifying whatever flowers they eventually put in. "I do know that some of these are planted in the spring, but certainly we will need our master plan carefully devised before we break ground on anything. Also, as an aside, the minimal beautification outside existing or future resident cabins is by design. We do not want people sitting on a cabin's rocking chair content to notice flowers planted beside the porch. That amounts to suburban living. Designated areas for wildflowers and other attractions are meant to get the occupant away from the cabin and on the trails."

Gina's phone sounded. She apologized, automatically glancing at Gabe. He didn't make any visible reaction. Not annoyance; not a small smile to tease her. That shouldn't be any surprise, though. He had a lot going on today. Gina looked at her notifications. Green background. A new text message, that was all. But now she caught the sender's name, Kristyl Floyd. "Just a friendly warning," it began, and Gina was unable to stop reading.

"Reuben Marks has seen social media pictures of you partying during Halloween, and this is not sitting well. His expectation is that you are portraying a plunge into seclusion and are staying wary of the people you are there to report on." Gina felt her face turn color. She glanced up quickly, hoping her change of demeanor hadn't been noticed. The wildflower topic was still on the table, and most everybody was looking at a phone or writing on paper. After the mention of foxglove and geranium, Gina threw in that she had liked Queen Anne's lace for as long as she could remember. Maybe Mrs. Madison would connect that to what she'd said earlier about including taller varieties.

Reuben had been monitoring her online? Gina knew she shouldn't be naïve regarding that, though. Social media was highly accessible by most anybody, and that was kind of the unspoken point of it for a lot of users, wasn't it, those who nursed hopes of "viral" fame? Not everybody who dove deep into Facebook accounts was really a friend who cared about an individual's home life, social life, or love life. Should she delete her posts and ask Emmie to do the same with hers? What good would that do? The pictures had already been seen. *Whatever. I guess I'll have to be more careful.*

The other thing bugging Gina was what Kristyl had said, or, rather, *hadn't* said, which was "the people *whose business* you are there to report on." In practice, of course, it might not matter whether this thing she had been hired for was described as rating the retreat or as rating the Madisons themselves. It was a bit difficult to separate the two. If you were evaluating a hotel or a restaurant, and the staff had been rude to you or unresponsive to complaints, then reporting on the people would be essentially the same thing as reporting on the establishment. In fact, the form Gina had been given to complete included questions on staff friendliness and professionalism. Kristyl might have chosen her words without much thought. Regardless, whether she had meant to or not, maybe she had sent Gina a valid caution. Liking the owners would have a tendency to make you rate their business better than if you disliked them. And hadn't Reuben emphasized impartiality a number of times? Gina finally raised her eyes and found Gabe watching her. She silenced her phone and put it away.

Conflict of interest. The phrase came calling, and once again Gina tuned the table discussion out. *Was* she going to be able to rate this place, this experience, impartially after getting so involved and attached? And yet, wouldn't it be natural for any authentic retreat seekers to find themselves deeply involved? Gina sighed involuntarily. This was getting confusing! The announcement of lunch break couldn't have come at a better time.

~

Apparently, while Gina had been so distracted right before lunch, the Madisons had finished their dialogue on flora, fauna, and any related physical structures. Now, during dessert (compliments of Emmie's handy spreadsheet, and the "chipper chocolate chip" cookie in Gina's hand tasted *sooo* good!), their agenda was the mental health aspect: what prompts could be provided for the thinking a guest might do. That, and possible developments in recreation. "No zip line!"

Gabe had announced earlier in the kitchen, over turkey club sandwiches.

During discussion of a supply they were calling key focus cards, Gabe's idea of virtual "cards," to reduce costs and minimize the risk of litter, didn't fly. "No, Son, I do not envision a QR code tacked to a tree or mounted on a wooden post. Remember, we are trying to convey and to champion experiencing this place with the human body's senses and not through electronic devices. This is a time and a place for tactile engagement. Therefore, *laminated cards* in the hands of our guests."

"True." Emmie was working her phone. "If you're accessing a PDF online, there is almost a guarantee that notifications, or just the irresistible temptation to swipe over and check social media or e-mail, will distract you...and it's goodbye to retreat thinking. So, we will need some kind of station to hold the prompt cards, and here's an idea on that. Look. It's essentially a birdhouse, but with a hinged lid and no other openings or perches." She turned her device around and showed a series of images.

Gina liked the idea. The wooden box was shown attached to a tall post. One view was with lid closed. Another showed printed material inside the box's cavity, the lid cleverly held open by a jute loop caught on a hook mounted above.

Chip threw in, "Produced by a local woodcrafter, I think we would prefer."

"Dillon has a friend trying to ramp up his Etsy shop, and I noticed these items last week." Emmie grinned. "We can support him and write it off as a business expense, too. Sweet. Though Dillon could probably make this for us himself if he had the time. Also, we will want age-appropriate prompts. I already know some elementary-level teaching resources that will give us some ideas easily adapted for children."

To prepare for her undercover assignment, Gina had done a fair amount of reading about retreat approaches. She volunteered to contribute some adult-level material. "Everything in that subject area seems to start with the letter R: rest, reflect, reevaluate, recharge, reconnect, relationships, et cetera. Even *resistance,* which some articles cover. Anyway, I'd be happy to e-mail y'all what I've found." She paused, then added, "If you think it will add some substance and length to your proposal." Some of them nodded at her, and Mrs. Madison said "thank you" as she made notes.

Recreation's first official comments came from Gabe. "Canoeing. Check. To turn our personal launch into one a visitor may use unaided may involve little more than an introduction to rules and methods – preferably by a handy video – and a sign indicating that life vests are mandatory." He shifted in his seat. "Also that users are expected to put the equipment back where they found it. For anything beyond that, we can check sources online, including the Boy Scouts book on canoeing badge requirements."

Put things back? Oh! Gina bit her lip. It had been four days since her watery run-in with Olivia Boggs. Was that yellow canoe still in the lake? And had Gabe seen it?

Chip turned his head and torso toward one of the bookshelves. "Uh, yes. We have a copy of that scouting manual right there." He straightened and smiled toward his nephew. In a somewhat softer voice, he said, "As a matter of fact, I remember how proud your parents and I and your Aunt Claire felt the day you earned your badge."

Gabe might have made eye contact with his uncle just now. Gina wasn't sure. But she did think his expression had softened.

From riding on top of the water the discussion moved to trying to bring fish out of it. Gabe immediately recommended they delegate that angle to Chip. Gina couldn't resist calling attention to the pun. "Angle? Especially appropriate word choice if your uncle is an angler." Her comment received mild accolades.

They moved on. While fishing was Chip's bailiwick, hunting was Gabe's, but he didn't give it a green light. "Absolutely not a thing we can offer to any guest on this land." Based on Gabe's tone, Gina wouldn't have argued with him for the world. And nobody else did, either. "Possibly, we could provide referrals to some of the area's hunting clubs, assuming our guest is experienced. And don't forget camping. Anybody who would rather not stay in a cabin would be free to bring in tents and sleeping bags, I guess, as long as we designate what areas and have strict guidelines for campfires – unless it's possible for us to personally supervise and monitor each one."

"Could you provide a basic archery practice range? I'll bet most people would at least like to know how a bow feels in their hands, and to discover how easy or hard it is to shoot arrows from one." Afraid that the silence answering her idea meant she had goofed, Gina faltered, "I mean, well, maybe suction-tipped arrows, and a *small* practice range."

"There is absolutely nothing wrong with the idea of introducing the skill of archery. I like it." Mrs. Madison looked at Gina approvingly.

"I like it, too." Gabe was giving Gina the first nice smile he'd had for her all day. Unfortunately, it faded right away when his mother introduced the subject of playground equipment. "You mean plastic forts and slides, and nasty sandboxes?"

Gina respected his opinion, but she had to hide some amusement. Maybe, once he was married with children, Gabe would feel differently about such toys.

"I hear you, Son. We can include something in general

terms, such as 'safe and age-appropriate activity apparatus,' agreeing in this room that any specific choices will have to meet with unanimous approval before being purchased and installed."

Emmie spoke up in favor of kid-friendly aspects, which wasn't surprising, given her line of work. "Bringing children into the woods and directing their attention to watching things like birds can train them to be generally more observant." Her face changed. "Oh, my goodness. I have a great idea! My teacher friends were saying last week that they wished they could put together a local outing for when their students get so antsy right before the holidays. Why couldn't we host one class for a little field trip? Maybe a half-day affair, factoring in a picnic lunch at some other spot in town? Even back at the school, for that matter. Unless we can do a campfire meal right here. Y'all decide on a number that's manageable, whether it be 10 children, 15, or 20. The teachers can require the kids to earn their chance for the trip by having model behavior between now and then."

Recalling Gabe's expressed attitude toward plastic playground equipment, Gina wasn't sure his sister's idea would suit him, but their mother promptly said they would take the proposal under advisement subject to school approval and if no unforeseen red tape such as potential liability got in the way on their end. "To pull that off just before or after the Thanksgiving break would be a feather in our cap as regards this legal business."

Gina said elementary-level field glasses could be ordered for the students at a cost of around three dollars a unit. Meanwhile, her phone vibrated, and a second later she found another text from Kristyl at Three Points. "Do not forget that you are there as a short-term guest." Gina stared at her phone. Obviously, this was a follow-up to the slap on the hand for enjoying herself too much. This new directive's timing felt especially cruel as she sat here participating in an important session that could make such a big difference to the Madisons' bottom line and to each of them personally.

Short-term guest. The words were like cold water flung on Gina, almost in a worse way than what had happened by the dock on Saturday. Yes, of course, she was aware practically every day that this temporary job would conclude, landing her back in her apartment and probably back at her old job. Her contract specified a termination date.

The previous message had referred to social media, and Gina couldn't argue against it. *This* one, though... It was almost as if Reuben and Kristyl had her brain under surveillance, knowing she might need a caution about getting too attached. Gina's throat grew tight. Yes, that was exactly what she had been doing: getting too attached! Still, though, maybe Kristyl had simply issued a standard caution sent to all of their reviewers at this point in their employment period. Three Points must have so much experience dealing with employees just like Gina that they knew the dangers inherent in an assignment like this. They weren't targeting just her with that kind of message, surely. But it was no less of a wake-up call, was it? Even though her retreat was a ruse, she wasn't immune to the allure of this beautiful country.

Come to think of it, it must be common for real retreaters – people who had acknowledged a high degree of stress (or a low degree of happiness) to the point of seeking a temporary break from established patterns – to find themselves wishing they could permanently escape what they had left behind. Gina held her breath. That was it! She had not seen it in herself until this very moment. *I never want to go back to the life I've been living.*

When Gina could again comprehend her present place

and present company, she felt as if she had awakened abruptly from a dream, with full memory of its details. No, she did not want to go back to her old life. But did that mean she could stay in this interlude existence, this temporary circumstance, instead? The answer to that question was so obvious she couldn't even bring herself to form it in her head. Her *aching* head. Her aching head that now was remembering something else. Olivia Boggs had said the Madisons were being nice to Gina just because they needed to be able to put on paper that they had hosted a retreat guest successfully. She surveyed the four around the table, one by one. At the moment, Gina might as well be invisible, her total detachment from this meeting going absolutely undetected. Mrs. Madison was writing. Gabe was looking at his phone. Chip seemed to be staring into space, and Emmie was looking at her watch.

Olivia could have been telling the truth. Well, in a way. The Madisons could have been treating her so kindly because they were naturally nice people...*and* because they needed her cooperation. Today, all of them had been pretty much "all business." Gina was adrift now in a mounting sea of doubt. Her eyes landed on Mrs. Madison. "*I* would have scheduled this meeting for yesterday," she had said hours ago. Gina relived the way that matriarch had handled Olivia, basically kicking her out of the house. Today, the woman was quietly but effectively asserting her authority from the head of the conference table. Furthermore, it was Frances Madison who had sent flowers to Gina even though her son had delivered them. It was she who had asked Gabe to see Gina out on that ironing Monday. And it was she, even more than either Emmie or Gabe, who had confided lots of family drama, playing on Gina's sympathy.

Now, Gina watched Gabe. He might be general manager of Madison Timber Farm, but his mother unquestionably occupied the driver's seat on this retreat thing. Was Gabe consciously or subconsciously doing his mother's bidding in seeming to pay special attention to Gina? Had she been reading too much into moments like the silly spider song, the special smiles and times of lingering eye contact, the spider incident itself, and the easy joking she and Gabe had engaged in since resolving their initial conflict? By now, Gina's value to this meeting was gone, and it wasn't going to come back no matter how long she sat here. She timidly owned up to her headache and prepared to excuse herself.

"Can we get you something for it?"

Which of the nice Madisons had asked that question made no difference. With her head lowered, Gina gathered her purse and said she had basic pain reliever in the cabin. She pictured her personal belongings – the medicine, her clothes, her groceries, her sewing machine, all of it – unpacked, organized, set up, as though she had been expecting to live there forever. Tears stung her eyes, and it took all of her self-control not to run to the front door.

Chapter 9

Sitting on the edge of the bed, Gina massaged her forehead and temples with the tips of her fingers, at the same time taking deep breaths, holding them, and exhaling. Over here, she could get herself together and try to sort things out. That conference had been interesting, even stimulating at moments. Nevertheless, this headache might be partly from the retreat discussion and not exclusively because of those unexpected text messages.

The boss had seen evidence that Gina was enjoying herself. So what? Her daily responsibilities hadn't been spelled out in excruciating detail, but Gina had the impression that, posing as a retreat guest, she could seek solace to a degree and also seek social situations sometimes, assuming some were available and might make her feel happy. If the hiring company wanted thorough feedback on this retreat, they ought to give Gina the freedom to immerse herself in it in her own way. Besides, she hadn't been out on the town night after night. Just twice, for Halloween, which was a holiday!

In spite of that very logical-sounding justification, a shadow of doubt crept in. Sure, in this empty room she could point out to herself how she hadn't been wrong, but the company was the one calling the shots. They were the ones holding out a stipend at the finish line, and Gina meant to cross that line in good standing as far as they were concerned, and with self-respect as far as she was concerned.

She had been a working girl for what seemed a long time, weathering coworker conflicts, bad managers, angry customers, annoying staff meetings – all of it, including the occasional mistake in judgment that she'd had to answer for. This situation today shouldn't be that difficult to get past. The standard "I'll survive" sigh escaped her. She pulled a jacket on over her long-sleeved gray T-shirt and went out to the side porch. Maybe the crisp air would handle the headache and she could skip the pain reliever. Her jeans were stretchy enough for sitting cross-legged, so she pulled her ankles in that way and unlocked her phone.

Kristyl Floyd had seemed nice in person, and just because her two messages today hadn't been cutesy and sweet, that didn't mean the sender had undergone a personality change. Gina tried to view the situation fairly. Ms. Floyd was a professional, wanting to help Gina walk the proper line so she could turn her information in successfully and receive her reward. That being the case, and if less evidence of partying was expected, then from now on there would be less evidence of partying. Gina smiled. Not necessarily less partying. She could always casually tell the Madisons that for her retreat she'd realized she could have been abstaining from social media long before now, and for the duration wasn't going to post anything. That should take care of that. (If they even cared.) Gina set her phone aside right now, symbolically, leaving it face down on the table. Anyway, Halloween was past, and her social calendar boasted nothing else of interest.

That left the rather blunt suggestion she keep her "short-term guest" status in mind. Suddenly, a jumble of names, faces, and memories paraded past: working at the craft store; strolling through the woods every day (while getting paid for it); Gabe; Scrabble and guitar; Josh; Gabe again; her small apartment; the Madisons' huge house; the cities of Auburn and Opelika. It was a mixture of things, most of them falling into one of two categories: things right here that Gina wished she could keep indefinitely, and things at home that she would prefer to stay away from longer. Either way, it was all *short-term*. What she wished she could keep longer wasn't going to last, and what she didn't care that much about returning to was going to pull her back to it. Bottom line: this temporary assignment, this interlude, would end sooner than she wanted it to, even factoring in her misgivings, just today, about the Madison family's motivations.

As for Gabe in particular, well...Gina couldn't deny how attractive he was. Might he feel the same way toward her? Under the circumstances, it was difficult to be sure whether he was developing an attachment to her, but she certainly had sensed that vibe from him a few times. He had even sat next to her at lunch today. Gina shook her head and accused herself of wishful thinking. Supposing Gabe *were* genuinely interested. What would happen if he found out she had been lying about why she came here? If all of the Madisons found out? Being a good listener would be reinterpreted as doing reconnaissance, hearing their expansion ideas would be considered investigation, and someone Gabe had seemed to be establishing a special rapport with would suddenly be a person he wouldn't know whether he could trust.

In her own best interest, Gina composed a text to Kristyl Floyd acknowledging the two messages received earlier. "Thanks for checking in. All good reminders. Be assured I have my focus on the goals agreed upon. In fact, I attended a retreat expansion planning session with the owners today that proved very informative. It should give me more areas to rate knowledgeably." That ought to satisfy Reuben Marks.

Gina eased her neck, then stood and stretched. The crisp air *had* taken the edge off her headache – surprisingly, given the weighty things she still had on her mind. But a nice, warm shower might help still more. She headed indoors. In the bathroom, she arranged her towel and such, then turned the bright vanity bulbs off, preferring the free and available daylight. She raised the window a bit for ventilation, then angled the blinds for an acceptable compromise between privacy and light intake.

Clearly, Emmie and Mother thought highly of Gina. Uncle Chip did, too. Gabe stopped now, still some yards away from the cabin. Chip might be fairly out of touch sometimes, but he would not have agreed to let Gina move in if he had had a negative feeling about her. Especially, *Mother* never would have had Gina or anybody else outside the family present at today's planning meeting unless she liked that person a lot.

He trudged forward, noticing the nice feel of a cool breeze on his neck and listening to the sounds of the woods. Gina *was* a very likable person. Levelheaded, with good ideas and the forthrightness to share them. And she sure had the forthrightness to tell somebody off if she had a reason to! Gabe grinned. Involuntarily he turned his head to look at the bench where he'd first seen her. Her long, straight hair had been pulled back, the way he'd seen it most of the time. Gabe had heard Emmie telling their mother Gina's hair was "mochaccino," a trendy name for a shade of brown. Color, schmolor; he just knew he liked it.

And here he was, about to go knock and see whether she

was feeling any better by now. Gabe looked at the cabin. The front blinds were shut. Maybe Gina was napping, trying to get rid of her headache that way. He could always tap lightly, then go away if she didn't answer. He took a quick breath and let it out, then stepped onto the porch. *What?* The shrill sound of yet another of Gina's mysterious and many phone alerts turned his head. Was she outside, down there on the side porch? Had he been saying any of his thoughts out loud?

Stealthily he peered around the corner. No Gina. *Whew!* Just her noisy phone. He might as well go silence it for her. He could do that by pressing a side button, and nobody could blame him. As the land's manager, it was practically his duty to keep that alert tone from drowning out the sounds of nature. Gabe strode ahead and reached for the device, which lay face down on the table. Before he could get his fingers on a side control button, he'd seen a lockscreen full of notifications. He silenced the current reminder, apparently regarding an e-book Gina meant to download. That notification disappeared from the screen, and Gabe couldn't help reading what was now in full view. Names stared up at him. Josh Larkin. Reuben Marks. Taylor no-last-name. Well, it figured, didn't it? If Gabe had been assuming Gina was unattached, he'd probably been kidding himself. He frowned as the display went black. Were some of these relationships what had been bothering her so obviously in the company office earlier? Gabe couldn't help himself. He put his finger to the screen, and the notifications came back. Josh had sent a video. Reuben, "Stick with it." Taylor had said, "How's it going?"

Surrounding noises somehow changed now, and Gabe suddenly realized where he was. *Water turning off.* His eyes flew to the window – the bathroom window! He couldn't see inside, but he instantly recognized the sound of a shower curtain rustling. Panicking, he put Gina's phone where he'd found it and bolted off the cabin's porch, practically diving for cover behind the nearest trees. *Oh, don't let her have seen me!* She'd think of him in the worst possible way. Worse, even, than that world's largest rodent she'd called him before. A peeping Tom! Had she seen him? Heard anything? She might be looking out the window right now. If so, he mustn't move. Gabe tried to calm his breathing and his thoughts. Now, he heard the hum of a hairdryer. Hoping Gina had her eyes closed (Emmie sometimes dried her hair that way), Gabe took his chances and darted farther away, in as straight a direction as possible, until confident enough to turn back and be sure there was no sight line between him and the side of the cabin. *If she never mentions anything, I guess I'm in the clear,* he reasoned, already trying to figure out when Gina's next opportunity for mentioning something might be.

~

Nobody in this new group text, except for Emmie (who'd initiated it), was in Gina's contacts. Therefore, it was a challenge to guess identities based on what people were saying and what area code they had. Dillon must be in here, probably that 205 number. Emmie had said he came to Auburn from Birmingham. Beyond that, it was too early in the morning for Gina to speculate more on the group that numbered four besides Emmie and herself. She could always message Emmie separately to get the lowdown. Basically, though, it was about going out on Saturday to eat wings and watch the Auburn-Mississippi State game together. "Unless any of y'all wind up with tickets."

Finishing her coffee, Gina tapped her laptop to open her folder called Madison Retreat. So far as she knew, no official name for the retreat site had been given or speculated upon. She opened the document of free-form paragraphs and bullet lists she had been amassing since the start, capturing impressions that would feed into the quantitative rankings she would turn in eventually. The most recent notes were those she had added during the weekend, based on that planning conference. Wildflowers, cards to prompt guests' introspective thinking, recreation, educational potential. Oh, and the information she had offered to supply on renewing and recharging. That task was still on Gina's to-do list. Surely, she could knock it out in under an hour.

She scrolled to the top, where her own status notation in a comment field on page 1 read, "Approximately 91% complete." That had been her vague assessment a few days ago when attempting to numericize how close she was to fulfilling her work contract. If she were truthful with herself, Gina already could have ranked everything. Ranked it, turned her information in with the click of a few buttons, watched for the direct deposit of her pay, and been packed and out of here. Only one category was giving her pause. That "nine percent" hole in her reconnaissance had to do with retreat staff. Staff friendliness; professionalism; responsiveness to guest comfort issues; size relative to guest population. *LOL. Roughly, four staff to one guest, at the moment!* Gina raised her head and stared unseeingly out the window above the desk. She had left the Madisons' house on Wednesday afternoon uncertain about staff friendliness. Staff sincerity. By now, her feelings had evened out somewhat.

Since those two brusque texts during the expansion meeting, the only new work directives had been from Reuben personally. The first had instructed Gina to stick to her task. That one had been on the same day as those from Reuben's assistant. The second message was sent yesterday. Gina picked up her phone to look at it again. "Hang in and keep listening."

Date stamp Monday, November 8. She rolled her neck around and eased her shoulders. His assistant would naturally have passed along to Reuben that Gina had been privy to the retreat owners' idea session. That development could be viewed as a win-win. Three Points wanted more information, and Gina wanted to stay longer.

She cleaned up after her coffee and scrambled eggs, then couldn't find her phone. Finally, when it sounded an alert to conveniently clue her in, she found it on the desk and discovered a new message from an unknown sender. Area code 334, and, yes, this number was also in Emmie's group thread. "I need to be over near the cabin later this morning and I just wanted you to be aware of it. This is Gabe, BTW."

~

"So, how's retreat life?"

Gabe had not volunteered yet what business had brought him toward the cabin. All Gina knew was that he had found her and that now they were taking a walk together. In an attempt at humor, she had shown him pointedly that her phone was on silent and would not be disturbing the peace. He had actually given her kind of a weird look, though.

She answered his question now, in an offhand way, referring to the latest nature poetry line she'd seen in her journal, about wishing for trees that their only enemies would be winter and rough weather. When Gabe didn't react, Gina elaborated, "I'm sure that would make more sense in context, though my guess is it's hinting at artificial dangers to trees, like being chopped down or accidentally burned." Still no response. "It's Shakespeare, though." (As if that would make her sound more intelligent.) But Gabe clearly wasn't impressed, nor interested at all. *So stop rambling, would you?*

"I'm sorry you had to leave our little idea fest last week. I could tell something had upset you."

Oh! Is this what he's had on his mind the whole time? Gina wondered how she should answer. Could it be that Gabe didn't truly have any work business here today, just personal business? A nervous sensation – the *good* kind of nervousness – took hold of her. But her original brand of unease came right back. "Oh, you know, the headache and all..." she ventured. There was nothing true that she could tell Gabe about what had brought her headache on. Not at any time since her arrival had she felt this much like an impostor. "Um…though, until then I was enjoying myself. I'm really glad y'all included me. I loved hearing everybody's ideas for expansion." Gina turned her head for a moment, toward the cabin, though it was no longer in view. "I mean, right now you have one cabin, a bench, a couple of trails, and a lake with canoes. But picture it the way it sounded during your meeting!" It was a beautiful lake, come to think of it. Gina honestly hadn't been able to relax and simply enjoy the view either time she'd been out on it. Was the lake where they were headed right now? A sudden idea took hold, and she voiced it immediately. "Would you consider installing a frame with a porch swing, near the water's edge?"

After a moment, Gabe offered a positive comment on her idea. Then he sighed. "Yeah, I guess expansion is going to happen. It's what my mother wants, regardless of why we're scrambling to get it going just now."

Yep. He was in a state of glum about that whole situation. Time for a change of subject. "By the way, I don't think you ever mentioned to me that you were a Boy Scout. If I had known that, I might have felt even safer in the canoe with you than I did." This was entirely true, but Gina hoped the rumored tendency of males to respond to female flattery would apply, improving Gabe's mood.

He stopped walking, and Gina stopped to see why. Suddenly, it occurred to her she still needed closure after Gabe's remark that guests were expected to store equipment after using it. "On that topic," he started, and Gina cut in to apologize that a canoe had been left in the water. During the weekend, she had had to have her curiosity satisfied on that. Down at the lake, she had found everything in place on the rack.

To her astonishment, Gabe lifted a hand and gently gripped her upper arm. "That's not where I was headed at all. Gina, I've heard from Emmie what happened with you and Olivia. And I apologize for not telling you sooner how sorry I am." Melting fast, Gina visualized herself fully in both of his arms. "I want you to know that if it had been me with you, I would not have let that happen." Gabe dropped his hand, but his eyes still held hers.

"I know you wouldn't have," Gina answered softly. She felt deeply warmed and...*cherished!* She smiled shyly at Gabe, then ended the sweet moment of eye contact before it could become awkward. Walking again, she said she had been meaning to ask why some of the trees had plastic tape tied around their trunks.

The simple answer, Gabe told her, was that the ties identified some of the oldest trees on the land. You didn't live and work in a place like this, he said, nor study for a degree in forestry, without developing a sort of "hybrid" interest in it all. "You are making your living off the trees and are approaching that aspect scientifically, but the conservationist or preservationist viewpoint is never absent. Nor aesthetics, which is another thing still. There is a mindset within this industry – and I know, because it's in my family, and it's in me – that is about valuing a tree as a living thing that deserves to keep living because of what it can inspire, what can be learned from it, and what ecosystems would be upset by its removal."

Gina practically tripped over an exposed root, focused as she was on Gabe's expression of what couldn't be called anything other than a passion, delivered so articulately. "Wow," she breathed. "Somebody needs to quote *you* in the next nature journal they publish!" She wanted him to keep talking, so she asked whether he really hadn't been out of town for a two-year stretch before the trip he'd returned from on the day they had first met. Reluctantly, and almost with humor, Gabe admitted he might have "rounded up" during his rant; in reality, it was maybe fifteen months.

"Tell me how you spent your time," Gina urged. "I don't even know where you went."

The sighs punctuating Gabe's description of his business trip confirmed to Gina again that he operated under a weight of stress virtually all the time. Observing a heli-logging operation in Oregon had been "really interesting," but the rest was a combination of field and classroom time on cutting-edge planting technology and dry presentations on tedious but necessary matters like contract law, road maintenance, invasive plant removal methods, and tax structure lobbying efforts.

Gina stopped walking, and Gabe did the same once he realized she had fallen behind. She said she couldn't imagine such a business trip not having had any side excursions factored in. "Now, for me, that would mean antique stores or museum tours." She smiled. "But what about you?"

He nodded and shrugged. "Actually, there *was* a side trail, and of my own planning. I did some hiking." He looked aside, then back at Gina. "It wasn't relaxing, though. I worked too hard at it, setting a goal in terms of distance and time. I lost sight of the difference between hiking and walking. Truth is,

I could have done better for myself by taking a leaf out of *your* journal and just letting myself enjoy the place spontaneously."

Gina laughed. She flapped her arms, remembering the baby bird bit, and she cheered inwardly when Gabe laughed with her. As they resumed their stroll, she just had to ask, "That hiking goal...did you meet it?"

"Almost," he said, and Gina looked over, afraid she had spoken insensitively. But Gabe seemed fine. "I came this close." He held his thumb and index finger half an inch apart.

They had walked the entire loop of the main trail and had started around again, but Gabe now led Gina in an unfamiliar direction. Both of them started a bit at the sound of Gabe's ringtone. "*Now* whose phone is not on silent?" Gina teased, watching as Gabe decided to take the call after a slight hesitation. Gina easily heard enough of the other side of the conversation (which was the side that talked the most) to gather that Olivia Boggs wanted Gabe to jet over, literally, on her family's private plane, to Auburn's next away game, against South Carolina a week from this Saturday.

Out of respect for her, Gina wanted to believe, Gabe didn't stay long on the call, politely saying the invitation was a kind offer but he already had plans. He apologized to Gina for the interruption and interpreted the matter in an offhand way. "Olivia cares much more about arriving and departing on her family's Cessna than she cares about football, especially Auburn football. She is a Bama fan through and through."

"You weren't tempted in the least?" Gina wanted to hear him say it straight out.

"I *was* tempted." His answer made her hold her breath. "For maybe two seconds." That sounded better. "The only temptation for me in that scenario has nothing to do with Auburn football and nothing to do with Olivia."

"Oh? Then it must be the private plane. You have a

fascination with the transportation methods of the rich and famous, do you?"

Gabe laughed and shook his head. "Not even close. There's a national cemetery in Columbia where longleaf pine has been cultivated, and I've heard from Uncle Chip and others that the trees are worth seeing."

Gina and Gabe smiled at one another until a buzzing sound drew their attention elsewhere. He said pretty quickly he thought it was another drone, and she could tell the idea bothered him. Neither of them ever spotted a device, but Gabe said a skilled operator could maneuver in and among trees even as dense as these.

Gina had been enjoying the walk so much, she didn't want it to end prematurely, and especially she didn't want it to end with Gabe feeling as bogged down as ever. She pointed out some Queen Anne's lace she had noticed while looking for the drone. "It has been said to 'brighten a weed-entangled way,' according to my information. My journal, I mean." She smiled, then spotted some light purple flowers the other direction. "I wonder what those are." She moved closer to take a picture.

"I admit I don't know, but send me the photo and I'll show you a little trick of the trade." Gina did, and Gabe worked his phone for a few seconds. "Here you go." He turned the device toward her. Her picture was on the left side of a split screen, beside it an image of the same plant, identified as gentian pinkroot.

"That's pretty cool!"

"The app is called FloraFile. It will give you an accurate identification most of the time. There are other apps like it, but I've found this one the easiest to use."

"Impressive!"

~

Saturday, November 13. So ends a full week, starting with Emmie's proposal that 6 of us go out for wings & football. That led to a text from Gabe, and then to – for sure – the best walk in the woods I've EVER been on with a guy. ♥ *Really comfortable talk...his eyes...a touch!* Gina stopped writing and pictured her time with Gabe. She looked down at the arm he'd held while telling her so seriously how he hated that she had gone into the water. She relived the pressure of his touch. Gazing at her open journal, but not seeing the words she had just added, Gina reminisced.

A little while later, the page came back into focus and she finished describing her week. She was the best kind of tired right now, and she wanted to drift off to sleep while her memories of the game date – a triple date that lost two of its couples along the way – remained vivid. *The short version is, Emmie & Dillon ended up with tickets to the game, and Gabe's college buddy Micah and his girlfriend had to bail early in the second quarter to catch her family's tailgate. So it was just Gabe and me for most of the time. Sweet! And fun! Very relaxing. The most mellow I've ever seen him, even though Auburn's team suffered some key injuries and lost the game.*

Not only that, but while I was text-joking with Taylor during the game (Gabe said he didn't mind my being on my phone; he was using his a lot, too), I suddenly realized something. Gina held the pen and remembered that moment in the Madisons' company office – how certain she had been about never wanting to go back to the life she had been living. *I thought of my good friend in Montgomery and realized I wouldn't wipe the slate of my "old life" completely clean even if I could. I would just want to feel completely different as I kept what mattered, cut out what didn't, and made room for something new and very special, if something like that came my way.*

Chapter 10

With Emmie's field trip approved for 3:00 to 6:00 on Friday the 19th, preparations for it had included craft supply shopping, food planning for a campfire meal, and script writing for the welcome speech Mrs. Madison would deliver shortly, standing beside the bench that was a memorial to her husband.

Gina had been recruited as a helper, and she had enjoyed the prep work for art and craft projects. Right now, she wished she could overcome her minor nervousness. Here the kids came, with their teachers and chaperones, from the area where their bus must be parked. Emmie led them into the clearing. Gina counted heads. Had Emmie and her teacher friends decided that 12 was the perfect number for this experiment, or had no more third-graders than that achieved the required model behavior?

Mrs. Madison's poise and speaking skill as she delivered her company's first official welcome to its first official day group did not surprise Gina at all. She had seen the woman in action as matriarch of her home and had heard about her volunteer work at the nature center. Gina watched the adults and the children. No doubt the speaker, too, was judging the audience's degree of interest. She did not drag out her remarks. After saying how happy she felt to have such a great group gathered here to enjoy the beauty of creation together, she briefly thanked her family, their friend Gina Wright, and the school's staff for all they had done to make the event happen. She said they would take a walk along the trail, have craft time at the tables right over there (borrowed ones had been set up), and eat supper by the fire after sundown. "So, let's get started. Gina?"

Gina was up. She asked the students to join her in a game of Follow the Leader, a trek meant to give the kids a physical outlet after their bus ride. She started out, explaining as she changed her gait or added arm motions that the outdoors was such a wonderful place – and space – "for stretching, moving, turning, jumping, and letting yourself feel free." Around the clearing she guided the activity, glad when a couple of the teachers joined the line, spacing themselves between the kids. Of course, Gina included flapping the arms, and she immediately pictured the one Madison who wasn't on hand. Gabe's Friday afternoon agenda obviously had him occupied elsewhere. To end the activity, Gina had the students step up onto the elm bench and walk across it, spotted by adults at each end. The second time, Gina asked the kids to pretend the bench was a bridge and to imagine what kind of brook or gully or road was below it.

Meanwhile, others had set out pinecones, leaves collected earlier in different shapes and colors, pieces of Tootsie Roll Pop candy on a stick, and glue. It was time to turn these materials into turkey decorations! Gina was right in the mix, helping as needed, when a boy called out to "Miss Emmie" excitedly, evidently spotting her for the first time since he'd arrived. He left his craft materials to go and see who presumably was his speech therapist. Gina couldn't decide whose face showed more animation, Emmie's or the student's.

"Isaac," someone called, and the boy turned his head, answering, "Mom!" Gina comprehended vaguely that a newcomer was entering the clearing; then, one of the little girls at the table wanted help gluing her turkey tail leaves. Gina stayed with the craft project until it concluded. Next, Mrs. Madison led a walk in the woods, drawing attention to different tree sizes, bark textures, and leaf shapes. She grouped the students, tasking each foursome with gathering a short "scavenger hunt" list including pine needles, a pinecone, a yellow leaf, a brown leaf, and more. As they compared their findings, if one group lacked something another had found, cooperative sharing made for maximum discovery. In the process, one of the more talkative children had to be asked to remember not to interrupt when a teacher was speaking. Soon after, Gina made an effort to personally encourage the little girl, named Sadie. Gina knew how it felt to be scolded for talking too much at school!

Mrs. Madison directed the regathered crowd to places around the cleared tables. She handed out samples of "Happy in the Forest" topic cards, which were the elementary-level version of the key focus cards the Madisons planned to house someday in a wooden box for grown-up retreaters. Gina noticed Emmie apart from the group, not with Isaac, but with his mother, the late arrival. Though her back was to Gina, she seemed familiar. As Mrs. Madison explained the art activity coming next, Gina had just enough time to casually ease away from the children and drift in Emmie's direction.

"After having had only e-mail conversations, I am so happy to meet you at last. You are my son's favorite person at school. He talks about you every day." The voice was one Gina certainly had heard before, but she couldn't place it. "When I adopted Isaac two years ago, they told me he had some catching up to do. You are a wonder worker, Miss Madison!"

Emmie's gracious response quickly took the focus off her professional skills in favor of complimenting the boy.

His mother laughed. "I tell him every morning before school, 'Do your work, be nice to people, and stay out of trouble.'"

"That advice seems to be working! I'm happy to have met you, too." The conversation done, Emmie headed to the tables, and Isaac's mother turned. Gina found herself face to face with Kristyl Floyd. Both were discomposed, and Gina felt her face growing warm. Besides the fact that she was pretty sure nobody here should discover the connection between Ms. Floyd and herself, Gina was confused. She had always assumed the woman lived in Montgomery, where Gina had interviewed.

Ms. Floyd leaned close to Gina and whispered, "This is all just a coincidence. Don't let *anybody* know you recognized me."

Gina nodded and moved aside. It was time to introduce the art project, anyway, which was simply to choose a flower from cut ones in several vases and use markers and paper to draw a picture of the bloom's "face." Each child's drawing would go home with a preprinted label affixed, reading "Every flower is making a different face at me." This was another idea sparked by Gina's journal.

As the students drew, laughed, and visited, Gina heard Ms. Floyd quietly bidding her son and Emmie goodbye, saying apologetically that she had to return to work to make up the time. How sad that the woman couldn't take the afternoon off on the Friday before Thanksgiving. She was going to miss the campfire. Was Reuben Marks that demanding? Or did she not have any vacation time left in the year? Today's event *was* put on the children's calendar without a lot of notice. On the other hand, maybe it was a second job, not Three Points, that Ms. Floyd had to get back to. Supporting herself and a son – she didn't have a wedding ring on – might take working two jobs. Gina's mother had had to do that sometimes.

Emmie called for the group's attention, showing examples of the little wooden souvenir each student would get to take home. Made from maple, these were plant identification sticks, but instead of words like *Basil* and *Mint* the students' names had been burned on. Emmie had imposed on her fiancé for this woodworking idea, telling Gina ahead of time that she had insisted on longer pieces of wood, not smaller print, for Anna Kathryn and Constantine and anyone else whose name had more than six or seven letters. A small hole drilled at one end accommodated a key ring. The kids grew animated about the personalized souvenirs as they finished their drawings. And now Mrs. Madison was announcing that a surprise entertainer had arrived. Gina looked around. There, with his guitar strapped on, was Gabe!

Gina had no idea what to expect. So, along with everybody else, she waited. In his oh-so-charming way, Gabe said that one reason he liked guitar was that "it doesn't take any electricity, wi-fi, and possibly not even daylight." He encouraged the kids and their leaders to find a favorite activity like that. "When your bus takes you back to the school tonight, I'll bet some of your teachers and chaperones can help you think of some." He led the group to a spot newly cleared and outfitted for a campfire circle. Torches had been stationed here and there at the perimeter for extra light, and the adults were ready with pre-cooked meal packets in foil that would be heated over the fire, plus marshmallows for dessert.

As Gabe strummed and sang, Gina couldn't decide whether his talent or his willingness to do this impressed her more. He sang something he called "Don't Needle Me" to a tune that sounded a lot like "Don't Fence Me In," cracking up especially the adults with lines like *Oh, I'm 'pining' for the trees again, Can't wait to 'leave' this city noise, I love a tree that's all 'bark' and no bite,* and *I 'wooden'...'wood' you?* Gina stole a look at the rest of the audience. Everyone's eyes seemed locked on the handsome, surprise performer. All surprises should be this nice! And now the musician's eyes were locked on her.

During the meal, Gina heard Emmie comment softly to a teacher friend, "The kids are in that perfect state right now: too tired to be fidgety but not tired enough to be cranky!"

Gina toasted a second marshmallow for herself, then started to sit down in a new spot, where the heat radiating from the fire was not as strong. Very unexpectedly she found herself caught by the arm.

"Whoa, there! Ants." Gabe's quick action had probably saved Gina from sitting on top of the frenzied insects, or stepping in them, or both, as they had a good little trail going from the ground to the split-log bench.

She thanked Gabe and said she was glad none of the kids had found their way to this spot. "Ant bites would be an awful way to end such a wonderful outing."

"I couldn't agree more. You know, this is the second near miss you've had with insect life. It seems I'm going to have to keep a close eye on you."

Gina grew warmer, and not from the campfire. "I'm okay with that, but I'm going to have to put you on report for an inappropriate comment." That got him! He looked really worried. "Don't you know, Mr. Forester, that spiders are not insects?" She gave him her most saucy look and hadn't a clue what it might provoke.

Gabe leaned close and said in Gina's ear, "All I know is, insects aren't the only thing you're attracting right now." He drew back, but he held Gina's eyes as the fire sparked in the periphery.

While the visitors prepared to depart, Gabe stayed fairly close. The last words she had from him happened on the porch of the cabin and were in the form of a question. Would she want to take a walk with him on campus tomorrow? As Gina nodded, it didn't bother her one bit that Gabe had just suggested he spend time in her company on the very day Olivia Boggs had wanted him a captive audience in her private plane!

~

"My sister says you were pretty awesome with the kids yesterday." Gabe glanced at Gina while getting the truck into reverse for parallel parking on College Street. "I'm sorry I didn't get to see more of that for myself."

The main campus library was across from them, and ahead on the right stood large, brick buildings Gina recognized now as the parking deck and hotel where she had met with Reuben and Kristyl. Pulling her thoughts away from that detail, she murmured a delayed reply over the lid of her pumpkin spice latté. They had swung by The Bean on Dean Road before heading downtown.

Gabe's compliment was highly gratifying. Furthermore, though he had attended only the tail end of the field trip, he had made good use of his time as concerned her! Gina thought back to that highly romantic moment by the fire (well, to be honest, seldom had she *not* thought about it since it had happened), when Gabe had whispered what clearly indicated his interest. She was tempted to ask right now what had prompted that, but maybe it was too soon for a conversation of such depth. Romantic impulses seldom stemmed from a coherent thought progression, so asking him to explain himself might embarrass Gabe. Still, it would be helpful to know his present thoughts and expectations.

"I'm glad you didn't mind getting a somewhat early start. You can never quite tell how crowded it will be around here at a given time, even with students out now through Thanksgiving weekend."

Gina undid her seat belt and reached for her purse, a slim but sufficient crossbody bag. It was one of the few she ever carried that wasn't of her own making. "Being morning people must be something we have in common," she offered as they climbed out of the black F-250. It looked newly washed, a fact Gina wanted to take as a chivalrous gesture. She'd heard Emmie call the truck's paint color "mud" based on Gabe's frequent treks along their property's dirt roads. "Yeah. From what I know about Iron Bowl, even though it's still a week away, I'm surprised the entire town isn't already crawling with tents and RVs."

Gabe smiled but didn't answer. He turned and pointed to where he said a popular barbecue place had been until it got torn down five years ago. "Price's, but everybody just called it The Barbecue House. They had the best Brunswick stew. People were really sad to see the place go, and I know for a fact that alumni came back to town from parts unknown to eat there one last time before it closed."

"Sad, I guess maybe except for whoever got the land and those who profited from the sale." Gina bit her lip as her remark was left unacknowledged. She'd accidentally reminded Gabe of land sale issues, hadn't she? *Idiot.* She finished her coffee and veered over to a trash receptacle near a small but beautiful brick church building. The historic marker identified it as Auburn University Chapel. So, this was where Emmie and Dillon would be married. *Gabe in a tuxedo? Wish I could see that!*

"Anyway, since Barbecue House isn't an option, why don't you decide where we eat lunch?"

"Okay!" Gina purposely made her tone bright. "Thanks."

"It just has to be roughly near Toomer's Corner so we can work a lemonade in. Deal?"

"Yes. Sounds fun."

Gabe directed Gina to a crosswalk that took them to campus near the brick sign reading "AUBURN UNIVERSITY Established 1856." Beyond that lay the huge green space and iconic clock tower building that appeared in virtually every set of Auburn campus pictures. Some of the engagement portraits Gina had seen by now of Emmie and Dillon had been taken in this area.

"Are you going home for Thanksgiving?"

Gina looked at Gabe and nodded. "Yes. I need to see my mother. It was actually shortly after Thanksgiving that my dad died."

Gabe stopped walking. They were on a wide concrete and brick walkway now. On both sides of it were large classroom buildings interspersed with more green spaces and landscaped courtyards. "I miss my father, too, Gina. All the time. I'm sorry you lost yours."

Standing near Gabe, Gina nodded. She appreciated the sympathy, and she noticed Gabe hadn't asked her for details. Maybe his sister had already told him. Gina was much more interested in seeing whether Gabe would open up any more about *his* father. Mrs. Madison had said he needed to.

"Will you be coming back after you go see your mom?"

Gina grew flustered. She looked away. She looked at her feet. She started walking. Finally, she stalled by trying to treat it lightly, answering the question with another question. "Why? Are you about ready to get your cabin back?" This conversation had gone far afield from the subject of grieving one's father. Maybe Mrs. Madison had put Gabe up to something again, come to think of it. Could the host family be wondering how long this retreat of hers was going to drag out? Unhappy thoughts took over. Was today one of the last times she would see Gabe? But Reuben Marks, when last heard from, had said she should "hang in and keep listening." Gina improvised, "Uh...well, I'm working from recommendations that I keep listening. I mean, you know, listening to what my soul is telling me, and that kind of thing." *Oh! So lame!* What would Gabe make of that?

He merely nodded, finally breaking the silence as he turned and pointed. "That area near Foy used to have little lily ponds with goldfish. I remember coming here and watching them with my dad. And he would tell me how he loved fishing as a boy."

Gina said the first thing that came to mind, asking Gabe whether he was fond of fishing now. Not really, he replied, saying nothing more about fishing or about his father. Gina imagined that the sport may have lost its appeal after Gabe no longer had his father to share it with. They walked in silence until they reached the corner of a huge, red brick building with white trim.

"Hey, isn't this the place everybody says they get lost in, no matter how long they have gone to school here?"

"Yes, that's it. Haley Center." Gabe laughed lightly. "I imagine every campus has its myths and legends, but this one seems to have a strong basis in fact."

"Speaking from personal experience?"

"Afraid so." They turned left. "What kind of things did you do with your mother when you were a kid?"

Gabe probably knew, again from Emmie, that Gina's mother had never seemed to get past her grief. If the same applied to Gabe, that might be why he needed to talk about this. The best she could do for him right now was to share freely. She stopped walking and leaned against the wall on the left side of this shorter concourse. Gabe followed suit. Gina described learning a few basics of sewing from her mother, "very sporadically, though. Later, I started taking store classes and watching a lot of how-to videos." What knowledge Gina had acquired of cooking, she said regretfully, came more by watching her mother than by the two of them working together. "I think the burden of having to handle everything – work, paying bills and taxes, calling plumbers and yard people, not to mention caring for me – colored her viewpoint through and through. It had to be hard for her. In a way, I had it easy by comparison. I really didn't know what I was missing. If that makes sense," she finished softly.

Gabe nodded. He appeared to be staring into space. So Gina went on to say she'd had to work all through high school to earn her spending money, and after that she had just kept right on working. "It was my way of life, and it made sense to me. Eventually I wanted a different environment, so I started sharing apartments with friends to split expenses. In fact, I've never lived by myself. Until now." The cabin was hers alone. Entirely hers! No wonder she wished so much that this could last. As a measure of self-caution, she added, "I've enjoyed your cabin even though I know it's temporary, so thanks again for letting me use it." She had just given Gabe a great opening for issuing an eviction order if that's what he had on his mind. Worried, Gina watched him and waited.

He was regarding her. *Scrutinizing* would be more accurate. "Does your mother know what you're doing right now? I mean, where you are, and why?"

"Oh, sure. She knows I took a temporary job."

"Job?" Gabe looked puzzled.

"Oh," Gina laughed nervously. What a stupid goof! "I guess 'task' is what I meant. The task of taking time to reflect for long enough to be sure what I want to do next."

"And the added task of helping *us* out quite a bit."

Gina smiled at Gabe and felt absolutely rotten inside.

"Let's go this way." Gabe inclined his head and started toward some wide steps leading down to more sidewalks and a huge, grassy plot outside the football stadium.

Gina's phone vibrated. She couldn't resist pulling it out. Kristyl Floyd had texted, "Surprising to learn yesterday that my son's beloved Miss Emmie is connected with the company you are reviewing for us. Isaac has been seeing her since the start of school, but I've honestly had so much on my plate that her last name never even got on my radar. Even if it had, I'm not sure I would have made the connection."

Gina murmured, "Sorry, I hope you don't mind if I answer this message." Gabe made no reply. She'd try to make this quick, but that wasn't easy since she wasn't sure what to say. She held the phone down by her side and just walked, noticing something in the trees that she wanted to ask Gabe to explain. Phone back up in both hands, she replied, "I didn't know you lived in Auburn." She hastily added, "I mean, assuming you do." With Gabe so tall, Gina had no idea whether he could read what was on her screen. She just had to trust that he would not blatantly watch.

Auburn and Montgomery were not that far apart. Kristyl Floyd might live here but work in Montgomery. Or she might commute there some of the time and do the rest of her work from home. Lots of businesses operated that way. Gina frowned and glanced to her left, the side Gabe was on. First of all, she didn't need to be getting into all this with him walking right here beside her. Second, maybe Kristyl didn't live in Auburn, but her son attended school here. Anything was possible.

"I'm sorry, Gabe." Gina put her phone inside her purse and asked the question she had been thinking of as they'd climbed the steep hill on Duncan Drive. "Why do so many of the pine trees have almost no lower branches? They remind me of those party toothpicks with crinkly cellophane on one end."

"Sometimes they naturally shed their lower branches with age, depending on sunlight and density of planting."

As Gina acknowledged Gabe's answer, she saw the School of Forestry and Wildlife Sciences on their right. She pointed. "And would this building be of particular importance?"

"Very good. Yes, this is where I spent a great deal of time as a student." They stopped on the sidewalk outside the front entrance. "Oh, speaking of forestry," he segued, "I wanted to tell you that with the kids out in the woods yesterday I got another glimpse into the mental health angle, if that's the right term. You, with all of your retreat reading, probably know that better than I do. I spend so much time with the business details I haven't often been able to see the aesthetic and educational aspects as alive as they were yesterday. It showed me what an added value of our land they are, and that gives me even more motivation than ever to fight this court battle and win it once and for all. On that topic, we received your list of R words that can apply when a person wishes to retreat and regroup. Ah!" He interrupted himself. "I don't think *regroup* was on your list. Did I just trump you?"

Gina grinned. "To quote from a certain Harrison Ford movie, 'More isn't always better. Sometimes, it's just more.'" Gabe gave an exaggerated sigh suggesting abject defeat, and Gina laughed. "You can find a synonym for almost anything in order to achieve alliteration, I've found. For example, *regard* to introduce that quote on looking up, in the stuff I e-mailed to y'all: 'Look up, up, up...to the highest leaves of the tallest tree. And do not stop there. Look higher still, to the trees' Maker – and yours.'"

"I like hearing you talk about words. English and literature weren't my favorite studies, but that was classroom. It's completely different when the information comes up in the course of real life."

Gina longed to exult freely in Gabe's praise, but she couldn't – not in view of his reference to "real life." As much as she wished otherwise, this situation wasn't real life. Something stirred inside her. Maybe, in spite of everything, she could have an impact on *Gabe's* real life for as long as she was here. "Another retreat suggestion I like is the one that says in order to achieve serenity you need to look at whether there is somebody you ought to forgive." Gina strove for a facial expression that was nonjudgmental, yet gently challenging.

Gabe didn't keep her waiting. "I've always assumed my father would have made better business decisions, had he lived, than my uncle has. It's impossible to know that, I realize now. I have unfairly compared my uncle to my father, and not just regarding the timber business. Uncle Chip knows this. The whole family knows it. We just haven't talked about it openly."

Gina leaned a little closer. "Well, it seems you've just talked about it openly to *me*. I think that's a great first step." She smiled warmly, and what Gabe's eyes started doing to hers nearly took her breath away. He finally lowered them, saying they should head to the truck and move it closer to Toomer's Corner.

On College Street, Gabe held the passenger door open for Gina. After she was in and while he walked around to the driver's side, she stole a look at her phone in case her last text had been answered. It had. "Our company has offices in multiple locations. Anyway, good work on your part, not letting on that you knew me." Gina quickly stowed the device. To make casual conversation as they drove, she said she had been using her portable machine to sew some Christmas presents in her spare time. Was that an odd look across Gabe's face as he'd nodded without turning his head? Maybe he wondered why she would bother distinguishing spare time from her other time here. "Um...you asked me a question earlier, about my plans after Thanksgiving." By now, the truck was parked in a diagonal spot on Magnolia.

"And you didn't answer." Gabe turned the motor off and looked at Gina.

"I was afraid you were maybe hinting that I'm in danger of overstaying my welcome." His expression didn't change. "I hope I'm not, because...I'll be honest with you, Gabe." *Oh,* it felt so good to be able to say that and mean it! "I'm not at all sure that my thinking right now is any clearer than it was at the beginning."

"I see." He nodded a little. "Is it possible you have found some *new* things to think about?"

Gina held her breath. Gabe hadn't said, "Like me?" But that seemed to be his meaning.

"I don't wish you to lack direction, so don't misunderstand me, but if you need more time in the cabin to sort things out, it's okay by me."

For some infuriating reason, Gina had a stab of uncertainty that made her break eye contact and start reaching for the door handle. It was along the lines of what she had been feeling right before ducking out of that planning conference weeks ago. Was Gabe encouraging her to stay longer because he wanted her to, or because his family needed her to? Both? He had been making moves pretty consistently. And she hadn't been giving him any reason to stop. Where would it lead, though? That this mutual interest, or budding romance, or whatever it was, would ever get safely off the ground seemed really against the odds.

Chapter 11

"Happy Thanksgiving to you and Claire!" Frances Madison held her phone with one hand while the other stirred sugar into the tea just brewed. She listened to be sure no footsteps were happening on the stairs, then said softly, "I suspect your instincts were good in agreeing to the retreat. I have felt the same way. But only time will tell. And you never know; the holidays may help to turn festivity into something more!" The conversation felt deliciously conspiratorial. Chip concluded the call, saying he and Claire should be arriving within the half hour.

The tea was done. Frances licked the spoon and set it in the sink. *Oh!* Rolls mustn't be forgotten as they had been, here and there, once upon a time. Frank had always been such a good sport regarding her little cooking goofs, even championing her in front of a holiday gathering once, reminding everyone to focus on all that they had, not on what might be lacking. A mistiness sprang to her eyes. She and the children had had to follow that counsel many times, and would again today, regarding Frank himself. Frances searched her heart for a sweet melody to minimize the possibility that she would appear sad when her children ventured downstairs again.

She found a song and began humming it as she put milk and flour together in a shaker container for the giblet gravy. In the process, her humming of a favorite old chorus turned into singing.

He's the Oak and I'm the ivy,
He's the Potter, I'm the clay;
For my Lord and me there'll never be
A parting day!

"I love that song, too, Mother. Let's do that one on our next family night." Emmie was the first of the children to reappear since the early hours of breakfast followed by serious meal preparation. Gabe's computer probably had him glued fast again. Emmie came over now with a proud show of newly polished fingernails.

"Beautiful, Dear. Dear Mary Elizabeth!"

Emmie laughed gaily, carefully taking a large spoon and folding together cornbread crumbs, torn biscuits, diced onion, and chopped celery thrown together in the kitchen's largest mixing bowl as the start of a second batch of dressing. The first pan, in the oven, had the room smelling wonderful. "If Dillon is free then, I'll get him to bring one of the wood block and mallet sets he's been learning to make. Unless you think a staccato beat would destroy this nice lyrical by turning it into a march. How does it start, again?"

Frances Madison wasn't sure at that moment which brought her more joy, the song itself or the fact that her daughter sincerely wanted to hear it. She started at the beginning, and Emmie joined in:

He's the One I love in the morning,
He's the One I love at noon;

He's the One at evening twilight,
He's the One at midnight gloom;
He's the Oak and I'm the ivy,
He's the Potter, I'm the clay;
For my Lord and me there'll never be
A parting day!

And here came Gabe, clapping his hands.

"You missed the singing, Son, but you're just in time to pull the hash brown casserole out and get those cornflakes on it that are in the small mixing bowl."

Gabe obeyed, but only after stopping to snitch a sample of the turkey that was already carved and under foil. "How soon do we eat?"

"Just as soon as your uncle and aunt arrive and I make sure you children have clean hands!"

Emmie laughed. "Oh goodness, Mother."

"Hilarious." Gabe poured some tea for himself. "I will fill the other glasses with ice when you say the word."

Some fifty or so minutes later, after the food dishes had been passed twice, Chip jokingly predicted that they would soon hear "the annual Frances Madison Thanksgiving soliloquy."

"Yes, you are absolutely right. And thank you for leading up to it with what you said in your prayer before our meal. Indeed, our God does give us even more joy than the harvest brings. I hope all of you were enjoying your food so much that you didn't catch me on my phone finding the Bible reference for that." She laughed. "It is Psalm four, verse seven. As we reflect on all that we have to be thankful for, we should also remember the great confidence we place in our God because He will always supply what we need." Some heads nodded, and some faces looked thoughtful. Frances sighed contentedly. "That's my soliloquy for this year. Joy, thankfulness, confidence."

"Hear, hear!"

"Thank you, Mother."

After Frances and Claire served the pumpkin pie and coffee, in some cases with whipped cream on top of both, banter and buoyancy gradually settled into quieter conversations in smaller groups. Frances heard Gabe address his uncle, and she tuned in immediately. "Drones," Gabe was saying. "I've spotted one on two separate occasions during the past month. I'm trying to decide whether to be concerned."

Frances let the men discuss the matter without her interruption. Drones, scones, or phones…any subject that had those two dialoguing this calmly would not rattle her. She felt certain that, whatever the sightings meant, it was something that could be handled. She must not succumb to fear today, especially after exhorting the rest of her family to confidence. *In peace I will lie down and sleep, for you alone, Lord, make me dwell in safety. Psalm 4:8.* She had seen that when hunting to find chapter and verse for what Chip had quoted.

~

Gabe ate his second piece of pie slowly, then deliberately waited through another set of downs each from the Raiders and the Cowboys. He intended to text, but he didn't want to appear too eager to learn how Gina's Thanksgiving Day was going. His had been low-key. The usual great meal, mainly, and probably too much of it. He yawned, then pushed the empty dessert plate aside on the coffee table and propped his feet up.

He could have wished for Gina to join this crew today, but she needed to be with her own family. She didn't live with her mom, which was more the norm for adult children her age and his. He hadn't moved out on his own, except for living on campus part of his undergrad years. It just made practical and economic sense to be here on the land. It would have been hard to add rent and utilities for another whole residence to the list of expenses coming out of Madison Timber Farm income. Besides, Mother had needed him and Emmie in order not to be alone. At least, he'd always told himself that. They hadn't let him take over the company when he thought he was ready, so he had done the next best thing. He had started considering himself man of the house.

The game coverage switched to a crowd shot, and the camera stopped on a cute girl wearing a very fitted Raiders shirt that was black with gray sleeves. Her hair color reminded Gabe of Gina's. It was fixed down and curly the way Gina had worn hers on Saturday for their day date. If a date was what it had been. Gabe stayed in front of the TV because it was the traditional Thanksgiving Day football game and not because he especially cared about these teams right now.

There was something about Gina. Something different, but something *different* from merely "different." Gabe didn't know yet what it was. He just knew he wasn't through trying to find out. He grinned. She sure seemed to have *him* pegged. His brow wrinkled. Was that why he couldn't stop thinking about her – the effect she was having on *him?* Gabe nodded, then craned his neck to be sure nobody in the kitchen could see him. Yes. How Gina had managed to rock his world from day one, subtly and surprisingly influencing and challenging him, was a big part of this. He stared at the television blankly and eventually comprehended that the score hadn't changed. When a commercial break started, he lowered the volume a little and leaned his head against the couch. *Gina.* She was undeniably intriguing, mostly in good and attractive ways. But she had some shadowy corners, too, same as he did.

Gabe opened his eyes, blinked, and eventually got his bearings. *Football game.* It was the middle of the fourth quarter with the Cowboys trailing. The volume was way down at 16, a sure sign Mother had passed through the living room during his nap. Gabe eased his long limbs, stood, and went to the little half bathroom on a circuitous route, first taking his dirty dishes to the kitchen sink.

Where's my phone? The football game wasn't the only thing he had napped through. Was now the right time to let Gina know she was on his mind? He spied the phone half hidden by the pillow he had had under his feet. The screen showed a new text notification. *Gina!* "Hey, Gabe, hope you are full of turkey and dressing. Is your mother going to sneak any leftovers into the fridge at the cabin? LOL"

Smiling, Gabe stared at his screen, reading the words two or three times. It seemed clear Gina expected to be returning, and that was the most important box checked. Besides that, she had texted him first! Another good sign. He touched the reply field at the bottom of his screen. "I will speak to her about that." *Send.* He knew he was grinning like a thirteen-year-old enjoying his first mutual flirtation. "Or handle it myself." *Send.* He meandered up the stairs to his bedroom, glancing at the phone a couple of times on the way.

Ping! Gina had sent a smiley face. Gabe stretched out on the bed, eventually writing back and launching what turned into an ongoing exchange covering what each had enjoyed about their Thanksgiving meal, how they thought the Iron Bowl would shake out on Saturday, and what "Black Friday" typically was or wasn't for each of them. Meanwhile, Gabe caught a tying rally by Dallas that quickly proved futile when Daniel Carlson booted a 56-yarder giving Las Vegas the three-point victory. Because it ought to be done, Gabe gave forth a "War Eagle" cheer for the former Auburn kicker.

Gina sent, "Mom and I plan to venture out a little bit for shopping tomorrow. We've really enjoyed each other's company this holiday, which I guess I'd been hoping for but hadn't known whether to expect. I know I told you before that I was no closer to any great clarity, but for some reason I've found myself feeling more equal with my mother in terms of looking at her more objectively and respecting what her journey has been apart from how I always saw it while growing up. It has been unfair of me to view her whole life mainly in terms of how she has dealt with loss. There is much more to her that I've been so blind to!"

Another message came in on the heels of that one. "I mean, I'm sure that's very normal. I had my own life to manage. In recent years I've believed I was handling life a lot better than my mother ever did, but I see now that my assumptions have been shortsighted. And prideful." Gabe took some time to ponder this message. It deserved better than a hasty answer or an offhand "like" or "love" or "exclamation" symbol.

Ping! "Also, I apologized to Mom for getting so out of the habit of calling and visiting."

Gabe's mouth quirked. Issuing apologies wasn't *his* strong suit, and even Gina had seen that fact firsthand. Earlier today he had been nudging himself in that direction. Gina's example challenged him. Could he step up soon and go the rest of the way? He visualized himself admitting to Uncle Chip, on the subject of hurriedly installing a test guest in a nonexistent retreat while Gabe had been out of town, "I guess I would have done the same thing in your place."

~

Sunday, November 28. What I told Gabe on Thursday about my good visit with Mom was kind of a drop in the bucket, and I wish I could tell him the rest. But that's impossible, of course. Not to mention, using the word "breakthrough" with him might carry connotations I'd feel pressured to live up to (as in, I'm "recovered" from something), and it would also suggest I'm done retreating and ought to be packing my things.

Gina held her pen and looked around her. A poignant sense of attachment, something both physical and emotional, took hold of her. She didn't want the day to hasten when she would be leaving this cabin she had come to cherish, especially with the little touches that had made it even better. More so, now. Yesterday she had gone by her apartment, empty since both roommates were away visiting their families, and had been inspired to bring a potted philodendron back with her, along with some extra clothes.

She straightened the pillows against the headboard for better support, then read where she had left off, so she could finish the thought. *Instead of a breakthrough, I would call my weekend discoveries an epiphany, and that's the part I can't really share with Gabe. On Thursday morning, Mom and I worked together on a dessert (pumpkin spice cupcakes; I've brought 7 or 8 back with me), which led spontaneously to trying another recipe we saw on the same website, Dutch apple bread. We decided it could go in her freezer for a girlfriends' gathering in December – a monthly thing I didn't even know she had going. Anyway, I may toss both recipe links Emmie's way and hint for some baking time in the Madisons' huge kitchen. All that to say, right in the middle of sprinkling the crumbly topping over the apple bread batter, it hit me. My "fake" retreat in the forest has turned out not to be fake at all!! Anything "pretend" about it stopped being pretend I don't know how long ago. I realized that, apart from the whole deal with Three Points, I have gained something far greater.*

Gina stayed with the journal even after her hand began to protest, explaining on the page how and why meeting Chip, then Emmie, then Mrs. Madison, and then Gabe, and living here on their land almost entirely free of scheduled commitments, had broadened her outlook and had made her believe in her ability to contribute to new situations (the idea fest and the field trip, but also – she hoped! – with Gabe and some of his personal struggles). Add in the special and unique things the Madisons had invited her to do, like experience their family night tradition, sew on that awesome antique Singer, go with them to their Halloween parties, and, though the wings place wasn't precisely a date, there was that, as well as the campus walk with lunch and lemonade. And just look at how much time she had been spending – really valuable time – with this journal. Here on her lap she had a meaningful record of ideas and feelings potentially worth sharing. With Taylor, for example. And with Mom.

Josh was acting true to form during the weekend, sending me links to things that aren't always as cute as their thousands of views would indicate. This particular detail of Gina's life needed that breakthrough she had been writing about. She looked at his name on the page and automatically compared the guy she had dated halfheartedly last summer to the one who apparently had been in the cabin during the weekend long enough to leave that vase over there on the desk. Gina closed her journal and reached for her phone, suddenly surprised at herself for not having done this already. She captured some pictures of the flowers, then of the card she would probably tuck into the crease of her journal in the middle of tonight's entry. The card read:

The cornbread dressing and turkey Brunswick stew
in the fridge are from Mother, but the flowers are
from me and me alone. Welcome back. – Gabe

~

"Happy Thanksgiving" was a belated e-mail subject line for a message dated today, the 30th, five days after the holiday.

The sender was Kristyl Floyd. Gina frowned and opened the message with a deft finger while deciding which of the protein bar flavors staring at her from the open cabinet sounded most appealing. Settling into the side porch rocker a minute later with a blanket and her phone, coffee, and Sea Salt Chocolate bar, she realized that the company had merely merged their e-mail list with a stock holiday message prepared and provided by an outside service. Below the holiday greeting (complete with a cartoon turkey's antics) were predictable seasonal topics, with links: "Beat Holiday Stress Before It Starts," and "Hottest Gifts This Christmas."

Even though Gina was almost done with her gift sewing and had already bought or ordered everything else, out of curiosity she touched the link to find out what somebody somewhere wanted her to believe the friends on her Christmas list would like. The screen of her phone got overwritten by an ad for Iron Bowl victory T-shirts. Fine. She hadn't been *that* interested in reading the article. She closed the browser and went to the e-mail message again. Maybe this was a new method of goodwill contact for Three Points and some glitches had caused the delivery to be at least five days late.

Five days. That long since the holiday, but it was only two days since Gina had returned to the cabin to find Gabe's flowers. Maybe he had been led to make the sweet gesture because he would be out of pocket for a while. His brief "have a good week" message Monday morning had been followed by an FYI regarding a trip on short notice, to see some forestland in Clay County. On impulse, Gina asked her phone to tell her about the place where Gabe was. A page loaded, and she read a description of Dewberry Lands, a family-owned operation in Lineville for "timber production, recreation, wildlife, and aesthetics." Photos showed a darling, rustic lodge with bedroom loft and a large, main gathering space that provided a gorgeous view out huge windows; wildflower varieties of all shapes in yellow, white, purple, pink, and orange; and wildlife including turkey, deer, fox, bluebird, and a bald eagle!

Gina browsed more photos. These landowners hosted small-group retreats…and school field trips. So, Emmie's idea had been spot on! Gina considered texting Gabe to suggest he take notes, pictures, and videos for inspiration since his family would be putting their expansion ideas into practice sooner rather than later. But she held back. Gabe was on a work trip as far as she knew, so maybe he didn't need interruptions. Come to think of it, maybe to take notes on the Dewberry place was precisely why he had gone there. Gina recalled the day she had met Gabe, that "unlucky" thirteenth of October. His fatigue and vexation had clearly betrayed how seriously he did take his job and how hard he did work. Her best move right now was to respect that by staying quiet.

She had barely set her phone on the table when a text alert made her pick it up again. *Gabe?* she couldn't help wondering. Okay, *hoping*. But it wasn't. It was Kristyl Floyd. Speaking of taking one's job seriously, Gina had better follow Gabe's example. What she read surprised her. It was almost entirely a message of encouragement, praising her for doing a good job. It had a decidedly different tone from prior communications. And it ended by telling Gina that if she found herself ready to send her information in earlier than deadline she was welcome to do that. Gina angled her head and reread the text. Had they tried buttering her up simply as a lead-in to asking her to complete and submit her material early?

What *about* that idea? Would she want to turn her work in before the December 20 deadline? Holding one edge of the blanket, Gina stood. She drained her mug and set it on the table. She rolled the blanket up and put it on the chair, weighing that option as she stretched her arms out wide and finally raised them over her head before lowering them. Well...she could get that stipend deposited all the sooner and maybe treat *herself* to some nice Christmas presents. That thought lasted maybe five seconds. She shook her head. Ever since Thanksgiving she had had a different idea brewing, and during a rather restless effort at sleep last night she had finally made up her mind. The thing was, this new idea would require *more* time on Madison land, not less.

Three Points was expecting – insisting on – middle-of-the-road numbers. Fine. She planned to do what she had been hired for, letting the research company process her believable, average review in their usual manner. But she was not going to finish here until she had composed a second review, one with no restrictions. In it she would rate accommodations a 5 if so led, likelihood to return to the site and to recommend it to friends a 5, staff professionalism and friendliness a 5, and overall satisfaction level a 5.

At about 2:30 a.m. she had finally turned the lights on to look through the journal she had been keeping since her arrival. The content of that book, combined with some of the things in her texts to Gabe on Thanksgiving Day, could be fashioned into a "Wow" guest testimonial. Gina had in her possession persuasive, emotive material that, once compiled and edited, ought to prove highly favorable – possibly even profitable – to the Madisons. It could be posted directly on social media, in search engine reviews, and, eventually, on the Madison retreat's own website. But, in view of what Kristyl Floyd had just said, Gina wouldn't put it past Three Points not to stop at inviting her to conclude things early. They might start insisting. She had better get busy on her *honest* feedback.

Chapter 12

Thursday, December 2. Social media still blowing up with Iron Bowl aftermath and SEC championship hype. Work coming along. Tempted to use fabric left from gift sewing to make a new zippered triangle tote for myself.

Christmas events on my calendar! 12/4 Chorale concert of "Messiah" with Mom; 12/10 Christmas in a Railroad Town (in Opelika; Madisons have invited me to go); 12/11 brunch at their house.

Gina sipped her gingerbread latté and forwarded ahead a couple of songs on the Christmas playlist she had going through her earbuds. Coming way over to Panera Bread, early, for breakfast and journal time had been an impulse born last evening during somewhat a marathon of Christmas movies. Maybe she felt restless for a new environment because she knew Gabe was away getting that for himself. He had been silent, as regarded Gina, ever since Monday's message telling her his plans.

She could appeal to Emmie for an update on Gabe in case he had returned already. But now was bound to be especially busy for Emmie at school. Gina had been rather busy herself on her critical, under-the-radar review.

Christmas season being everywhere "in the air" was a much more festive thought. Come to think of it, the mall was right across Opelika Road. It might be fun to enjoy a second coffee until the mall opened, then wander through that gift shop where she had found the note cards for Mrs. Madison. That seemed forever ago! Plus, she could look for something especially nice to wear to the festival thing next Friday. Gina ordered a plain Americano this time and resumed one of the movies she hadn't finished last night. It had been authentically filmed in cold weather, so she didn't have to waste energy noticing that the actors' breath didn't show in the air even though all of them wore coats, hats, scarves, and mittens.

Working carefully on her hair for tonight's outing, Gina watched herself happily in the mirror as Gabe's text from Sunday night replayed in her head. She'd finally heard from him after a week of silence. "I know the Opelika thing this Friday is a family affair, but I'm hoping you and I can distance ourselves and take a carriage ride or something. I want to tell you about my time away." And so their plans had been made, to ride together in his truck to Christmas in a Railroad Town.

She hadn't seen Gabe once since his return, gathering from his mother that he was heavily involved, hands-on, in routine burnings for site prep in one area and for benefit of longleaf pine in another, besides being a little behind on clearing the roads and trails of the usual fallen limbs and displaced rocks. Gina applied her makeup either side of some urgent texts to Taylor asking the best eye shadow colors for her outfit, the focal piece of which was a gray, figure-enhancing sweater embellished with rows of red "garland" scallops and ornament shapes. She wanted to look her very best!

An hour later, during the drive, Gabe told Gina of his sudden decision to go away to Clay County to see a place he'd heard about through AFA. It was work, in a way, he said, but he'd also had a personal agenda. Gina didn't tell him she had looked the place up and had at least a starting idea of what it was like. Gabe had to focus now on the Friday night traffic as he maneuvered off 85; he said the rest of his story would have to wait. Gina contented herself with watching the sunset and anticipating an evening of delights. Unlike the sets of all those movies, no snow was expected to fall on this holiday gathering, but Emmie's description of the event had mentioned virtually everything else one could hope for, from carolers to a gingerbread house contest to local dance troupes performing. Not to mention the carriage rides!

Gina smoothed her sweater as Gabe came around to her side and helped her out of the truck. This was a real date! Gabe's strong arm watching out for her safety was such a happy contrast to that other occasion. No water hazards, no unfriendly family "friends" should endanger Gina tonight, nor ruin her hair! Besides her jeans and boots, she wore a thin and low-necked thermal top under her Christmas sweater so she could do without a coat. In other words, so Gabe could see her outfit.

They took a leisurely stroll to get familiar with where everything was, each of them saying what interested them. For Gabe, that was the carriage ride (he'd already booked their appointment time, he said), the hot chocolate, and – he teased – the face painting in case Gina thought he needed livening up. She seized that opening to tell her date she wouldn't change one thing about the way he looked. In fact, she'd become almost apathetic toward her own carefully selected attire, so dashing was Gabe in that forest green V-neck sweater with white shirt under it, the untucked variety whose hem fell just below the waistline of his dark jeans.

As they waited near the carriage ride departure point, Gina shared her theory that the song "Sleigh Ride" ought to be "Hayride" for the southern climate. Just now, a very different type of music, "The Hallelujah Chorus," drifted over from somewhere, reminding her to describe the concert she had attended last weekend with her mother, after which the two of them had spent time framing some old pictures with her dad in them.

"Speaking of family…" Gabe pointed out his mother and Emmie and Dillon in the crowd some distance away. Turning back, he checked the time. "Our turn."

The sparkling surroundings temporarily dimmed for Gina as she focused on stepping up gracefully for her very first horse-drawn carriage ride. She and Gabe settled into the upholstered seat of the all-white rig, and he quickly returned to the subject that obviously was uppermost in his thoughts. "Sometime, you should see the place where I stayed in Lineville." He turned toward Gina and described the Dewberrys' impressive stands of longleaf pine at different ages, a distant view of the crest at Mt. Cheaha, and even "the certified oldest chestnut oak in Alabama, practically right outside the lodge's front door." Those were some of the highlights of his week, which had been an effort to correct having achieved no real R & R during his trip in October. "This time, I remembered the difference between hiking and walking. I saw three wild turkeys one day. And, believe it or not, I binge-watched Food Network shows at night. I never do that!" The childlike delight on Gabe's face was something to see! Out came his phone now, and he showed Gina pictures of plants he said his mother would be thrilled about: bear's foot, blazing star, thickleaf phlox ("Try saying that five times fast!"), and rabbit tobacco.

When the carriage turned a corner, Gina waved at some

Victorian carolers. Those who saw her gesture smiled back. "I stayed," Gabe continued, "and tried to 'unplug' for as long as I felt I could distance myself from" – was there a slight hesitation? – "work, and everything." He stopped talking now, though Gina felt sure he had more to say. He might be gathering his thoughts. Or his courage. She waited, looking aside so as not to make him too self-conscious. Stations for face painting and for donating Christmas toys caught her eye.

Gabe reached for Gina's hand. "Based on…based on a lot of things, mostly having to do with you, I decided to take a careful look at my own status quo, trying to figure out honestly what I want the next phase of *my* life to be like. Admittedly, my attempted retreat wasn't nearly as long as the one you are having, but I was determined to try to follow your example."

Gina gazed into those brown eyes with all of her heart, shunning a nudge of worry over the words *honestly* and *example.* The means didn't matter so much as the end, and the end was that something really helpful was happening before her eyes, to a special man who wanted to express himself to her against the most enchanting background either of them would probably experience this year.

"And," Gabe's crooked grin did not change how serious he still sounded, "recalling what might have been a subtle hint a couple of weeks ago, I considered who I need to forgive."

Gina nodded at Gabe, then squeezed his hand and surrendered herself to the moment, settling back and leaning her head against him. Wouldn't you know it, though? The carriage was slowing to a stop. They climbed out, and Gabe asked Gina to wait on a bench while he went to get hot chocolate for them. Around her, the trees sparkled with little white lights. Before she had reveled in the setting for one minute, Emmie messaged her, "Hey, you guys seem to be enjoying yourselves. Dillon and I are, too! ☃❄ I think this is a great time to let you in on a little secret from football season, assuming you haven't figured it out already. My brother concocted that whole triple date thing so he could go out with you. He had me send the group text so it would conveniently give him your number. He knew all along that Dillon and I had tickets and would be going to the game, and he pulled Micah in for long enough to make things look legit." Gina put the phone away and tried to turn her grin into a casual expression as she accepted the tall, red cup being offered.

They meandered past vendor booths offering Christmas-themed merchandise and other gift items. "Oh, my friend Taylor would get a kick out of this!" Gina stopped and pointed, laughing. The oversized coffee mug was imprinted, My Boss Told Me To Have A Good Day, So I Went Home. "Sense of humor goes a long way in the workplace, as I'm sure you must know." Gina reached for the mug. "Like you, Taylor takes her job seriously. She's the best store manager I've ever worked under."

After a short silence, Gabe said, "Wait. Taylor is a *she?*" He looked puzzled but also pleased.

"Yes." It was Gina's turn to feel puzzled. "Why?" She sipped her hot chocolate for something to do.

"At any rate, that's good news to me. Strike Taylor. I hope this means I have only *two* unknown men who are probably my rivals for your affection."

Two unknown men? Gina stared. Who on earth did Gabe mean?

"Hold on, Gina. Let me back up." He looked very conflicted. But that was nothing to how confused *she* was. "Look," Gabe said, "I have a confession to make." Where this was going, Gina barely had time to wonder. "A while back, actually on the day you left our planning meeting with a headache, I came over to check on you and got derailed by your phone beeping on the side porch. I went to silence it, which maybe was the wrong thing to do. Anyway, I– I saw your screen." Gabe gave her a look she took to be apologetic. "It was lit up like a Christmas tree with notifications."

Gina bit her lip. "Okay..." What had Gabe seen?

"Gina, I'm sorry I looked. I wasn't purposely spying. But I guess it's my punishment that I've been agonizing over who my competition is. Josh? And Reuben?" Gabe's expression had a vulnerability that touched Gina in different ways. It was very sweet, and somewhat serious, what he was admitting. He liked her! Enough so that he didn't like the idea of her being involved with any other guy. But...he couldn't truly expect her to feel obligated to explain, could he?

"Before you answer, there's something more." Gabe shook his head and closed his eyes. He opened them again and now adopted an expression that might be called anguished. "By the time I put your phone down, I think I figured out based on sounds coming from the window that..." He hurried through the rest of it, though dropping his volume: "That you were in the shower. I ran! And I didn't look, and I didn't see anything!" He exhaled audibly. "I've been hoping all this time that your silence on the matter means you didn't realize it happened." Gabe looked almost as if a firing squad were taking aim at him. "I didn't mean to spy on your phone or on you. Please believe me!" He reached for her hand. "I want this off my chest. I don't want it hanging between you and me."

Gina's stomach started hurting. Had the rich beverage disagreed with her? As much as she wanted to hope it was that, she knew otherwise. "First of all," she finally got out, even managing to laugh a little as she imagined Gabe's ordeal on the cabin's porch all that time ago. Suppose he had twisted an ankle while scrambling away as he'd just described. He would have had an embarrassing time explaining his injury! "First of all," she repeated, trying for a sincere look that would bestow some absolution, "I had no idea you were ever there. So don't worry." If only the rest of what to say could be that easy. "And thank you for telling me. I realize you didn't have to own up to it."

Gina sipped from her cup again, and Gabe lifted his, too, not taking his eyes off her. Could she muster a degree of honesty to match his? She was going to try. She wanted him to know these men were not his rivals! "Josh is a friend. I mean, we dated for a while, but he was more interested than I was. Period. He's simply not for me." Gabe seemed to relax at that, but Gina couldn't skirt the fact that there was one more name he wanted to know about.

Hey. Interrupting a conversation to look at her phone was fully justifiable right now. Gina quickly opened her text messages to try to figure out what Gabe had seen from Reuben on...what day was it? Reuben hadn't sent many texts. Mostly, his assistant seemed to handle everything.

She found the message. Wednesday, November 3. "Stick with it." *Think, Gina!* The idea of lying to Gabe about this was misery. Maybe, sometime, she could and would explain, even though it would be a slippery slope to confess that Reuben had been an employer paying her to evaluate the Madisons' retreat without their knowledge. For now, she had the advantage. Could she manage it cleverly? Gabe had accidentally invaded her privacy and had confessed it. He was not due any information beyond what he had seen. "As for the other," Gina stalled with a little laugh, "it's nothing, really." She smiled and shrugged. "Just another friend encouraging me on my retreat." She held her breath.

The colorful choo choo train Gina had noticed during the carriage ride sounded its whistle. Someone called, "Hey! Miss Gina!" A child on the train was waving. Gina waved back, recognizing a girl who had been at the field trip before Thanksgiving. She tried to remember the girl's name, but it wouldn't come to her.

"And here I've been thinking all along I made a hit with my guitar that day. But 'Miss Gina' steals the show."

Gina shook her head and told Gabe *he* was the rock star from where she sat. "That child remembers me because I helped her glue her turkey together. Up close and personal. That's the only difference. Except for the fact that I wore a name tag. Did you?" She grinned at him.

"I have no idea." Gabe took her hand. This time, his strong, tanned fingers laced themselves between her smaller, softer ones. In spite of her inner turmoil, Gina's best dream moments seemed to keep happening. She and Gabe walked without conversation. Amid the holiday bustle, Gina realized a bit belatedly that they had stopped on a street corner not far from the city's official Christmas tree. Gabe stood looking at her in almost a mischievous way. In answer to her confused expression, he leaned his head back, raised his eyes, and pointed upward.

No. Not really! But it was. Had Gabe seen the mistletoe before now? Had he stopped under it intentionally? Their eyes locked, and Gina waited. Gabe lowered his head and brushed Gina's lips with his. It was very sweet and very romantic. *Scent of that "Steel Courage" body wash?* Gina reveled in a mixture of sensations. *A spare bottle in the house?*

Gabe was looking into her eyes now. Naturally, he wanted to judge her reaction. It must have pleased him. He repeated the move, placing a hand against her back, and this second kiss was not just for the sake of the holidays. It lasted longer, and it was not what anybody would call merely sweet! Gina knew she would record the moment, not necessarily in her journal, but in her memory. Forever. Her beverage cup landed on the sidewalk. They looked at it, and Gina's face grew warm. "Okay, you've got me flustered. I admit it." She retrieved the cup, muttering loudly enough to be sure Gabe would hear, "Mr. Unbelievably Romantic." Her words got her a look from Gabe that was almost as stirring as his kisses had been!

"Gabe!"

They looked toward the sound. Emmie and Dillon were beckoning urgently and calling for Gabe. Mrs. Madison was with them, looking more dignified than the others, but smiling. Gina could only imagine what they were up to. Regardless, the interruption wasn't unwelcome. She wanted a private moment to gather herself. She gave the excuse of wishing to check her face in a mirror, leaving Gabe free to go and see what his family wanted. Curiosity got the better of her, though, and she hoped that with her powder compact in front of her face the Madisons wouldn't notice her gradually easing close enough to hear.

Emmie giggled as her fiancé ribbed Gabe, "Eh...you want to tell us what was going on under the mistletoe?"

With his back to Gina, Gabe claimed to have no idea what Dillon meant. "And, even if I do know what you're talking about, the only information you'll get from me is my name, rank, and watershed."

All of them laughed, and Gina relished Gabe's quick humor. She felt no embarrassment or offense over the way his close-knit family was kidding him. It was natural. Obviously, they had seen the kissing, and their manner didn't suggest that they thought Gabe had made a mistake or had stepped out of line. Mrs. Madison commented softly, so softly that

Gina could barely hear her, "Is it possible we have over there an ivy that has found her oak?"

~

Gina stretched out on the bed and stared absently at the ceiling, unable to focus on capturing anything in her journal. On the desk she had set the funny coffee mug, her purse, and some cookies from Tart & Tartan Bakery. The box of cookies ought to go into a plastic storage bag. Later.

Tonight's date had ended a few minutes ago, without a parting kiss, on the cabin's porch. Those moments under the mistletoe, plus holding hands, had been enough to make the evening magical and memorable for Gina. Had Gabe felt that way, too? Maybe he hoped that *she* would hope for more of the same on another occasion. *He did say I looked very nice tonight!*

As for the awkward other stuff, well…she could talk to him tomorrow, confess everything, and make it right. Maybe, if she explained how she had really come to be here, emphasizing how wonderful everything *was* here, and omitting the part about average review numbers... No. Impossible! For one thing, voluntarily blowing her cover would absolutely violate the terms of her contract. For another, what kind of integrity was it to explain "everything," yet leave something out? That would never do. Tonight, Gabe had spoken of following Gina's example by honestly taking a good, hard look at his life. No matter how this whole situation had started, she understood that honesty now. She had experienced it in spite of the way she had begun, merely *pretending* to retreat.

~

Gina dressed with care for the Madisons' Christmas brunch, pairing the leggings she had bought for her first dinner at their house two months ago – two months ago to the day, in fact – with a long Christmas sweater designed with green snowflakes and red reindeer on a brown background. Pulling her outfit and boots from the closet a few minutes ago, she'd been struck for some reason by images of the clothes that had been in there between the day of her arrival and that Friday a week later when Gabe had retrieved them. The other garments didn't spark vivid memories, but those she had mended she felt intimately acquainted with: the camo jacket with its heavy zippers and its large, gusseted, exterior flap pockets that had hand-warming linings; and the blue plaid flannel shirt on which she had not only restitched the torn patch pocket, but also tightened up that pocket's button plus three more loose buttons – two on the front placket, and the one on the right sleeve cuff.

Gina finished her hair, brushed her teeth, applied lipstick lightly, and started to gather her things for the walk over. Her phone showed a couple of text notifications she would check later, and one new voicemail probably from a rejected spam call she had received while showering or drying her hair. She glanced at the printed transcription, frowned, and determined it to be a misdirected message, nothing to do with her. Someone was saying "sigh" over annoyance having to do with prescription medications. Gina deleted the voicemail without listening to it, then headed out.

Soon, the smells of maple syrup, coffee, and fresh-baked biscuits were welcoming her back into the home where she had formed some lasting memories this fall. "Merry Christmas!" she called, and Emmie led her past the huge, decorated tree in the living room. Gina definitely planned to take a closer look at the ornaments later.

In the kitchen, Mrs. Madison was waiting along with Chip and Claire. "Dillon is working today, unfortunately." Emmie explained her fiancé's absence. That meant a party of six including Gabe. He evidently would be the last one downstairs. Gina automatically counted the plates on the table. Only five! Her heart sank. Come to think of it, no footsteps or closet doors or hairdryers could be heard overhead. If Gabe was going to be absent, would somebody explain why? Trying to keep her face looking happy, Gina ordered herself not to bring the matter up.

"I'm sorry Gabe won't be joining us," his mother said right after voicing a prayer over the meal, and that much of Gina's question was answered. Mrs. Madison lifted a bowl of grits with two hands and started the dishes going around the table. "He has worked so much these past two weeks that he decided a day off to go hunting would suit him." Gina couldn't read Mrs. Madison's mind, of course, but it appeared she wished that her son had chosen to be here. Claire Ensley started complimenting the food and comparing the coffee cake to the recipe she planned to take to a dinner club gathering one night next week.

Gina tried to suppress her disappointment by focusing on the meal. Last night, Gabe hadn't mentioned his plans for today. Maybe going hunting had been an impulse like his recent getaway trip. Or maybe a buddy had messaged him late last night or early this morning to set it up.

Suddenly, it seemed that everybody else had gone as quiet as Gina had, so she spoke up about how interesting it had been to explore the historical resources in the company office. She wanted to be sure that Chip, especially, knew the value she had found in those materials. She mentioned the quote she had shared with Gabe the day they had gone canoeing, about outdoor recreation building receptivity into people's minds; also, an opinion piece treating forest "therapy."

"Anyway," she finished while using a nearby serving fork to transfer a slice of bacon to her plate, "that article started me referring to this place as the Madison Forest Therapy Trail in my journal. The dual meaning of *trail* is nice." She drew from the five-star review in progress on her computer. "A retreat site is obviously more than mere trails in the woods. To me, a 'therapy trail' through beautiful trees like these can help a person along their trail in life. Their journey." Some at the table began looking at each other oddly, but none of them were looking at Gina. Had her little speech embarrassed them? Sounded stupid?

"What did you say?" Chip broke the silence. "I mean, about a therapy trail?" The man's mouth was practically hanging open.

Gina let herself breathe again, but only because she had to. "I'm not sure I can repeat all of it, word for word."

"This sure beats all. Young lady, you have just delivered an address on par with our Frances Madison soliloquies!"

"We don't mean to embarrass you, Gina. I believe my brother is trying to say that you have inadvertently offered a solution we have been needing."

Emmie looked at her mother, then at Gina. "Right! Oh, I *love* that name! Madison Forest Therapy Trail. Gina, you are a genius!"

Emmie's mother added her enthusiasm by way of a sound that was probably the most emotion Gina had seen the woman display. Normally, she seemed to be the "poster mom" of calm. "We have become so focused on specific expansion plans that we have neglected one of the most daunting tasks of all: giving our retreat a worthy name!" She actually clapped her hands together.

Chip nodded his head. "Agreed, Frances. Every one of us seems to have forgotten about floating any ideas for an official name for this enterprise." He turned to Gina and bestowed almost a...*holy* expression on her. Gina wondered at it. "Not only that, but your timing is nothing less than miraculous! Emmie, you're quick with a phone. Get that proposed name down and e-mail it to the rest of us, please."

Now, Gina felt gratified by the affirmation. "But I don't really understand you. What do you mean about my timing?"

Chip explained not only that Silas Connelly's appeal would diminish in strength with every additional piece of documentation the Madisons could place before the judge, but also that the official name of the retreat had to be on file by a set date. "That deadline is the fifteenth. I suppose it's likely my nephew the manager has this date noted on his calendar with a big red flag and one of those audio alert tones, but the officers of the company haven't had a single meeting to discuss the name."

"Maybe that's part of the work he's been so busy with lately." Timidly, Gina voiced her thoughts. "Maybe he won't like my idea."

Emmie seemed to have a secret reason for smiling at Gina's words. Chip shrugged. His wife, who wasn't an officer of Madison Timber Farm, remained silent. But Mrs. Madison turned toward Gina. "Dear, my own opinion is that my son will be on board, as the rest of us are, and will be just as relieved to have a name ready to turn in not just on time, but early. The judge will notice that kind of thing. And, supposing we do decide later to tweak the name, which I doubt, well..." she winked at Gina, "that's what God made Articles of Amendment for."

Emmie quoted a Bible verse she said was appropriate for the moment. "God knows our needs before we ask."

"*Now* who's sounding like Frances Madison?" her uncle quipped. Then he sobered. "And to have the name come from the perspective of a guest instead of from any eggheads within the company – myself the greatest egghead, I imagine – that is a stroke of business savvy I don't think anybody could miss."

Emmie scooted her chair back, stood, and asked who wanted a refill of coffee. She rounded a corner of the table and stopped to place an arm around Gina's shoulders. "I'm going to order you a dozen cookies all your own!"

Chapter 13

Monday, December 13, 2:25 p.m. Had lunch today at Jim 'n' Nick's Bar-B-Q on South College...with my mom! That was a surprise. If ever Gina needed her journal time to be therapeutic, it was now. *The greater surprise was why Mom called me yesterday and asked me to meet her. In her mailbox on Saturday she found an "urgent and confidential" letter for me. An anonymous urgent and confidential letter. However, I didn't know it was unsigned until I read it two hours ago.*

The letter lay next to Gina on the bed. She stared at it as though it might do something besides lie there, something extra to frighten her even more than it already had. Burst into flames, for instance. Or sprout wings and fly out the window, like something in a Harry Potter book. Those scenarios couldn't be much more absurd than the letter itself, which was actually very short. Gina knew now that a bombshell didn't have to be large or long to make a huge impact.

"Dear Gina," it began in plain black type on white printer paper. "As a friend I want to warn you that the man who engaged you for your present assignment is not to be trusted. He has been subtly, or not so subtly, pressuring you to return a dishonest evaluation, telling you that high ratings are not acceptable. The truth is, this man has personal reasons for wanting to obtain from a disinterested party (you) a negative review of the Madison Timber Farm retreat site and plans. I strongly urge you to use caution as you conclude your dealings with this man. He is crafty and resourceful, with any number of people in his pocket."

That was the whole letter. Just one paragraph. Somebody wanted Gina to believe she had been working for a man who not only had a specific conflict of interest in this current situation but also had a deep pattern of shady dealings. Gina shuddered and bent down to rest her chin on one hand. The other forearm was wrapped tightly around her middle, protectively. How long it had been positioned that way, she had no idea.

What did this strange development mean? Was it even safe to stay here, to turn the work in and accept money for it? What if that wasn't the end? These people knew where she was staying. They knew her home address.

Speaking of addresses, the return address on the letter's envelope was a Montgomery post office box. Maybe it wasn't even a real box number. Any person sending an anonymous letter probably wouldn't put anything on the envelope that could be traced. Gina climbed off the bed and walked to the kitchen. An afternoon coffee might help. She set the pot brewing and sank onto a kitchen stool, resting her elbows on the small table.

Who could have done this? What kind of person sends unsigned letters? "A coward" was the standard answer. That, or someone convinced that revealing their identity would change the effect of the letter, would compromise their safety, or would embarrass certain people. And wasn't the very start of the letter, "as a friend," a red flag? Anybody who made a point of saying "I'm your friend" might *not* be a friend. True friends never had to remind you that they were; their actions proved it.

It was impossible to stop puzzling over this, yet Gina didn't want to overreact. If the statements in the letter were not from a friend, they were not to be trusted. The image of a certain face came clearly to mind. "Not to be trusted" ought to be the middle name of Olivia Boggs! Could *she* have sent this to derail Gina's plans, or, at the very least, to upset her? Someone who would in effect push Gina into the lake might do almost anything. Could Olivia possibly know that Gina had come here undercover, hired by Reuben Marks and Three Points? If she did know Reuben, she certainly couldn't know that Gina was his employee. Unless she knew him quite well.

"I've heard you are pretty competent in a canoe." That's what Olivia had said in the clearing that Saturday. Had she really heard anything from the Madisons about Gina's canoeing? Based on Gabe's and Emmie's professed opinions of Olivia Boggs, that scenario seemed unlikely.

Gina poured peppermint mocha creamer into a mug. She covered it with the strong, hot coffee whose aroma and brewing sounds had been rendering a necessary measure of comfort. Setting the mug on the table, she watched steam rise from it and went back in time to an earlier canoeing date. The one with Gabe. They had spotted a drone in the air. Could that be how Olivia knew Gina had been canoeing? Maybe that was a slim possibility. Still, though, video of two people on a lake couldn't tell Olivia anything regarding Gina's work situation. That degree of drone reconnaissance would involve hacking Gina's phone or her computer! Was Olivia – wealthy, manipulative Olivia Boggs – resourceful to such a degree? What could be her motive?

The more likely sender might be Reuben's assistant, Kristyl Floyd. During the field trip, Gina had wondered what kind of boss wouldn't give an employee Friday afternoon off for a child's school activity. One possible answer: a selfish, unreasonable boss. If that person was Reuben Marks and not some other boss directing Ms. Floyd at a second job she held, might she be the person describing him in this letter as untrustworthy, manipulative, self-serving, crafty, and resourceful?

Gina drank from the mug, then held it while she thought. Something else had happened that day besides Ms. Floyd's saying she had to make up missed work time. The woman had met Emmie Madison in person, discovering that she was the "Miss Emmie" Isaac could never say enough good things about. Might these factors, added together, have led the assistant to throw her boss under the bus this way? Sometimes, a mounting pile of long-held frustrations could be called "enough" after a single word spoken with a sneering attitude, or by just about anything if the pile were high enough and already teetering. Most important to Kristyl Floyd in this matter might be the connection to her son's health and social progress. A motivation such as that definitely could have prompted the kind of communication lying over there on the bed.

The problem was, what should Gina do? Should she allow herself to be caught in the middle of employer-employee drama – assuming the letter was from Kristyl Floyd? In the interview, Gina had liked Ms. Floyd, and Reuben Marks, too. If this letter could be believed, liking Reuben on first meeting didn't say much for Gina's judgment of character. She squeezed her eyes shut and shook her head a little. What of Ms. Floyd's somewhat odd text message shortly after Thanksgiving, the one with an "atta girl" tone? Had that been a precursor to this letter? Had Reuben's assistant been trying even then to support Gina in whatever way she could? If Gina had taken the hint about sending her report in early, pocketing her pay, and checking out, could she have avoided whatever trouble the letter seemed to say might be coming?

She stayed with it, trying to put the pieces together. That letter had come to Mom's address. Not to Gina's apartment. It hadn't been slipped under the door of this cabin. *Wait. Mom's address!* Gina's eyes grew wide. There was only one place she had given her mother's address in anything to do with this: the space on the job application for emergency contact. The letter *had* to be from Reuben's assistant. *Application. Interview.* Gina pictured the progression. Besides herself, three people had participated in the interview: Reuben Marks, Kristyl Floyd, and the Chief Financial Officer, Garry Wyatt. Would the CFO send such a letter? Use "Dear Gina" as the salutation? That would be a bit creepy. And Gina couldn't very well telephone Three Points and ask these questions.

How about some uplifting Christmas music? Sitting at the desk, Gina launched a playlist and warmed her arms with the tan cardigan that had been draped across the chair. Classic "Holly Jolly Christmas" by Burl Ives with backup singers was a sure and comforting foot-tapper until the line "Ho, ho, the mistletoe, hung where you can see." That set her right back to stewing on her troubles. She advanced one song. "Sleigh Ride." Nope. Too close to carriage ride. "O Tannenbaum," instrumental. Fine. She let it play.

The gentle music sounded nice, but it didn't ease Gina's mind. It merely made a setting for continued speculation. She certainly hadn't needed a big, new upset at this stage of the game. She would be out of here in a week, and that fact was discouraging enough. What was her departure going to mean with regard to Gabe Madison? By now, both he and his family seemed to accept her, value her, and...trust her. Gina winced.

It had been three days since that romantic date with Gabe at the Christmas festival, and she hadn't heard much from him. She killed her music altogether as soon as she recognized "What Are You Doing New Year's Eve?" And she'd been thinking this playlist would cheer her up! Did work have Gabe so busy he should apparently cool off this way? Was he attempting to continue some kind of retreat, wanting to avoid distractions? Was he upset because of the evasive way she had identified Reuben?

A line from a song ran through Gina's head. Funnily enough, the words weren't from "Holly Jolly Christmas," "Sleigh Ride," or anything else she had just been hearing. They were part of a little chorus sung at the Madisons' during their family night late in October: "See me over every sin and sorrow." Gina said the words to herself two times, three times, and more. They'd come to mind just now for a reason, hadn't they? Sin wasn't a clear issue in these present worries, but sorrow definitely applied. Or, she felt sure, it was probably *going* to apply, and sooner rather than later.

Running out to grab dinner had been a thought earlier in the day, but Gina's gas gauge was low after the drive to meet her mother at lunchtime. Besides, she had brought smoked wings, potato salad, and mini cheese biscuits home in a to-go box. The leftovers had gone into the freezer, but that didn't mean they couldn't be pulled right out again. Gina gathered her sweater closer around her. Best to hunker down and study more on this matter.

~

Melancholy though the mission must be, Gina couldn't deny herself some last looks in Auburn. It was five days until her deadline, but she'd pretty much decided to take Kristyl

Floyd's text message suggestion and turn the review in before the 20th.

She started out with a vanilla latté from Starbucks on South College, delaying the pleasure of those first delightful sips until she had found a parking space downtown. The decision to basically retrace the path she and Gabe had taken together seemed to have made itself. Gina paused outside the Chapel, taking a photo of its historic marker, both sides, so she could read the information later. Next, she broke with the former route by going in J&M Book Store to buy a university logo sweatshirt as a souvenir, coming away with an Aubie the Tiger Christmas ornament as well.

She took more pictures. A lot of pictures, of the official Christmas tree on Samford Lawn, of painted Santa faces and holly sprigs on storefront windows, of a light pole wrapped in green garland topped with a red bow. How long she would keep the pictures on her phone was anybody's guess. On impulse, she held her new ornament up and photographed it against the white brick wall painted WAR EAGLE in orange and blue. Then, before she could chicken out, she texted the photo to Gabe with a simple "Good morning" caption, determined that he should know she was thinking of him.

Suddenly Gina was maxed out on melancholy. Yeah, enough was enough. She dispensed with the last looks tour and drove back to the cabin. Agenda: proofread the review one last time and try to decide exactly when – *or whether* – to send it on its merry way (to throw a Christmas word in, even though it didn't fit the situation).

She put her purchases away, bundled up a little, and headed straight for the elm bench. Why couldn't more of life's nearly perfect, temporary realities, like this time in Auburn, not be temporary? Why couldn't they last? She sat down and ran her fingers along the surface's texture. *A cheater's balance beam*. She hadn't felt like walking the length of this bench lately, and certainly not like pretending to be a baby bird.

After dinner, Gina showered and indulged in some of the pampering that wasn't everyday routine, putting a mask on her face and tea tree oil on her feet. That left her hands okay for computer work, and work she did until time for nightly exercise videos and a few minutes' journaling, the latter of which turned out to be mostly staring at the pages with nothing cute, clever, or coherent to write. Ultimately, she gave up on that and went back to her computer, working far into the night. Too keyed up for sleep after editing her review, she started deleting old photos, browsing recipes, and reading sewing posts.

She dragged out of bed after eleven on Thursday and was hungry enough by early afternoon to prepare and eat a large meal of rather assorted things on hand. That made her sleepy again, and she crawled back into bed around three.

Ping! Gina opened her eyes and got her bearings. Her phone – *Ping!* Now she had two new alerts at least. She groaned, stretched, and reached to unplug the device from its charger cable. *Gabe!* She saw his name first and only deigned to register Kristyl Floyd as the other sender. Gabe had apologized for taking until now to answer her, and he'd even implied some chastisement that she had ventured downtown yesterday without him. Wasn't that a good sign?

Gina read the message again, scrolling higher to smile at some earlier ones, too. But, as much as she wanted to stay right here under the warm covers dwelling and speculating on matters Gabe, it would not do to ignore the other message. Here came that feeling of dread, the one that hadn't truly left her since she had opened that unsigned letter three days ago. She inhaled, exhaled, and touched the Back arrow on her phone. Gabe's text thread closed, and Gina entertained the merest flicker of hope that Kristyl Floyd hadn't sent something worrisome.

Was this all? A link? Gina automatically hesitated. You weren't supposed to open links without caution, even links from a known party. She frowned at the URL, which started off appearing to be the website for Three Points LLC. The "dot com" had extra characters behind it. Gina didn't touch the link. Instead, she climbed out of bed and went to the desk, carrying with her the Christmas throw that had been a nice Black Friday doorbuster find. She turned her computer on and carefully typed the entire URL into a search field. Maybe this was no less risky than opening the page on her phone, but her computer had good virus protection. Besides, she just had to know what this was about! She carefully verified each character: https://www.threepointsllc.com/officers/430832_veracity/.

Holding her breath, Gina touched the Enter key. Nothing that looked suspicious went scrolling over the screen. Thank goodness! Instead, a normal-looking web page loaded, and Gina studied the simple photo gallery of just two images, head shots of Reuben Marks and Garry Wyatt, the officers of Three Points LLC. Gina had seen these pictures when deciding whether to apply for the job. Garry's first name had only one R on this page, though, and it was supposed to have two. As for Reuben's...Gina's brain registered the photo ID under his picture in slow motion: Silas Connelly, alias Reuben Marks.

Gina stared, open-mouthed. Silas Connelly? The land developer? Could this be true? Her hands trembled and her heart pounded as she kept staring at the name. She looked at the URL again, catching the word *veracity* at the end of it. Was that a clue? And had Ms. Floyd sent this information by way of an unpublic web page, giving only Gina its online address? Gina opened a new window and pulled up the Three Points home page she had accessed on previous occasions. It looked correct. She clicked the drop-down and went to Officers. A page loaded, looking virtually identical to the other one, but the names were what Gina had been told at the outset, same as what she had seen on company name tags worn by those men during the interview. Reuben Marks, President. Garry Wyatt, CFO.

She bolted for some cold water to drink, then opened a third browser window and searched "Silas Connelly Alabama." Here came the results... LinkedIn. Facebook. CCC Development Corporation. All over the Internet: Reuben's face, but Silas Connelly's name! Gina got the letter in hand and read it again. "This man has personal reasons for wanting to obtain from a disinterested party (you) a negative review of the Madison Timber Farm retreat site and plans." Oh, how could this be? *Silas Connelly* had interviewed and hired Gina? *Silas Connelly* was Kristyl Floyd's boss at Three Points? Gina swallowed. She felt hot all over.

As if in some kind of "out of body" state, she located telephone numbers for Better Business Bureau and Auburn Chamber of Commerce. How fortunate that this hadn't happened after 5:00, or on the weekend, when these offices would be closed! Afterward, Gina couldn't account for how she had managed it. But she had. Without crying, without whispering, she had placed her calls. And it was just as she had feared. Neither of those places had record or knowledge of a company called Three Points LLC.

Now, just for good measure – and with a simmering belligerence beginning to drive her – Gina phoned CCC Development Corporation and stayed on the call just long enough to recognize Kristyl Floyd's voice on the recorded greeting designed to screen and route calls to the correct department.

Gina had thought she had come here undercover to evaluate the retreat for a research firm. In reality, she had been helping the Madisons' enemy, a land developer. It was absolutely unbelievable! She took a series of deep breaths, holding each before exhaling slowly. That didn't help to calm her, though. She took a second water bottle from the fridge and pressed it against her forehead, behind her neck, and on each wrist. She had been absolutely tricked. Used! Her eyes flew around the room. *Silas Connelly.* "He has any number of people in his pocket," it said right here in black and white. Gina was frightened. What was she going to do? Her tremulous sigh echoed through the room. *Sigh. Sigh...* She frowned. *"Si."* Short for Silas?

Gina's lower lip began to tremble. "Sigh here" was part of that weird voicemail transcription from last week. She grabbed her phone, fumbling it and dropping it loudly on the floor. She tried again. Opening the Voicemail app with unsteady fingers, she scrolled to the bottom of the list. *Yes!* The option for Deleted Messages. She touched the screen. There near the top was the unknown number. She set the message playing on speaker and listened, also trying to make sense of the misheard and misspelled words in the transcription. It absolutely was the voice of Reuben Marks. Correction: the voice of conniving Silas Connelly.

"Guerre. Sigh here." Right. That was the "sighing" bit Gina had misunderstood on first glance. "Si here," the caller had identified himself. Silas Connelly. No more proof was needed. Reuben's voice and Silas's name. "Gar" is what he'd said at the outset, addressing his financial officer Gary Wyatt. Gina checked the number of origin against the one Reuben had been texting from. They were different, of course. Sure. With a fake name, Connelly would also be using a dedicated phone to communicate as Reuben Marks. Probably a burner phone. *A crafty, resourceful man.*

Gina read, listened, listened, and read, her heart beating ever faster. This wasn't anything about prescription medicines. It was *Madisons!* Why, even she had seen in her own dictated texts to Taylor that the name Madison would come out "medicine" half the time and would have to be corrected. And "Patsy," whoever she had thought that was during the first couple of listens just now, wasn't a proper name at all. The message referenced a "patsy girl." And that patsy was her. Gullible, naïve Gina Wright.

"Gar. Si here. The Madisons are all I can think about night and day. How sweet it's going to be when we've squelched their interference once and for all. Impatient for that on-site info from our patsy girl so you can get your hands on it, spin it our way, and get this show on the road."

Silas Connelly planned for Gina's information to go to the CFO. Probably, she hypothesized, because that man knew how to work a computer better than the company president did. And Garry or Gary Wyatt's job was to spin, or alter, or whatever it took, to use Gina's review against Madison Timber Farm.

A patsy. She pulled the definition up on her computer to get the full force of it, even though doing so was probably going to add insult to injury. *"A person easily taken advantage of, especially by being cheated or blamed for something."* Her mind flew back to the interview session. She had feared that the long list of jobs on her résumé would be a red flag, especially because they were unsalaried positions, mostly in retail. But these people had told her, "That is an asset as far as we are concerned. After all, this *is* a short-term assignment, and your varied job experiences will give you a wide perspective." And she'd believed them. In reality, they had been hoping Gina wouldn't be smart enough to see what they were up to. And she hadn't been. *How humiliating!* Her face burned with shame.

She had feared the company would lean toward applicants with degrees, but Reuben's attitude on that point had been surprisingly offhand. "We need someone for this job who can come across as easygoing and casual," he'd said, even suggesting that Gina ought to be good at pulling the wool over people's eyes with her cute looks and bubbly personality. He had spoken of wanting her to go on the land and pretend to "stare off into space" while actually staying on alert for anything that could be a point of guest inconvenience, discomfort, or danger. In retrospect, Reuben's, or Silas's, choice of words seemed insensitive, even sardonic. How had this escaped her at the time?

That man's manner of describing how she should pass herself off as a retreat guest had been dripping with sarcasm, though, again, Gina hadn't registered it then. "Let them hear you refer to 'gathering your thoughts,'" he had smirked, even making quotation marks in the air with his fingers. "We can send some sketch pads with you, or an easel and canvas, so you can try your hand at painting landscapes." As if Gina, with absolutely no knowledge of art, would have been willing to look that ridiculous in the eyes of the land's owners! She practically threw her phone onto the desk as tears filled her eyes. *This* was how she had "risen above" those other applicants. By being taken advantage of. By being a pushover, by being easily fooled and manipulated. No wonder she couldn't believe her good luck. The situation had seemed too good to be true because it *had* been too good to be true. She was a stupid, *stupid, stupid* girl! Gina's body convulsed with bitter sobs. *Suitcase...where is my suitcase?*

Chapter 14

Gina awoke beside her open and empty suitcase. Last night she had been too distraught to do anything besides pull it off the closet shelf and set it out. Physical and emotional exhaustion had probably played in her favor there. In the first shock wave from all of this upheaval, the dark of night hadn't been the time to rush into anything. She sat up now and pushed the covers below her knees, automatically turning her head toward the direction of kitchen and coffee.

Exactly. Rushing into something had landed her in this mess to start with. She was not going to depart a totally whipped dog, crying and running for cover. Yes, they had deceived her, but they would not utterly defeat her! She was not going to run home out of control, out of breath, out of options. Not Gina Wright. Her faux retreat that became real along the way had taught her better than that. This much she held to, and before caffeine, even. She took a deep breath, pushed the covers all the way down, and got to her feet.

Showering while her coffee brewed, Gina pondered the facts at hand. First, how had that call even ended up on her phone? Eyes shut, she leaned her head back to wet her hair under the spray. *Address book.* She pictured scrolling through contacts. That had to be it. Silas Connelly had missed Wyatt's name by one line, probably, touching Wright instead. He'd been in a hurry, no doubt, or distracted. Paying no attention while a robotic voice told him what 10 digits he'd reached, he had left his smug and gloating message after the beep.

By the time Gina was indulging in the comforts of warm clothes and hot coffee, she had recalled more details from the job interview. "Reuben" had crossed the line of appropriateness, ignoring most of her legitimate aptitudes and even using the word *pretty* in reference to what she could bring to the task. *Booo!* How could she not have seen so many warning signs? She'd just wanted the job so badly.

If these were that man's true colors, it was easy to see how his assistant could reach her breaking point. If Kristyl Floyd were on Gina's side now, that could be a big plus in terms of what ought to be done. Such a big *if!* The warnings and sudden "honesty" in both the letter and the text message could be grand measures meant to scare Gina into pulling out of the project and forfeiting her stipend. Fear gripped her. Maybe CCC Development alias Three Points *already had* their information from her! Maybe they had hacked her computer. *Oh, don't let that be the case!*

Gina would lose her stipend, she now knew as a desperate resolution took form in her head. She wouldn't take the money now even if they sent it, which they wouldn't, according to the terms of the agreement. She was *counting* on forfeiting it, and that knowledge had her this moment feeling defiantly, self-righteously satisfied. What she would take away from this experience wasn't money. It was self-respect, and changes of attitude, and everything else this genuine retreat had resulted in.

Gina was going to give Three Points exactly what they deserved: the opposite of what they had schemed to get from her. And the Madisons were going to get exactly what *they* deserved: a glowing, raving, five-star review. Silas Connelly would probably destroy the report once he got his dirty hands on it. Maybe that wouldn't happen, though. Not if Kristyl Floyd was still handling the paperwork, and not if her allegiance truly had changed.

As for the personal side of this matter, Gabe and his family were going to learn sooner or later that Gina had lied to them. From the sound of things, this Silas Connelly would probably be sure to tell them, to rub in how he had duped not only Gina, but them as well. Gina ached to think how Gabe, Emmie, their mother, and their uncle would feel about her, not just because she had been deceiving them, but also because of how gullible she had been. The name Gina Wright would mean to them a deceitful and stupid person.

She had to stop herself from sinking again into the inconsolable remorse and self-pity that had had their way with her last night. No matter what anybody else came to think of her in the days ahead, at least *she* would know that she had not benefited financially at the Madisons' expense. Three Points, or whoever these people were, weren't going to get any "average, middle-of-the-road" data from this reviewer. The only feedback they would ever see from Gina Wright was going to be 100% true and 100% positive. Why? "Because character matters." Gina answered her question out loud and found herself nodding. "Where is that quote?" She had seen it in one of the old periodicals borrowed from the company office a few weeks ago.

Gina scrolled through her photos until she found it. The paragraph had caught her eye as she was paging through technical and persuasive articles. It was a short, stand-alone item used as filler. She stretched the view larger and read out loud to give the words greater force: "'The first condition of success in any job is not brains but character. Over and over again, people of moderate intelligence have come to the front because they had courage, integrity, self-respect, steadiness, perseverance, and confidence in themselves, their cause, and their work. Which of these qualities comes first it is not easy to say, but certainly courage, perseverance, and self-respect rank high.'"

What a difference a night's sleep and a great statement of truth made! Gina was doubly glad she hadn't fled last night in a storm of emotion. Head held high, heart full of the courage and perseverance she had just read about, she went straight to her computer. She deleted the average, moderate review of the Madisons' retreat from her folder, scorning any consideration of the time and effort she had invested in writing it. Out of the Recycle Bin she booted it, fairly shouting "Good riddance!" Then, she started a new e-mail and attached the document that reflected her true retreat experience. She carefully addressed the message to Kristyl Floyd and sent it.

One hour later almost to the minute, Gina's belongings were packed and loaded. It was time to land this plane. Her trip was over. At the first red light she hit, she checked her phone and replied without hesitation to a text message from Taylor. "Yes, I can work tomorrow. What time do you need me?"

~

"I'm working until three," Gina wrote cautiously, thumbs working the letters on her phone back in the stock room. Kristyl Floyd had asked to meet her! Meet her today, as soon as possible. *Send.* An answer came without delay: "Can you meet me at Wintzell's on Commerce Street at 4:30? I'll have Isaac with me, and a friend who will sit with him at a separate table so you and I can talk. Please come. I think you'll want to hear what I have to say."

Was there even more warning to be given? Something the woman wasn't comfortable putting on paper or handling in a phone call? Surely, bringing others with her and requesting a public meeting place meant no risk of danger to Gina. So she went, taking care to share her location with her mother and with Taylor.

Young Isaac was sweet, and he remembered "Miss Gina." Julie, the friend, seemed nice. But Gina had been down the "seemed nice" trail recently, with poor results. Ms. Floyd herself appeared approachable, calm, and believable as she laid before Gina a series of statements starting with, "I am no longer working for CCC Development Corporation, nor affiliated with Silas Connelly in any way. That decision has been a long time coming, and I'm only sorry I didn't reach it soon enough to stay out of this whole, sordid business involving those nice Madisons and you."

She described how the field trip had tipped the scales for her, confirming Gina's suspicion that Emmie's connection with Isaac had been a deal-breaker. "I'd been conflicted over this Madison situation already, including how Silas was using *you,* but the things I saw and learned that day opened my eyes. I worked as Silas Connelly's assistant for four years, which was about three years and ten months too long! He is unscrupulous, unreasonable, and verbally abusive." Kristyl stopped to take a sip of water, then shook her head with subtle movements, finally leaning forward. She spoke in tones still softer than the guarded ones she had been using from the start. "I am *so glad* I will never make another pot of coffee for that man, nor waste another ounce of energy being annoyed that in these *four years* he has never figured out that my first name doesn't start with a C!"

Gina had to laugh. In spite of all that had happened, her first instinct about this woman had been on the mark. She had liked her then and now was liking her even more. Gina looked over at Isaac. His plate of popcorn shrimp now disheveled and set aside, he was using a pencil to do phonics exercises in a workbook, appealing occasionally to "Miss Julie" for help or approval.

"Silas fussed at me for printing Isaac's field trip permission form at work even though he knows full well that I reimburse the office supply account for every copy I make."

Gina nodded, commiserating in a general way to try to encourage the woman.

"I'm not certain Gabe or Frances Madison would know my face, but they very likely would have recognized my name if they had heard it the day of the field trip. That's why I made my exit early, after putting in an appearance for Isaac's sake. I mean, no apology is due for my having a son who happens to be a client of Emmie Madison's, but I know it would have upset her family to have me around." She inhaled and exhaled audibly. "Let's get down to cases. You deserve a full explanation of what's been happening."

This ought to be interesting, to say the least! Gina reached for her glass of sweet tea, not taking her eyes off the source of information.

"Silas and Gary cooked up the customer review ruse after some failed attempts at reconnaissance by their cohort, Miss Olivia Boggs." Again, Kristyl dropped her volume. "Naturally, the first strategy occurring to these men would be the *femme fatale* bit, with Gabe Madison as the intended victim." She rolled her eyes. "It gives me pleasure on a couple of fronts to tell you that that shallow excuse for a woman never even got a toehold."

Gina's mouth had dropped open at the mention of Olivia Boggs. Now, her heart sang a little song at the news that Gabe had never fallen for Olivia's wiles. He had demonstrated that fact himself, hadn't he?

Quietly, Kristyl owned up to the fake company Three Points LLC complete with website, trident fork logo, and imprinted name tags. "Only Silas felt the need to use an alias, a decision I credit more to ego than to reason. We held our interviews in this city, away from CCC Development's offices in Auburn. And, by the way, the phone call you thought you placed to AFA for your cover never went to Montgomery or involved that organization at all. You spoke with Gary Wyatt that day. He was using his own 334 number, a put-on voice, and the name Gordon Oakey."

Gina stared at the space between herself and Kristyl Floyd. Was there no end to the trickery those men had come up with? No doubt they had found their scheme highly amusing. She shook her head. *I can't even...*

"Also, there is more to say concerning Olivia Boggs and the matter of reconnaissance while you were the Madisons' retreat guest."

"Drones?" Gina wanted to show that she hadn't been entirely clueless.

Kristyl nodded and said Connelly had hoped to get useful video but would have been satisfied just to worry and intimidate whoever saw the device. Gina remembered Gabe's unease over the drone sightings. What a lowlife this Connelly was!

"Miss Olivia 'Boggs you down' did her best to antagonize you, but she eventually took herself out of the picture, having simply lost interest, especially with Crimson Tide football getting into full swing. She toes the family line, but only so far, at which point the job of appeasing Silas Connelly goes back to her father. At any rate, Silas told Olivia that his drone saw you and Gabe Madison in a canoe."

So! The girl *had* heard; she hadn't lied to Gina about that. But her information hadn't come from anyone named Madison. Good.

"The drone was almost an entertainment to Silas as much as anything serious. He liked its being a high-tech and trendy gadget. He had to have a paid operator for it on the front end and a consultant on the back end. All in all, the effort cost him a bundle and gained him almost nothing." Kristyl rolled her eyes again. "Serves him right. His question about how much time you were spending indoors versus outdoors was almost baseless, not prompted by any drone footage, from what I understand. He just meant it to keep you uncomfortable. He wanted to make your experience as unenjoyable as it could be without actually arousing suspicion of anything underhanded."

She went on, "Not to suspect deceit in other people is natural for trustworthy people like you. Silas Connelly has deceived and manipulated *many* people, myself at the top of the list, alongside some ex-wives. You definitely are not the only one, so do not let this setback destroy your confidence.

"Something else you should know: Silas never saw any of your off-time activities on social media the way he had me say to you. The Halloween parties were reported by Olivia, who was miffed enough by her failure to entice the son that she kept showing up to make mayhem when and how she could. She is no fan of Silas personally, by the way. He just knows things from his business dealings that he holds over her family."

It was Gina's turn to inhale and exhale loudly. She felt the sudden need to push her dinner plate away from her. How fortunate that Kristyl Floyd had stepped up, choosing to stop the charade before Gina had fulfilled Connelly's assignment and had accepted money from him!

"About your report, now. You sent it to me earlier than your deadline, which is exactly what I had hoped for. This has given me time to stop some damage before it happened." Kristyl looked very satisfied. "And I won't deny that it is giving me great pleasure to get the drop on one of the most disrespectful, condescending, demoralizing excuses for a man that I have ever had the misfortune of knowing." She leaned forward again. "Yesterday afternoon I hand-delivered copies of your beautifully written review to the judge and to the attorneys who are representing the Madisons in this court case. *Silas* still thinks he and Gary are going to get their mitts on something you'll be submitting on the 20th." She laughed shortly. "Little do they know that even if you did, it would bounce back. I've already deactivated my company e-mail address, besides emptying my desk. Silas also thinks I'll be working until 5:00 on Christmas Eve. Instead, I will be curled up on the sofa with my little boy, watching *A Charlie Brown Christmas!*"

Gina felt as if *this* were a feel-good movie moment. She wanted to burst into applause!

"You want to know what I left Silas as a going-away present?"

Gina smiled. She could imagine! A boxed rattlesnake? An open jar of red ants...or banana spiders? Her smile became a grin. "Sure. Tell me."

"He loves to call environmentally-conscious people *tree huggers* and *tree lovers.* He thinks it is so cute to say that those opposed to clear-cutting are afraid the Keebler Elves won't find a hollow tree to do their magical baking in. I'll bet I've heard that crack from him a hundred times or more. *So...*" she raised and lowered her eyebrows, "when next he arrives at work, he's going to find a package of Keebler fudge stripe cookies on his desk." She folded her arms and sat back. "And he will have *no coffee* to wash them down with."

Gina laughed out loud. And she did applaud this time. Very small, and silently, just above the tabletop.

Kristyl nodded and seemed pleased by Gina's reaction. "I have maybe kept you too long already, but there is something I mustn't leave unsaid. I realize how self-protective this may sound on my part, but I hope you will distance yourself from this fiasco without contemplating any kind of revenge, Gina. Please hear me: people think of revenge as ruining somebody else's life, when in fact it is ruining their own. What you have done for the Madisons – denying Silas Connelly what he wanted from you – proves to me that you are their friend. That being the case, I don't think it will help you to have lingering issues with the man whose interference they are trying to be forever rid of."

Was that some subtext, pertaining to Gabe in particular? Or was Gina imagining that? Did Kristyl know about the times Gina and Gabe had spent together, beyond canoeing? About the mistletoe incident, even? She and her former boss seemed to know everything else.

"Please don't lose hope."

Maybe it wasn't imagination. Maybe Kristyl did have good intelligence. Gina gave a wan smile and uttered some things to Kristyl, mostly without eye contact, describing the good that had happened. "I've learned a lot. I've been helped – in spite of everything."

"Gina, I have hated doing this to you. I've hated many things about my job for a long time, and until now I haven't mustered the courage to break away. Mostly, because the pay has been very good." She lowered her eyes and appeared ashamed of herself. "When I met my son's 'Miss Emmie' that day in the forest, it was like a slap in the face. I admit to you, Gina, that it took my desire not to hurt Emmie Madison or her family to drive me to action on this, because their welfare mattered more to me than yours did. I hope you can forgive me."

Gina didn't know what to say to that. She kept her head lowered, eventually nodding and whispering, "I understand."

"I will be confessing the entire scheme to the Madisons via an e-mail to Emmie, apologizing for my role in it, throwing myself on their mercy, and letting them know I am permanently severing all connection with Silas Connelly. That e-mail is still in the works. Naturally, it will come from my personal mail. That account of things will serve a dual purpose: confession, which I hope the Madisons will take well; and documentation, so I will have in writing the facts I am privy to, in case I need them. At any rate, my plan is for them to have this information by Christmas – a little something for under their tree, so to speak. What they will do with it, well...I'm hanging my hopes on what I know of their track record; their good reputation."

Hours after the meeting, Gina replayed parts of it in her head over a mocha latté, dine-in. She was still reacclimating to the joys of city life after so many weeks away. *Huh.* Yet another R word, this one applicable to post-retreat life. Gina closed her eyes and shook her head. The Madisons' reputation and character went a long way with Kristyl Floyd. The woman was taking a huge risk, confessing the fraudulent scheme to everyone affected by it. She must feel extremely confident that things would turn out okay. Or else she just knew that this was what she had to do, no matter the consequences.

The Madisons would learn what Gina had come on their property to do and how she had fallen for Connelly's scheme. Neither of those actions was going to make them want to associate with her. *"Do not let this setback destroy your confidence."* She needed that advice desperately! It would go into her journal later, underlined in two colors of ink and flagged with a page marker.

Besides urging Gina not to despair, Kristyl had called her trustworthy. Could the Madisons possibly agree with her on that? It was one week until Christmas. All Gina could do now was wait.

~

Gabe frowned at Gina's reply rejecting his suggestion of a simple Sunday afternoon stroll around the loop trail. As far as he knew, both of them had always enjoyed those walks. He looked at his phone and reread her texts. "I won't be able to," was the first message. She had added, "I'm really sorry, Gabe." No explanation of what business had her tied up or for how long. He went to his truck and left the driveway, headed to the access road. Was Gina not feeling well?

Sure, he'd been pretty busy lately. Maybe Gina had misread that. He wasn't uninterested, if that's what she had been thinking. In fact, he was so interested that he wasn't greatly confident what to say to her or how to act. He hadn't wanted to move too fast in case that wasn't what *she* wanted. After all, she wouldn't be staying here indefinitely. Once she found the direction she was searching for, what would that mean for the two of them? Had she been wondering the same thing? Was she worried that a greater attachment would ultimately result in a greater hurt? What if her new direction took her far out west or across an ocean?

Gabe parked. Gina's car wasn't here. So, she'd gone to get her weekly groceries or something. Or had met up with friends. Since she *was* out, this could be a good time to check on things at the cabin. He should. It was the proper thing to do. He climbed out of the truck.

~

During her first week in Auburn, Gina had told Emmie and her mother, "I stay pretty connected to my phone." Right now, she wasn't any too fond of the device and would prefer to have it far from her. Like left-at-work-by-mistake far. But it was in her hand, as usual, and she looked at her text exchange with Gabe from a few minutes ago. At a doctor's office they always asked you to describe your pain level as a number between 1 and 10. Hers while answering Gabe had been 7 or 8, but now it was at least 12.

Same as when Gabe had wanted to know about "Reuben," there was nothing more she could tell him right now. The truth as to why she couldn't go walking with him would be, "I'm actually not in Auburn anymore. And, regardless, I should not see you. We should not move this relationship along, because I know you're soon going to regret ever having met me." Regretting Gina, assuming Gabe did have feelings for her, was going to be an emotional blow. A loss. A new grief, and right when he'd seemed to be making some progress in dealing openly with his father's death. Tears filled Gina's eyes as she realized something more. When Gabe did learn all, he would probably blame his uncle for the "mess" Gabe had called her situation that very first day. And Gabe would be right. It would turn out to have been another misstep by Chip, and then those two would be right back at odds with one another!

"See me over every sin and sorrow." The music came wafting toward Gina the way it had done on Monday when this disaster – this mess – had started blowing up. She lowered her head, and her heart cried out, *See me over this sorrow, oh God!*

~

Things looked normal as Gabe approached the cabin. On the porch, he headed for the right-hand corner. He leaned around it and looked at the table and chair where he'd had those terrifying but comical moments when Gina had turned out to be just feet away from him, in the shower. Grinning, he headed for the door.

Hold on. Something was different. Gabe frowned. His eyes scanned the porch floor, the railings, the posts, the door. Was something missing? *"That's fresh basil. Your mother gave it to me."* The memory of Gina's voice saying some of the first words she'd ever spoken to him answered Gabe's puzzlement. Where were the little bags of DIY pest control she had pinned along here? He nodded. Sure. Mosquito season was past, so she'd taken those things down recently.

He extended his hand to the keypad, then stopped. Best to knock and be absolutely sure Gina wasn't inside. He definitely didn't want a worse goof than that last one. He couldn't risk walking in on her! "Gina?" he called, rapping on the door. He listened, waited, and did the same a second time, calling a little louder and knocking a little harder. No answer. He entered the code and opened the door, calling out once more. Still no answer. Moving inside and flipping the nearest light switch, Gabe saw immediately that Gina's large, colorful cloth square was gone. Her "accent wall" was bare. Gabe flinched. Could she have taken the fabric down to wash it? He called her name again, alarmed at the urgency he heard in his voice.

The bedroom door stood open. Gabe peered in before entering, comprehending the neat covers in place on the made bed before he got any light on in the room. *Closet.* He rushed to check. Gina's clothes were gone. All signs of her were gone, inside the cabin and out. Was there a note she had left, maybe, explaining? He turned his head toward the desk on the front wall of the bedroom. Grouped together in the center of the writing surface were several nicely wrapped Christmas gifts. He went closer, frowning. The tags told him these packages were for himself, his sister, his mother, and his uncle and aunt. Gabe picked his gift up, held it, stared at it, fingered the bow, and set it down again.

Maybe Gina had left her explanatory note on the kitchen table. Gabe turned toward the doorway, stopping as a light fragrance hit him. Gina's perfume? She hadn't ever struck him as wearing any. *Wait.* It might be the scent of some hair product she used. Yes, that was it. He'd noticed it the first time when leaning in close to her that night by the campfire, then again in his truck the day he had driven her to campus. Under the mistletoe two weeks ago...not so much, with competing aromas in the air, like cinnamon and fir and freshly baked cookies. Not to mention competing sensory alarms within himself during those kisses.

Finding no note in the kitchen, Gabe reversed his path. Slowly. The blank wall hit him harder this time. All he could do was stare at it as though expecting the fabric to magically reappear. Instead, the empty wall was like a movie screen where flashed images of Gina's face – in the canoe, across the meeting table, in the front seat of his truck, beside him in the horse-drawn carriage.

It wasn't just Gina's face he recalled now. It was the sound of her voice and the things she had said. Gabe exhaled a little laugh. Nobody talked like Gina. Nobody had ever made him stop and think the way she did. During one of their several walks through the woods, he had said something offhand about timber being a slow-growing asset. And what was her reply? Gabe's mouth pulled back on one side. Nothing to do with economics, or even with trees themselves. "*Patience* is a slow-growing asset, too," she'd said with a little laugh. He wasn't sure whether she had meant that observation primarily as a word of wisdom to him or as a reminder to herself. *Connections.* That was the thing with Gina. She always seemed to be making connections between one aspect of life and another. And she seemed to have an insight into *him* that he hadn't encountered from anyone, maybe ever in his whole life. Gabe kept staring at that huge, plain, empty section of pine board wall.

Finally, he wandered back into the bedroom, where the only signs of Gina remained: the presents on the desk, and that fragrance in the air. Now that Gabe was in search of the scent, he wasn't sure he could detect it again. Another little while, and it would be gone forever.

Exactly when had she left? Should he call her to find out why? If she'd wanted him to know something, though, wouldn't *she* have called, or texted, or left a note? He sank onto the bed, and his shoe hit something that went clattering. Down on hands and knees, he reached and retrieved what turned out to be a spool of gray sewing thread. Gabe sat on the bed again, holding the small item and turning it, examining it from every angle. This might be the thread she had used to mend his jacket. *"A stitch in time..."* she had mocked him that first day, before they had become friends. Before they had become more than that. Gabe stood and shoved the spool into a front pocket. Not counting whatever was in that box with his name on it, there on the desk, would this thread be his only memento, if that was the right word for an object that might prove too painful even to keep? He needed to get out of this room.

The breathing was a little better outside, but not much, and the gait taking Gabe out of the clearing was slow, bordering on despondent. He couldn't stop himself from turning to look back at what would never again be the same uncomplicated and happy haven it had always been for him.

Chapter 15

Emmie lowered the volume as her playlist Christmas Instrumental served up a song a little too peppy for the work at hand. With Mother out delivering festive packages of muffins and cookies to assorted friends and neighbors, Emmie had the big kitchen all to herself. Best to keep the music level underneath the more important business of thinking things out before Gabe showed up. He had gone outdoors after grabbing a late-morning coffee from the pot and deigning to say to whoever might be listening that he didn't know what his lunch plans were. That had been more than an hour ago. Emmie checked to see how close the oven was getting to temperature, then pressed the tines of a fork against the top of each peanut butter cookie dough mound on the baking sheet.

It had been five days since Gabe had discovered Gina's things gone, three since he could force himself to get the Christmas presents and bring them over here. Few words he'd given when setting the packages on the living room coffee table, as though he needed the women to take charge and decide what to do with them. Later, when his melancholy had taken him elsewhere, Mother had placed the gifts under the tree. Emmie was excited about what might be in the boxes. Gina possessed remarkable sewing skill. It wasn't unreasonable to hope for something along that line, and Emmie needed some bright prospect right now to pin hope on. Mother planned for them to open the presents after dinner. Years ago, they had established the custom of opening one gift apiece on Christmas Eve. That process was bound to be poignant, not just for Gabe, but for all of them. However, though Gabe couldn't know it now, poignant reminders of Gina might be a minor concern to him once Kristyl Floyd's tell-all e-mail was unfolded to him.

Beep! Emmie set the cookie sheet inside the preheated oven and shut the door, less aware of future dessert joy than of her brother's present heartache. She murmured a prayer for Gabe, not just because he was hurting over Gina, but concerning how he would react to tonight's news.

The e-mail Emmie had received early this morning was unsettling, even shocking. It was a good thing Gabe hadn't been around much today, come to think of it. That had given her and Mother a chance to talk the situation over and agree on a plan of action. Taking the information to her mother immediately had been a no-brainer. For as long as Emmie could remember, Mother had always been able to help her children make sense of what felt like earth-shattering drama, whether a girlfriends' quarrel or a college registration glitch or an ongoing workplace tension. She managed to bring to the forefront a focus on victory rather than defeat; on thankfulness instead of disappointment; and – perhaps more important than either of those – on raising or rehabilitating the oppressor instead of seeing only the insult or the hurt that had come at the hands of that person. *"Overlook an insult."* That instruction was all but written on the doorposts around here.

With some six minutes' baking time left, Emmie stored the sugar and flour canisters and wiped the countertop down. "Madison Kitchen" wasn't even on her spreadsheet, but it ought to be. A list of the best cookies in town should not exclude homemade ones! This dozen soon coming out of the oven would go with Emmie tomorrow to Birmingham, where Dillon and his family were eager for her to join them.

She rinsed the empty coffee carafe, remembering the pumpkin-shaped shortbread cookie that had made for a conversation starter the day she and Gina had first met. They surely had been drawn to one another for a reason. Mother felt the same way about Gina, and so did Uncle Chip. Dillon, too, and even Micah. All of them had seen the impact of her personality and, especially, they had seen her effect on Gabe.

In fact, Gabe himself had not tried to hide his interest in Gina. It remained to be seen whether that interest would survive the coming storm. Out there in the car somewhere, Mother likely was fashioning at this very moment the counsel she would give with regard to Gina. And with regard to Silas Connelly, a man Gabe already held in great contempt. How would her brother cope with tonight's reveals about that man? That aspect certainly was important, but Emmie remained more concerned with how Gabe would react in terms of Miss Gina Wright. *Wright.* She almost laughed out loud. How had she not made this word connection before now? Was Mary Georgina Wright "Miss Right" for Gabe?

Out came the cookies, and Emmie let them rest on the baking sheet while she pulled a cooling rack from a lower cabinet. There was so much to debrief in what the e-mail had divulged, with potential fallout for all of the Madisons, Gina, Ms. Floyd herself, of course, and her little boy. So much depended on the collective response this family would give.

Emmie used a spatula to transfer her beautiful cookies one by one.

Five hours later, she set *White Christmas* playing on the TV as background noise that might help. Gina's opened gifts were in the foreground, and Mother was at the helm. The time for action had come. Mother informed Gabe that she had news concerning their court case. "It's *good* news, in the final analysis." Her voice had that boardroom tone one might assume when giving a statement to the press. "Kristyl Floyd sent your sister a rundown of some desperation tactics Silas Connelly has tried to perpetrate against us in recent days. Tried *and failed* – including being behind that drone you were discussing with your uncle." Gabe was all ears.

"I have Ms. Floyd's permission, Gabe, to say that her son is one of my clients." Emmie took the floor as prearranged. "That's a big part of why she wants this trouble out on the table and resolved, with cool heads prevailing." Not surprisingly, her brother reacted, catching the subtext about his hothead history. "She has chosen to sever her employment and all association with Connelly. Her conscience has become more important to her than her paycheck, Gabe, and I think you know that that is a difficult step for people to take."

"So, she told you..."

"E-mailed me. Right before emptying her desk and stepping out in faith."

"She e-mailed you to say that Connelly has had drones over here?" Gabe's expression grew dark. "Did she tell you what information was collected?"

"She said virtually *nothing* was obtained, other than that the device spotted you and Gina canoeing." Emmie's plan was to gradually bring in Gina's involvement and the way Kristyl had attempted to exonerate her. "And she said Silas has been using Olivia Boggs to try to spy and report on us in general."

Emmie watched her brother's wheels turning. Was he picturing Olivia's recent visits, wondering specifically about her behavior toward Gina? Mother now reminded Gabe, and he was nodding throughout, that Connelly had ways of persuading various people to do his bidding, and why that was the case, at least according to rumor.

Gabe stood and started pacing the room. Emmie summoned her nerve, eager to plow ahead and get this over with. She was going to try, in one quick speech, to cover Gina's deception of them, Connelly's deception of Gina, and Kristyl Floyd's praise of Gina's actions and character. If Gabe heard all of it at once, maybe the last "paragraph" would be what he remembered the most, the way it was supposed to work when one read a news story.

"Gabe, listen to this part, please." Emmie held her phone and took a deep breath. "'Having fully believed herself to be employed by a legitimate, independent, and disinterested research firm called Three Points LLC, Gina Wright arranged a stay on your property under the guise of pursuing a personal quest for retreat. Her assignment was to provide to this research firm a review of your site's staff, facilities, and activities. Upon arriving, she had absolutely no knowledge of the legal dispute between yourselves and Silas Connelly, nor the identity of Connelly himself.

"'Her contract of employment was with a man she knew only as Reuben Marks. The end result of this ruse perpetrated against Gina is that, after learning the facts, she broke the terms of her agreement and forfeited her stipend by turning in data that paints Madison Timber Farm in a highly positive way. Connelly, under the false name Reuben Marks, had emphasized repeatedly to Gina that this research firm would reject any feedback containing very high numbers. For weeks prior to her departure, Gina had been documenting her true impressions of your land and of its potential and actual effect as a place of retreat. I am certain you will want to know what this young woman has said about your site, so I am attaching what she turned in even knowing it would nullify her contract and would alleviate the other party of the obligation to compensate her.'"

~

"We need the Christmas spirit now, as on no other Christmas Day since your father's passing." Standing, Mother was strategically positioned between the Christmas tree and her children, as though using the promise of presents to entice good behavior. "Furthermore, we are not going to get today's family time off the ground, not to mention honor the reason we celebrate this holy day, until the matter at hand is resolved." She folded her arms. "And I, for one, do not intend to wait until the new year to open my gifts!"

Gabe watched her go to her phone and remove it from its charging cable. She worked the screen, then held the device to her ear. "Chip?" You could tell she was impatient to get past the standard holiday niceties being said on the other end. "Merry Christmas to you, too. Look, could you come right over? We have a little family situation I need your help with."

Gabe heaved a sigh and looked at his sister. It was obvious she and Mother meant to railroad this thing through, and he honestly didn't have the fight in him to buck them on it. Surely Christmas Day was the worst possible time for a family blowup, and he wanted this one over and done as much as the women did, though they might be thinking otherwise based on the way he had been stewing and fuming ever since Emmie's dramatic reading yesterday.

What bringing Uncle Chip into it now ought to accomplish, Gabe couldn't begin to guess, unless Mother and Emmie simply wanted a man on their side. He put his fingers to his temples and massaged. Who cared? Two against one, or three against one. What difference did it make?

How he wished Christmas hadn't been ruined by Silas Connelly! How he wished Gina Wright had been what she had pretended to be, wanting the natural wonder of these woods to relax her, speak to her, and help her find the calm that should eventually produce clear direction for next steps. If only Gina were here now, with things going the way Gabe had believed them to be going. If only she had been with all of them yesterday as they had opened and admired her handmade gifts.

Gabe wandered over to poke at the fire. Its power energized him yet worked to settle him at the same time. He watched the flickering flames. Like a breeze through the treetops or the pounding of an ocean tide, a blazing fire always had that constant repetition, but never the exact same action. It never got old.

Emmie was setting a mug of hot chocolate on the coffee table for him. She laid a hand on his shoulder for a second before going away. Gabe straightened up, put the poker away, and sank into the sofa's cushions. He watched the steam rising and finally reached for the Christmas mug designed with red dots and green holly leaves. Ranting for the past hour about suing Silas Connelly eventually had begun to sound irrational even to his own ears, especially in view of the rebuttal Emmie and Mother absolutely would not back down from. And they hadn't been argumentative with him; just patiently listening, loving, and calmly answering. Basically, they had been acting out their point about Connelly and himself: it takes two sides to sustain a fight.

Mother had carried her point, that "we are not going to sue anybody. We are going to show ourselves to be of better character than those who have mistreated us." Nothing that perpetuated belligerence and anger was going to get any of them anywhere, Gabe had finally conceded. The hothead, the angry young man – *that* Gabe Madison – had been a lot scarcer during the past couple of months, and nobody had missed him. Nobody wanted him back.

Still, it was impossible to know what to think about everything, and that fact must account for this headache. Gina…spunky, sometimes a little quirky, smart, funny, perceptive. Gabe actually had wanted to follow her example, yet she had been acting a part the entire time! "Clearly, you can't trust *anybody!*" he had shouted earlier, but Mother had quickly shot that down.

"Yes, Son, you can. The challenge isn't that nobody can be trusted. The challenge is being willing to *place* your trust in those who are worthy of it. That young lady has done absolutely nothing that has hurt any of us, yourself included, with the possible exception of having run from here frightened at the prospect that all of us might hate her and never want to see her again. And all three of us know that that is not true. Don't we?"

Ultimately, Gabe had read the entire e-mail and the review attached to it. Gina had given the Madison retreat site five stars out of five for staff friendliness and professionalism *(in spite of the way I treated her on day one!)*; check-in and check-out process; housekeeping and cleanliness *(even though Gina took care of that herself, and better than I ever do)*; amount and quality of recreation and other activities (she had listed canoeing, city festivals, university campus tour, and group activities, writing of "a homey atmosphere in the hosts' private residence with the kind of flavor most people know only from the pages of vintage books, complete with singing, guitar strumming, and wholesome parlor games"); affordability; overall satisfaction level; likeliness to return; and likeliness to recommend the venue to a friend.

"Hang in there." Mother took a seat on the sofa beside Gabe. "Let's not forget the meaning of Christmas. Jesus came so that God and sinners could be reconciled, as the familiar carol puts it. *Forgiveness* is the message of Christmas. At last," she ran her thoughts together as the doorbell sounded and she sprang up, "we are going to get this train back on the track."

Here we go. Leave it to the Madisons to have a family meeting even on Christmas Day. Mother ushered Uncle Chip in, and Gabe decided to stand and be polite rather than sit and continue to be the object of everybody's concern and the target of their counsel.

"Chip, will you please explain what's been happening this past week?" Apparently, this was either so urgent or so simple it didn't even require all of them being seated. Or else this business had Mother so disconcerted – in spite of her outward control – that customary courtesies were off her radar.

"Gladly, Frances." Chip turned toward Gabe. "Your mother has brought me up to speed since yesterday morning, Gabe, and I can't tell you how I hate what has happened for our sakes, and for the young lady Silas decided to manipulate in his attempts to get the better of us. But here is something *you* don't know. Steps have now been taken to end the original dispute. Silas Connelly is off our backs at last."

Gabe frowned. "What do you mean?"

"Frances and I have come to a settlement with Connelly, Gabe. Out of court. We have called a truce. We – Frances and I – have sold him a tract we jointly owned, personally, near Society Hill Road. It's a good move for us financially. It is a tax liability removed, for starters, also a better location for Silas's development goals. A win-win." Chip folded his arms and looked very satisfied.

"Furthermore," Mother took over, "the income from disposal of the tract's timber will be ours. Not only timber, but smaller species I intend to transplant either to the Madison Forest Therapy Trail or to the Kreher property, pending approval. Purple coneflower, for example." She looked radiant. "We have some work to do, immediately after the holidays!"

"It's done, my boy. Signed, sealed, delivered."

"As a matter of fact, this sale is a decision your uncle and I have been contemplating for some time. The proceeds are going to help both of us as we enter our retirement years."

"I, for one, am greatly relieved to have this thing settled. Silas and I used to be friends, you know. I'm not sure he has any real friends these days, only people he tries to control. That's sad, because people with good intentions, not evil, will always have more resources available to them."

Mother nodded. "The power of the Holy Spirit, and prayer, you mean, on top of human help."

"Precisely. Also, remember that if we could have found a way sooner to get this matter resolved, Silas would have felt no need to concoct his elaborate reviewer plot, nor to sic his dubious *local* spy on us...speaking of controlling and manipulating. Rumor has it that a certain Miss Boggs has opted to spend her Christmas holidays in Cancun."

Hmm. Uncle Chip *was* in the loop, more than Gabe would have imagined.

Emmie muttered, "Good riddance."

"A piece of land is greatly valuable, especially in this county at this time. *Peace of mind,* even more so."

"Amen and hallelujah to that, Mother! I certainly want to

head out of this county later today, to see Dillon, with more peace of mind than has visited us lately."

"'Sorrow and sighing will flee away.' Remember that verse from our family night in October?" Mother expected nods and got them. "But do you think God's removing sorrow is going to hold if *we* are holding on to anger? Or if we are fearful? 'Fear not: for, behold, I bring you good tidings of great joy'! Luke chapter 2, verse 10. More of the real meaning of Christmas: joy, because we need no longer fear death or the grave. I told all of you last month that I expected this challenge would stretch us and would make us stronger as a company, as individuals, and as a family."

"Another 'amen'!" Chip said. "And I can't help but add my own wisdom, though I'll never be on par with your soliloquies, especially when I'm only quoting somebody else. Our longleaf expert Rhett Johnson once said something so profound I've never forgotten it, even though it was way back when he served as Director of the Solon Dixon Center. His meaning had to do with propagation by prescribed burnings, but it couldn't have been a more perfect metaphor for life when he spoke of 'the renewal that comes after fire.'"

How appropriate that his uncle's words seemed to echo through a room silent except for the logs crackling in the fireplace. Gabe made the connection and immediately thought of Gina. *Connections.*

"As long as we are clearing the air, sorting things out, and getting back on track, let's remember how Joseph's brothers misused him so terribly. Literally years later he told them in Egypt, 'You meant it for harm, but God used it for good.'" Mother moved a step forward and directed a look straight at Gabe. "Don't stand there, Gabriel Madison, and try to tell me *you* don't know of some unexpected good that has come out of this fiery trial." She folded her arms and challenged him, not the least bit shy of putting him on the spot. She wore as stern an expression as it's possible for anybody to use on someone they love. Gabe knew exactly what she was getting at.

"Every romance has its challenging moments, Son. Remember that what has been told us about Gina in that e-mail, and what she said herself during the brunch you missed due to hunting, or due to mysterious reasons of your own, amount to this: that young woman is our friend, not our enemy."

"Right." Chip weighed in again. "Look at the facts. Gina took that job in good faith, with no intention of harming anybody. We've been told that by Silas's assistant – who, don't forget, has burned her bridges with respect to him, same as Gina has. True?"

Gabe shrugged and nodded.

"And, while pretending to be on a retreat, Gina found herself truly engaging in one. That fact by itself legitimizes Madison Forest Therapy Trail. We were scrambling and almost pretending, ourselves, at the start of this business, and now we can hold our heads higher about it all."

Again, Gabe couldn't argue with his uncle. Not about retreat expansion, especially not with Mother standing right here, pure satisfaction written all over her.

"She gave up the pay due her for ten weeks' work. She broke the rules, broke her contract...all to benefit us."

"That's true," Emmie murmured.

"And we all know why she did this, don't we?" Chip pressed. "She grew to care about this land and about all of us."

Mother reached for the box holding her apron accessory Gina had made. "You don't spend hours sewing gifts like these for people you mean only to deceive and injure."

By this time, Gabe was almost smiling. "Look, I don't know why all of you are ganging up on me this way. What if I told you I'd already come to the same conclusions and you could have saved your breath?" He gave them a sassy look that took the place of sneering, "So there!"

Chip was nodding and grinning now. Mother and Emmie started making the kind of sounds they always did during the last five minutes of any of the gazillion Christmas romances that would be on TV from now until Valentine's Day.

"That leaves only one question, Nephew. What are you going to do about it, and how soon?" Uncle Chip looked happier than Gabe had seen him look in a long time.

"That's *two* questions, Uncle Chip."

Kudos to little sister for getting the last word in. Gabe let her have it. He was already making his plans.

~

"Gina, it's Gabe." He started right in without a script. He hadn't wanted voicemail, but it was what he got. "I really want to talk to you. Will you call me back, or text me a time that you'd be free to answer?" Maybe she and her mother were in the middle of Christmas dinner. He didn't even know what *his* family was doing right now except wishing him luck with this. "I've missed you," he finished. He touched the red circle to disconnect, exhaled loudly, and set the phone aside. If Gina felt afraid, the way everybody was predicting, he hoped his message would reassure her. Of course, this was assuming she hadn't gone back to that Josh bloke.

I am not going to stalk my competition on Facebook. Not going to. Even though I have time to kill. He reached for the phone. What was Josh's last name? Gabe opened the app and started by browsing his notifications. A call alert popped up, and the name at the top of his screen made Gabe forget Facebook, Josh, and basically everything else. "Gina?"

A little breathless, she told him she had gone for a walk

with her mother and they had left their phones in the house. Later (assuming this was going to go well), he'd have to confess his disappointment that coming in from a walk, and not excitement over listening to his voicemail, accounted for how she had sounded.

"I'm so glad to hear from you! Merry Christmas."

"Merry Christmas." He'd say it again under some mistletoe given the chance.

"Gabe, I'm guessing you've been told by now why I left when I did. It wasn't what I wanted. I was just so upset. I was embarrassed and conscience-stricken. I was afraid to face you and your family."

Gabe hurt for her. Wanting to put her mind at ease, he said the first thing that her mention of his family made him think of. "In that case, I have a message for you from my mother." He laughed, hoping Gina would remember the first flowers he had brought to her. "She says one of the main themes of Christmas is 'Fear not.'"

After a silence, Gina answered, "That's nice." More silence. "And what do *you* say? Not that I'm not interested in a word from your mom, too." She giggled. It was so great to hear that!

"*I* say I'm parked at a rest area about 20 minutes your way from Auburn, with the grill of my truck pointed toward Montgomery. And I say I'm hoping you'll tell me it's okay for me to keep heading in that direction. Will you see me?"

He could hear her breathing. "There is only one answer to that question, Gabe, and I'm hoping you know what it is."

~

"You're wearing it!" Gina pointed to the phone holster belt she had made from camo fabric and waterproof lining.

Maybe sewing talk would calm these nerves. Gabe stopped a few feet from the front porch steps and patted the accessory. "Of course I'm wearing it. It's great. *So* great, in fact, I may never take it off!" He moved a little closer. "Uncle Chip loves his, too. And Mother and Emmie and Aunt Claire have gone bananas over those kitchen towel things."

"Boas." Gina informed him of the correct term for the apron-like accessory made from a fabric strip with a pleated kitchen towel attached to each end. "Emmie texted me a picture of her and your mother wearing theirs." Gina had already added the image to her Gift Sewing album, pleased with the colors she had put together: blue dish towels for Mrs. Madison, attached to a floral fabric featuring hydrangea blooms; and a bright green, pink, and white stripe for Emmie, with white towels.

"Boas." Gabe nodded and folded his arms. He probably knew exactly what he was doing, keeping his distance this way, looking into her eyes this way, increasing her suspense. "Do you never tire of proving to me how smart you are?"

Smart? Gina's train of thought crashed. Her face fell as all of her recent anguish came storming back. She cried, "Oh, Gabe, I am so sorry! I am *so sorry* about the whole thing!"

He was on the porch and next to her in an instant. "Gina." Gabe's tone was so gentle! He took her two hands in his. "Gina, you don't have anything to apologize for. One villain engineered this drama, and that person is not you. You accepted that job in good faith. My family and I understand that. As far as we are concerned, you are our friend, beyond doubt."

Gina's voice broke. "Beyond doubt, Gabe?" Her eyes stung.

He leaned near and brushed a tear from her cheek. *"Yes."* Gina fell into his arms.

A few minutes later, hand in hand, they entered the house. Gina introduced Gabe to her mother, thrilled by his good manners and by the response to those manners. The three visited until Mom said, "I expect the two of you have things to talk about."

"Let's go scare up some hot chocolate." Gina led the way toward the kitchen, passing by the Christmas tree Gabe had already remarked on. It had turned out well with its long, vertical spirals of wired ribbon and its blinking, colored lights – lights that radiated even more joy now, come to think of it! "Unless you'd rather go somewhere. I'm not sure what's open on Christmas Day at 4:00."

"I'm good right here. Especially if you have a sandwich or something." Gabe patted his stomach. "Peanut butter and jelly? Anything. This Christmas is one for the books! I don't know what the dinner lineup was that I skipped out on at home. I just know my breakfast cereal is long gone."

After Gina fixed something for him a few levels above PB&J, they carried their hot chocolate outside. He suggested they take the walk together that he'd been counting on, the previous Sunday. "Have I really not seen you since Friday the tenth?"

Gina agreed it was hard to believe that. "I had expected to see you again after that night. But it didn't work out that way." They left their mugs on the porch and started out.

"I'm wearing the shirt you mended, in case you hadn't noticed."

Gina was really glad Gabe wanted to be wearing something he associated with her. She attempted a flirtatious smile and said, "I noticed." Oh, yes, she had noticed the shirt. She'd noticed how well it looked under his dark gray zippered vest, and she'd noticed how that ensemble, combined with some other things, were working on her. His eyes definitely had that charm thing going on that he was so good at. The Brawny paper towels guy was back. *Totally.*

Probably because she'd been prevented from telling Gabe so many things in the past, Gina let him know that one task she had accomplished lately was clarifying with her former boyfriend how things stood. "I told Josh I definitely was interested in somebody new. I think his silly text messages will stop soon." She imagined Gabe taking a delightfully territorial stand such as, "*Soon?* I can put a stop to it sooner than 'soon.'" Her heart laughed and thrilled!

"You're interested in somebody new? Is it anyone I know?"

Gina grinned. "I will give you a hint. He is tall, dark, and extremely handsome. He works very hard, but he has an appointment with a forest therapist in the near future, and she is going to give him some lessons in pretending to be a baby bird."

Gabe laughed and put an arm across Gina's shoulders. "As for this new guy, Gina..." He stopped walking and turned her to face him, utterly serious now. "I want to tell you something about him. He's been learning lately about the virtue of forgiveness. He's trying his best to forgive the wrong actions of a man called Silas Connelly in order to be more worthy of this girl that's interested in him."

Gina managed not to cry. "You can do it, Gabe. I have faith in you."

He told her his uncle and his mother had made a new contract of sale for a different piece of land, settling the legal dispute. His mother, Gabe said, was thrilled over expansion plans, especially without the recent pressure and scrutiny. Gina's relief was too great for words! She and Gabe looked at one another, eventually grinning, relaxing, and resuming their ramble.

The neighborhood was a holiday wonderland, its houses

trimmed in lights, their lawns sparkling with moving characters, bright trees, shining stars, beautiful nativity groupings, giant candy canes, and red-nosed reindeer. Even so, "You know, suburban streets with sidewalks are great, especially this time of year" – Gina gestured with her arm – "but I've missed spending time on the wooded trails at Madison Timber Farm. And I've missed those little extras like the occasional vase of flowers and the odd visit from the general manager."

"Well, the GM is right here, and he has a question for you."

"Yes?" They had stopped again. Gina didn't remember stopping.

Gabe's eyes wandered ever so briefly downward, then up again. "What are you doing New Year's Eve?"

Gina decided she'd had all the suspense she could take, of a certain type. She lifted a hand and touched Gabe's face for the very first time. "Would it be okay if I act out my answer?"

He nodded almost imperceptibly. "It's okay."

So Gina kissed him, remembering the festival in Opelika. But she discovered, as Gabe wrapped his arms tightly around her, that his kissing under the mistletoe that night had been rather restrained!

Finally they parted, but with a look that said neither of them had wanted to. After a moment, Gabe grinned at her. "Hey. How about one of your famous nature quotes to commemorate this moment?"

This wasn't at all the quadrant Gina's focus was in, but she would do her best to please Gabe. "Hmm…" She stalled. *Poems… Gabe… Forestland management.* She turned her head and looked around until a smile broke across her face. "Yes, I have one." She clasped her hands together in front of her and recited, "'Poems are made by fools like me, but only God can make a tree.'"

Madison Forest Therapy Trail

Key Focus

presence

Become aware of what is present around you in this moment. What do you see and hear? Pay attention in different directions, including up and down, with your eyes open. Next, do the same with your eyes shut.

Did you notice or feel anything with your eyes shut that you did not notice with them open?

Think about people and events currently important in your life. Is there someone you would wish to have the kind of experience you are having here? Are you capable of being more present with anyone, or on any work task, than you have been lately?

Madison Forest Therapy Trail

Happy in the Forest

look down, around, and up

Look down so you do not trip on anything!

Look around to watch for trees, flowers, birds, butterflies, squirrels, or bigger or smaller surprises! Do the plants and animals seem happy in the forest?

Look up to the highest leaves of the tallest trees. Are they very high? How much sky do you see? What color is the sky?

Keep Me On the Straight and Narrow
Keep me on the straight and nar - row, Je - sus,
Lead me in the path I ought to tread;
See me o - ver ev' - ry sin and sor - row,
Feed me with the liv - ing bread.
©2021 See Acknowledgments for the origin of this chorus.

Discussion Questions

<u>THESE CONTAIN SPOILERS</u>.

1. Gina decides in chapter 8 that she never wants to go back to the life she has been living. However, in the last paragraph of chapter 9, she is adjusting her prior sentiment. Read that paragraph and discuss how a person can make real changes without attempting to "start over from scratch."

2. All of this book's main characters have had a significant loss followed by a unique grief journey. Gina says her mother never achieved grief recovery. Mrs. Madison says her son Gabe has seemed perplexed by her evident peace after loss. Discuss this in light of your own experience of grief as one knowing loss or as one observing someone who has been through a loss. After loss, have any of the following made an impact: certain individuals; later blessings; scripture verses; comfort directly from the Holy Spirit? Explain your answers to the group if willing to do so.

3. Read Genesis 1:26-31 and Psalm 8:3-8, then discuss this statement: "Each of us is a part of nature."

4. Chapter 2 finds Gina convincing herself that it will be safe to post a certain photo on social media (safe in terms of her job success) because the picture likely won't generate much notice anyway. While writing that scene, I had to ponder why people often do post their average-quality pictures of fairly common sights. One reason is the habit (and the fun) of "checking in" – in other words, of telling one's audience, "This is where I am right now and this is what I am doing." What other reasons can you think of?

5. After hearing it earlier, Gina recalls a song excerpt about "sin and sorrow," sorrow being her greater connection point. Read Psalm 119:1-5 and Psalm 139:23-24. Should the possibility of sin enter our appraisal of worries and situations more often than it does? Do you think most people have an adequate willingness to look for sin in their thought patterns, their talk, and their track record (including the more "minor" decisions) so that those sins may be exposed, confessed, and forgiven?

6. Chapters 14 and 15 refer to a glowing review Gina gives the retreat site. Bits and pieces of it are given in the novel, but the following is presented as "bonus material." Read and discuss this summary segment of her review:

   ★★★★★

   Pursuing Permanent Heart Change

   A retreat site is more than mere trails in the woods. Spending adequate time among beautiful trees like those at Madison Forest Therapy Trail can help a person along their trail in life; their journey.

If you want to discover peaceful paths, you might start by exploring these woods. Suggestion: leave your phone behind. Also your "wisdom," because it has been said that truth is discovered sooner by those with hearts like little children.

Retreating involves more than a wish to relax and more than a drive to regain energy and focus for the goals you already knew about when you arrived. Chances are your retreat experience here will be better if you humbly subject your goals and attitudes to some real examination.

Does your journey to permanent heart change begin at Madison Forest Therapy Trail? Mine did. – M.G.W.

7. Gina sends the Madisons a set of R words connected with taking oneself aside for a retreat. Such a list might include words like these: review, rejuvenate, renew, etc. These concepts focus on an internal "makeover," so to speak. Consider another set of R words: rescue, raise up, resuscitate, reconcile, remake. These words evoke the idea of an *external* process at work upon the individual, achieving things one cannot do for oneself. For example, a person lying unconscious on the beach does not resuscitate himself. By definition, *rescue* involves another party coming to one's aid. Furthermore, seeking God's healing of wounds and weariness is very different from engaging in a self-directed renewal. Most important, we cannot raise ourselves up in terms of attaining access to heaven without a Savior, who is Jesus Christ. Discuss these statements in light of the following Bible passages: Isaiah 64:8; Romans 12:1-2; and John 10:9.

8. After the death of John the Baptist, Jesus "withdrew to a solitary place" (Matthew 14:13). Later in the same chapter of the Bible (verse 23), we are told that, after the miraculous feeding of a large crowd, Jesus went to a mountainside to pray. Mark 1:35 describes an occasion when Jesus arose very early in the day and went off alone, to pray; the Bible text implies that Jesus may have been there for hours. Discuss how followers of Jesus can and should "withdraw," and how often, in order to follow the Savior's example. Do you have a habit or a single experience of this nature that you are willing to share with the group?

9. Gabe makes an observation in chapter 15 about his mother, regarding outward control in spite of inner turmoil. Discuss situations where this effort seems to be required of you. How can brief "retreats" throughout one's day help in the area of managing inner turmoil? What else helps with this challenge that faces all of us on an ongoing basis? Prayer? Specific Bible verses? Counseling? Friends?

10. Gina musters some unusual courage or adrenaline that enables her to speak up for herself in an early scene. Later, she regrets getting pressured into an uncomfortable situation with a different character. Do you recall feeling frustrated or conflicted about doing something or going somewhere because of someone else's insistence? Discuss the difference between being nice and letting yourself get pushed around.

11. In Mark chapter 8 we are given an account of Jesus feeding a large crowd using seven loaves of bread and a few small

fish after He gave thanks for the food that was found (rather than complaining about how little was found). Characters in this novel express thankfulness for having had a loved one in their lives for a period of time. Can you name a circumstance in your own life that required you to decide between the "glass half full" attitude (rejoicing over what is or was) and "glass half empty" (grieving or complaining about what is lacking)? Give some everyday and theoretically "minor" examples of this attitude challenge, keeping in mind that how we behave – and how others observe us behaving – in "minor" circumstances results in major character substance.

12. Have you trusted Jesus Christ for the forgiveness of your sins? Prayerfully read the following Bible passages and consider your response to what the only Son of God has done to provide the way of reconciliation between the Father and yourself: Isaiah 55:6; Philippians 2:7-8; Ephesians 2:8-9.

About the Author

A unique and fresh voice is what reviewers said of Betsy Lowery's debut title *Pause: Everyday Prayers for Everyday Women* (Baker Publishing Group, 2004). Now, readers are consistently hailing her novels for vivid description, "real" characters, chuckle-out-loud humor, and communication of important and biblical values. Southern style and a Christian worldview are prevalent in her debut novel series *A Stranger's Promise* and *No Doubt It's Love* (WestBow Press, 2019), set in Tennessee and Georgia, respectively.

Personal experience as a Southern Baptist pastor's daughter later called into ministry herself allows the author to speak through fictional events and through characters whose spiritual journeys cover a broad spectrum: some are solid and mature; others, indifferent or uninterested; still others, listening and receptive. Themes include sacrificial love, malleability in the hands of the Potter, self-image, and forgiveness, but the overall message is that of salvation by grace, through personal faith in Jesus Christ.

Lowery holds a bachelor's degree in business administration from Mars Hill University and a master's degree in Christian education from The Southern Baptist Theological Seminary. Her ministry passion for adult Christian education drives her interest in providing discussion questions in the final pages of her novels.

Born and raised in North Carolina with brief residencies in North Dakota and Virginia during childhood, Betsy Lowery moved to Alabama in 1985 and happily considers it "home." Now retired, she and her husband Jeff divide their time between Birmingham and Auburn. The couple have two daughters, a son-in-law, and one granddog.

Since entering the world of Christian fiction, the author has found speaking about her books, their characters, and their themes with library audiences and book clubs energizing and delightful. Her speaking engagements typically include Q & A regarding the writing and publishing process; analysis of literary techniques; and plot-related door prizes. On June 24, 2021, *Opelika Observer* ran a half-page feature on her first two novels. Find her posts, photos, and video author talks on the Facebook page Books by Betsy Lowery.

A great admiration of prolific author Grace Livingston Hill is evident in Lowery's previous novel *No Doubt It's Love,* a hybrid romance and mystery. With the release of *Love Ever*

Green, she has stepped fully into the Christian romance arena, fashioning her first book of that genre with the acknowledged goal of mimicking Grace Livingston Hill. "I want readers to find this novel worthy of comparison to that iconic name in the genre yet in its own right earning 'keeper' shelf space for romantic tumult and plot originality."

CPSIA information can be obtained
at www.ICGtesting.com
Printed in the USA
LVHW100542080422
715542LV00001B/39

9 781664 251045